P9-CFF-146

"I disturb you. Why?" Jared asked as he slid the pad of his thumb over Erin's lips, sending little fissures of electric heat to her breasts and below.

She should move, scramble to the front seat of the SUV and get out of range. But she didn't; she stared into his iridescent blue eyes as if mesmerized. This was not happening. This injured, delusional stranger was not hitting on her, he was not pushing her hot buttons, and she was not responding to him.

Erin cautiously ran her gaze over Jared. A six-foot-something hunk of power thighs, pumped pecs, and piercing blue eyes didn't walk by every day. The man was so potent that even his light touch was a heady aphrodisiac. The sensations he drew from her were stronger than anything she'd known, or at least could remember. It had been a while.

You don't know him from Adam.

Eve didn't know Adam either—at first.

"If you love dark fantasy, you'll love *Touch a Dark Wolf.* Jennifer St. Giles creates a fresh new world populated with innovative creatures of the night."

—Lori Handeland, *USA Today* bestselling author

"A unique take on the werewolf world, and a thrilling ride."

—Lora Leigh, bestselling author of *Megan's Mark*

Praise for Jennifer St. Giles's
His Dark Desires

"Riveting . . . a sexually charged romance that satisfies whether [you're] seeking suspense or passion."
—*Romantic Times Book Club*

"Powerful and emotional, with complex characters . . . an excellent journey into the past you won't forget."
—*Rendezvous*

"In an era of overwhelming sameness when it comes to historical romance, *His Dark Desires* easily stands out from the crowd."
—All About Romance

"Gripping . . . a wonderful Americana suspense thriller."
—The Best Reviews

"With its dark, dangerous hero and sexy storyline, this historical romance will appeal to contemporary romantic suspense fans who enjoy danger and intrigue."
—*True Romance* magazine

"Teeming with menacing atmosphere. . . . St. Giles captures that Gothic essence with a sinister plot complete with unusual twists and turns, while maintaining a strong sexual tension between the protagonists."
—Fresh Fiction

The Mistress of Trevelyan
Winner of the Daphne Du Maurier Award

"Full of spooky suspense. . . . [St. Giles'] story ripples with tension. This tension and the author's skill at creating the book's brooding atmosphere make this an engrossing read."

—*Publishers Weekly*

"[An] intriguing, well-crafted romance."

—*Library Journal*

"[An] excellent debut novel. St. Giles does a masterful job of evoking a Gothic atmosphere, and updates it nicely with smoldering sexual tension. . . . The story is compellingly told."

—*Affaire de Coeur*

"Jennifer St. Giles must definitely be a descendant of the famous Bronte sisters. The story is enthralling, and the characters are captivating. *The Mistress of Trevelyan* is destined to become a classic romance novel, one readers will reach for again and again."

—*AromanceReview.com*

"This is an engaging gothic romance with all the classic elements. . . . The story line will touch readers."

—Harriet Klausner

Also by Jennifer St. Giles

The Mistress of Trevelyan
His Dark Desires

Published by Pocket Books

Touch a
Dark Wolf

JENNIFER ST. GILES

POCKET BOOKS
New York   London   Toronto   Sydney

The sale of this book without its cover is unauthorized. If you purchased this book without a cover, you should be aware that it was reported to the publisher as "unsold and destroyed." Neither the author nor the publisher has received payment for the sale of this "stripped book."

An *Original* Publication of POCKET BOOKS

 POCKET BOOKS, a division of Simon & Schuster, Inc.
1230 Avenue of the Americas, New York, NY 10020

This book is a work of fiction. Names, characters, places and incidents are products of the author's imagination or are used fictitiously. Any resemblance to actual events or locales or persons, living or dead, is entirely coincidental.

Copyright © 2006 by Jenni Leigh Grizzle

All rights reserved, including the right to reproduce this book or portions thereof in any form whatsoever. For information address Pocket Books, 1230 Avenue of the Americas, New York, NY 10020

ISBN-13: 978-1-4165-1332-2
ISBN-10: 1-4165-1332-9

This Pocket Books paperback edition September 2006

10 9 8 7 6 5 4 3 2 1

POCKET and colophon are registered trademarks of Simon & Schuster, Inc.

Art by Franco Accornero
Cover design by Anna Dorfman

Manufactured in the United States of America

For information regarding special discounts for bulk purchases, please contact Simon & Schuster Special Sales at 1-800-456-6798 or business@simonandschuster.com.

Acknowledgments

I first have to say that my family deserves a big hand this year. Writing consumed me, and they kept everything going at home when I couldn't. So my loving and heartfelt thanks to Charles, Ashleigh, Jake, and Shane. I love you and am so very proud of you all. Keep reaching and growing to make your dreams come true.

This book would not exist without the unfailing patience of editors Micki Nuding and Selena James. So, ladies, thank you for going the extra mile with me on this rocky road.

Many thanks to Maggie Crawford for believing in her authors and for looking to the future of the publishing market.

To Deidre Knight: Your support, advice, and encouragement see me through the darkest moments of my writing journey in life. Thank you for being the fantastic woman you are, and kudos to your hard-earned and well-deserved success in all things.

To Jacquie D'Alessandro and Wendy Etherington, forever friends through thick and thin, without you two by my side I have to wonder how I'd make it through. Your TLC, champagne, chocolate, lobster, and filet mignon are the best lifesavers a girl could have. (And thanks to Joe and Christopher for the great music and hospitality.)

To Sandra Chastain, Wendy Wax, Karen White: Your input and support has been invaluable. Thank you. Rita

Herron, thanks for finding me in the rabbit hole and knowing just what to say to shed a little light down there. Rachelle Wadsworth, I can't wait for your paranormal to hit the shelves. It's been a long time coming! To all those in GRW and RWA, who keep the dream alive—Never, never, never give up.

To Dayna and Annette: Fans and friends don't get any better! You two alone inspired a great many things in this book! Enjoy! BYS will be a great success. Stef, you are a goddess! Risa, you're fantastic and so very much appreciated! To all the GALS out there! I can't thank you enough for all of your much needed support. The fun and the laughs keep me going despite the hurdles, and The Muse is as hot as it gets! To Mo at GBUSA! You're a dream. I'm waving a big high five and thanks to Barbara, Beanie, Sarah, Bethy, Susan, Mish, Abrock. Mods extraordinaire.

To my parents, Ron and Diane Powell, thank you for understanding when I fell off the face of the earth this year. You've given your all and have never failed to support me my whole life. Thank you. To Tracy Clark and Ron Powell, I can't wait to see your books in print. And to all of the family, who gave me the best Thanksgiving book signing ever, and to Tracy for making that happen! To Colleen Blackmon and Luke, Alec, and Jordan: Thanks for making it possible by doing all that you do.

Thank you, Nancy Berland, for your wise help! I look forward to a great year! And finally, to all of you romance-reading fans around the world: You are the ones who make a writer's dream come true. Thank you for your love of story and your support!

In memory of fellow author Virginia Ellis,
whose heart, soul, and passion will live on
in this world in her fantastic stories and
in the memories of those who loved her
for the wonderful woman she was.
May your spirit soar,
my friend. We will miss you.

There are more things in heaven and earth, Horatio,
Than are dreamt of in your philosophy.

William Shakespeare (1564–1616),
Hamlet. Act 1 scene 5

Chapter One

T HE MIST FILLING the Tennessee mountain pass was either fate's middle finger telling Erin Morgan she was screwed, or a beckoning finger from the grave letting her know that sooner or later she was a dead woman. Sooner, if the budding sixth sense tingling her scalp and twisting her gut was proving itself true yet again. She'd been trying to shake the feeling, but couldn't. It was more than just the Sno-Med billboards lining the road, advertising, "Let us enrich your life. We care for you." Somehow Erin felt that Dr. Cinatas was tracing her escape from Manhattan into no-man's-land, realizing she was after his jugular rather than hiding.

She'd never dreamed—make that *nightmared*—that Dr. Cinatas was a murderer. She'd worked for the devil for months and hadn't had a clue until this morning. A sudden cold sweat made her shiver. How many people had she unknowingly helped kill during that time? How big a pawn had she been? What evil plan was Cinatas playing out, and why? From what Erin had seen, four people had been murdered to bring one back from the edge of death. Multiply the number she'd help treat by four, and the death toll was . . .

Oh, God. She gripped the steering wheel tighter, her nails biting into the leather padding. A cold sweat broke out all over her body, and her stomach churned with a sickening dread that she could hardly face.

Don't think about it! she told herself, trying to force her mind away from the scene that had greeted her that morning, but she couldn't erase it from her mind. She couldn't stop seeing everything in vivid detail.

She could still smell the antiseptic and the scent of the blood lab at the Sno-Med Clinic in Manhattan. The beautifully pristine marble floors, snow-white walls, fluorescent lights, and gleaming state-of-the-art equipment were all blindingly bright in her eyes. Even now it was hard to imagine that the perfection of it all had been marred by death. But she could still see the bodies on the stretchers. A middle-aged man and woman, and two teenage girls, all dark-haired and wearing colorful clothing, as if they'd dressed that morning with a celebration in mind. The girls had been wearing delicate gold jewelry, crosses at their ears, saints at their throats, and white rubber sports bands on their wrists. The older couple looked as if they'd spent many years toiling just to survive every day. They'd not had an easy life . . . nor death.

Even before she'd walked across the icy, off-limits lab, she'd known they were dead. Her sixth sense screamed it at her, and her clinical eye had quickly registered the unnatural paleness of their skin and the utter stillness of their bodies. Her panicked breath had frosted in the air and her gut had wrenched with dread as she'd touched them, checking for signs of life—first the young girls, then the middle-aged couple. They'd been strapped to stretchers and drained of their blood. The bags still hung on the hooks above them, tagged for the future recipient: the king of Kassim, Ashodan ben Shashur. Shashur, a close friend of the president's, had been waiting upstairs for Erin to administer the first of four transfusions that were to take place over the Fourth of July weekend.

Kassim was the smallest but most oil-rich country in the Middle East, and Shashur's security team, a force equal to the president's Secret Service, had arrived early this morning. They'd required the skeleton staff at the clinic—her, an aide, and a lab tech—to take a scary oath of secrecy. "Cross my heart and hope to die" didn't even scratch the surface of what they'd said would happen to her if she told anyone about the king. If word of his cancer reached the wrong ears, it would start a war nobody wanted.

But why murder for the blood? Surely there were

plenty of donors willing to support Dr. Cinatas's investigative treatment for cancer. She herself gave blood for the cause on a regular basis. She'd been hired by Dr. Cinatas to care for his "special patients," so all of the clients she'd transfused had been ultra-rich. Now she wondered if the diseased rich were feeding off the poor.

How many others had been lured to their deaths?

Don't think about it.

She shut her eyes, her body rigid as her SUV barreled into the fog. She wished she could press the gas to the floor and meet her death at the bottom of a rocky ravine. It was no less than she deserved, but she'd see Dr. Cinatas in hell first. Suddenly an icy shiver ran down her spine. Something was very wrong—

Thunk. She opened her eyes at the hard slam against her windshield. The glass cracked from the center outward, like a spiderweb forming right before her eyes. On the other side of the webbing was something huge and black on the hood of her car. She swerved wildly.

Pulse hammering with dread, she slammed on the brakes. The seat belt cut into her neck and her pounding chest. Her chin smacked into the steering wheel, ramming her teeth into her tongue. Pain slashed like a hot knife through her, dimming her vision and cutting off her breath. Something had hit her windshield, but it was hard to see what, between the black of the night, the dark of her car, and the mists that hovered just above the ground like ghosts bound by short chains. What had she hit?

A person? No, she told herself as she strained to see through the splintered glass. The thing was too black all over, and she didn't see anything to denote clothing. An animal, then? A bear, perhaps, but not a person.

Thank God. She sucked in relieved air and prayed she hadn't seriously harmed the animal. Fog whirled so thickly, she couldn't tell if the thing was moving or if it even breathed. She didn't have a weapon to protect herself, so she beeped the horn several times to rouse it, with no result.

Leaning closer to the glass, she hunched over the steering wheel. Maybe she could drive to the nearest town with the animal on the hood and get help. Swiping her hand over the uncracked portion of the glass, she tried to see through the quickly fogging windshield.

The black form rose up and snarled at her. She screamed, jerking back as a pair of blood-red eyes with yellow centers stared at her from a jet-black face. Black hands and red, dagger-sharp nails splayed menacingly against the glass. She rammed back in her seat, pressing the door lock button.

"What the hell?"

The creature smiled, its lips snarling back to reveal an even row of teeth shaped like ice picks. Evil, as palpable and throbbing as her pulse, hit her, and another scream rose deep inside her.

She couldn't look away. She couldn't move. It was as if icy death had frozen everything but her mind. The creature's eyes flamed like an ocean of fire, but its gaze centered a cold burn inside her, making her feel as if she'd never be warm again.

Clunk. Something from behind the creature had flattened it against the windshield. It screamed with rage and struggled against the glass, as the claw of a glittering silver wolf, which seemed to glow against the dark creature, raked across its face, snapping its head to the side.

Suddenly Erin could move, as if released from a spell that the black creature had somehow placed on her. Every fiber of her being shouted at her to get the hell out of there, to escape the wild creatures fighting on the hood.

She stomped on the gas, lurching the Tahoe forward and slamming the creatures against the glass so hard, Erin thought they would break through into the car.

Through the cracked glass, Erin saw the wolf-like thing had the black creature by the throat. It turned to her. Slivers of moonlight reflected off its metallic coat and made its eyes eerily glow. Its gaze, a bright, clear blue like the hottest part of a flame, met hers, burning itself into her mind, making a connection she couldn't even begin to describe. An otherworldly feel with a primal edge seeped deep inside her, as if a greater spirit resided within the animal, but one just as deadly as that of the other evil creature. She shivered.

The black creature reared up and sank its teeth into the wolf's chest. The wolf shuddered and howled, its scream chilling her soul.

Looking her way again, the wolf opened its fanged mouth. LEAVE NOW!

Erin heard the words as clearly as if a man had shouted in her ear. She put the SUV in reverse, pressed the gas pedal to the floor, and flew backward, bouncing the tangle of black and silver from her car hood. Then she shifted into drive and plunged forward, determined to leave what she'd seen behind.

It's not real. It's not real, she told herself. Yet her hands and body shook so violently, she had to fight to drive. She careened wildly across the road, barely able to see through the fog and cracked windshield. Her sweat-slick palms slipped along the leather steering wheel, leaving only her embedded nails to help her grip. Her stomach whirled with nauseating fear that seemed to worsen rather than ease as she escaped the creatures.

Then she hit a wall of thick fog, one that blinded her. Suddenly, the road disappeared, and she went flying into a black void.

Chapter Two

A WAVE OF GRIEF tore through the Shadowmen as Jared's howl reverberated into the spirit world, piercing the souls of those fighting for Logos. One of their brethren, one of their valued warriors, had fallen prey to the bite of a Tsara. Worse than death itself, the rabid, unclean infection would spread evil throughout the host, taking control of his mind and rooting into his heart. It was fatal and irreversible. And in the wolf's howl they could hear the echoing horror of the one who'd been damned.

It was just a matter of time.

As the Blood Hunters, the elite warriors of the Shadowmen, crossed into the mortal realm, a stormy wind swirled, whipping down through the atmosphere. Whenever in the mortal realm, the Blood Hunters appeared in their mortal forms, warriors of muscle and might and substance with the ability to shape-shift into their wolflike Blood Hunter cloaks at will. Inside the remote Tennessee mountain cave, the warriors gathered around a fire, silent as it flared hotly then flickered feebly, casting deeper shadows on faces already darkened by sorrow. The cold mortal ground was a filthy place for so great a warrior to have fallen.

Sven had brought Jared's fallen body to the mountain cave, not far from where Jared had killed the Tsara before falling unconscious from the pain of the assassin's evil poison. Grieving, he'd waited on his knees beside Jared as the other Blood Hunters arrived.

Aragon, the leader of all Shadowmen, stormed about the cave, stirring a whirl of dirt to cloud the air. He stopped and gazed at Jared's fallen form, agony tearing though him. "You should have executed Jared the moment you reached him. Maybe his soul could have been spared." His harsh voice sliced through the silence. "It's too late to save his soul now. I already feel the poison in his heart. By Logos's justice, what were you thinking, Sven? The millennium of Jared's sacrifices will now end in ruin."

Groaning, Sven shut his eyes but forced himself to his feet, ready to bear Aragon's wrath. "I couldn't kill him. I'd but hoped the legend was true."

"Hoped! That is your excuse for cowardice? We'd decided after Pathos was poisoned that we'd rather die than stake our souls upon a legend!" Aragon shouted.

"Kill him now," Navarre said. "I cannot bear to watch what will come when he wakes."

Aragon lifted his sword, yet rather than slicing through the unconscious body of his brother, he hesitated, recalling the many years he and Jared had walked through time fighting Heldon's forces. How many sacrifices had Jared suffered, saving them all from the deathly consequences of their mistakes? Aragon's stomach turned, and a cold chill ran through him. Resolved to save Jared from Pathos's fate, he let his sword fall.

"Wait!" York flung his sword out and up, deflecting Aragon's deathblow. "What if it isn't just a legend? It's been a millennium since a Blood Hunter was bitten. How do we know there is no hope?"

"Pathos was the last to be bitten and is now the most powerful werewolf for the damned." Breathing heavy, Aragon forced out words rather than the cry of frustration he wanted to vent. He didn't know if he had the strength to lift his sword against Jared again. "That is proof enough. There is little that can be done for a spirit once in the mortal world." Rather than finding his salvation, Pathos had joined the Vladarian Order and preyed upon the Elan in the mortal realm. "Jared and I made a pact to never let a brother cross the line again."

Sven fisted his hands. "Weren't there others before Pathos? Blood Hunters who did find salvation?"

Aragon sighed. "Yes, a long time ago, before the

earth became so vile, the Vladarian Order so strong, and the mortal seed of the Tsara so evil. Heldon's influence has grown. We all know that. It is better to die than become one of the Fallen and serve Heldon and the Vladarians."

"I say we give the legend a chance." York eased his sword to the ground.

"Why?" demanded Aragon. "Why take the chance?"

"Because Jared deserves it," said Sven.

"He was defending a woman, one of the Elan?" Navarre asked.

"Yes," said Sven.

"And she saw Jared in his Blood Hunter's cloak?"

"Yes."

"Rather than leaving Jared to awake and wander the mortal world alone to find salvation as was done to Pathos, why not leave his mortal body with one who is Elan? They are special within the mortal world. Perhaps it will help."

"I agree," said York. "Jared is lost to us, but he deserves the chance of having his soul redeemed by finding love within the mortal world."

"What if we're wrong?" Aragon said harshly, hands fisted around his sword.

"Then I will kill him," Sven said, stepping forward. "I will descend into Heldon's freezing fires and hunt him if need be, but I won't let Jared serve the Vladarians or fight with the Armies of the Fallen."

Aragon nodded, and prayed to Logos's mercy that he was wrong and that the power of human love could save a spirit from being damned. Because if he was right, Sven had just committed himself to a death sentence, and Aragon, too. As leader, he wouldn't let a Blood Hunter journey there alone, nor would he leave Jared's fate in the hands of another. No Shadowman had ever survived Heldon's fires.

Aragon held up his sword. "Then there is only one thing left for us to do." Lifting his blade high to a point in the air, he waited for the other Blood Hunters to join the points of their swords to his.

His sword glowed blue, like the purest heart of a flame, and he brought the broadside of it against the gaping wound on Jared's chest, where the virulent poison of the Tsara had already spread and sealed the evil inside.

From inside his pristine New York City penthouse overlooking the Hudson, Dr. Anthony Cinatas reclined on a white divan and sipped a supple merlot from Chateau Petrus, his preferred vineyard for smooth red wines. He'd been trying to soothe himself after the day's disturbing events, but had been rudely interrupted by Kassim's king. Cinatas watched with growing irritation Ashodan ben Shashur's righteous pacing across the snowy carpet, white robes billowing with each angry step. His sandaled footprints marred the pristine carpet's nape, destroying the perfection of the white sea. The man, if you could call the beast such, was livid over the Morgan incident. Were it not that Cinatas himself had suffered at Erin Morgan's hand, he would be pleased by Shashur's distress. He hated the man's arrogance.

Shashur's only endearing quality was that he was dependant on Cinatas's genius, unless, of course, the man wanted to abandon his refined, leisurely life to feed like a ravenous beast—to spend his every night groveling in the filth of the masses, desperately searching for Elan blood.

Cinatas shuddered at the vision, thankful that he was above the squalor of having to feed like an animal. By the time his life on Earth ended, he'd have the key to immortality without having to be dependent on a frequent infusion of Elan blood. But until he held that key, he'd play the Vladarian Order's game, feed their hunger, and take their money until he could take them over.

There was satisfaction in having the Vladarians dependent on him, even if they didn't realize he was their god. After one transfusion of Elan blood, Shashur had returned to vigor from death's door, and by the end of the treatment regimen on Sunday, the man's forceful energy would be virtually unstoppable for the next three months.

Cinatas would never forget his own brush with death on a dark night six years ago. The bridge his car had plunged over, the icy waters, his bursting lungs. The sudden peace and floating toward a brilliant light as he watched the incompetent idiots who'd pulled him from the water resuscitate him. They'd somehow managed.

And that night, in an isolated Appalachian hospital, a creature had made Cinatas's rebirth complete. In one excruciatingly painful bite from a Tsara, Cinatas was set on the path to discovering his greatness. Led by Pathos, the Vladarian Order tapped into his genius and paid Cinatas well for their transfusions of Elan blood.

It wasn't until the Vladarian Order's cloaked "research grants" had made him rich that the world stopped treating him as a bloodthirsty Frankenstein and saw his value as a hematologist/oncologist whose experiments with blood proteins were at the cutting edge of the bioscience frontier. There was power in blood, and someday his Sno-Med Corporation would be all-powerful. Cure a handful of people from cancer, and you became a god. Erin Morgan couldn't touch him, but she was a messy detail that needed cleaning up.

Cinatas tightened his grasp on the gold goblet. He shifted his gaze to the screen on the far wall showing a video of a gutted building, the smoke and ash remnants of the damage Erin Morgan had forced him to do.

Why did people always choose to make things difficult and messy?

Today was but a minor setback. A Special Elan or not, Erin Morgan had bought herself a one-way ticket to his private—pleasurable for him, painful for her—hell, just as soon as *his* men, and not Shashur's, caught her.

Cinatas's neck still throbbed from the damage she'd caused with her syringe, and his body was just recovering from the aftereffects of the drug she'd plunged into him. But the damage to his pride and reputation was worse.

"The wrong word from her to the wrong people, and I'll have to beat back the cursed Irmans again to reestablish my power. It'll cost me another year or two. I can't believe you let this happen," Shashur said, his dark eyes full of fire as he stabbed his finger in the air.

"My fault?" Cinatas merely smiled. Wine and the dregs of morphine made a heady and almost fearless cocktail in his bloodstream. "You're blaming me for a woman you and the rest of your kind personally requested to have service your transfusions? I warned you at the time that it wasn't smart to let someone besides me administer your treatments."

"Had you not left four bodies to be found, she wouldn't have become a problem."

"Your insistence upon fresh, unfrozen blood, warm

from the vein, necessitates the donors be brought here. They refused to come and had to be forced to do their duty. If a man cannot keep order among those who serve him, then he deserves to die."

"It doesn't matter why. Pathos will be displeased when he arrives for the Vladarians' Gathering. Your purpose in serving us is to minimize, if not eliminate, the body count, not add to it."

Cinatas paused mid-sip. Serve them? Wine spilled down his shirt, sending a stab of rage though him so sharp that he barely restrained himself from tossing the wine into Shashur's face and shoving the glass down his throat. The transfusions were to keep beasts like Shashur from having to live like an animal, constantly searching through the masses for Elan blood and feeding in violence. Transfusions were so much more aesthetic, like a trip to the spa. Pathos had been the one to realize that to gain more power, the Vladarians had to spend less time scavenging for food and direct their energies toward building influential empires. They needed to stay longer in the mortal realm. They needed to establish themselves among mortals to expand Heldon's reach.

Elan blood was very hard to find among the millions populating the world, and the hundreds of people Sno-Med Corporation screened every day for blood donations made that task easy. It had taken Cinatas an entire year to isolate and identify the special protein that made Elan blood different from that of most people. The rest was . . . glorious history. Cinatas established Sno-Med, and the Vladarian Order went to work. Identities were bought, corporations established, and regimes overthrown.

Shashur had taken over the oil-rich Kassim in a quick and brutal military coup, replacing a despot who wasn't near the beast Shashur was. Shashur just knew how to conceal it better. The Vladarians were very adept at concealment.

But still stupid. Didn't the beast realize that Cinatas held its existence in his hand? One little additive to a transfusion and . . . well, who knows what could happen.

"Why bother Pathos with today's trivial events?" Cinatas said. "I've already taken care of any problems."

"Pathos considers it an offense to be uninformed of any matter. He will also be the one to determine Erin Morgan's fate once we've captured her."

"Why?" Cinatas asked, feigning indifference. "What makes her so different from any other of the Elan? Why was it necessary for her to administer the transfusions?"

Kassim frowned, clearly disgusted. "There's no satisfaction in a meal if all you can smell is trash. Your Elan blood is polluted, my friend. And Erin's Elan blood is the sweetest on earth."

Cinatas refrained from commenting on Shashur's

insult, but he put another mental mark against the man. One day Cinatas would be in a position to decide who from the Vladarian Order was allowed to stay longer than the single month, or "moon phase," that Elan blood made possible. Once he has passed through the spirit barrier to walk among mortal men, a Vladarian's vitality wanes, and his body eventually decays, feeding off itself like a cancer unless it gets mortal blood.

The purity and power in the proteins of Elan blood delayed the dying process for three months. When Vladarians fed on ordinary blood, they had to have it on a daily basis; and the longer the Vladarian was upon the earth, the more frequently feedings were needed. Eventually the Vladarians had to constantly kill and eat to sustain life, a problem that rendered them useless to aid in Heldon's battle.

Cinatas decided to have the lab examine Erin Morgan's blood a second time, wondering why Shashur considered Erin's blood sweeter than any other. Perhaps Erin's blood had a higher concentration of proteins. He kept samples from everyone, blood and pieces of their tissue as well as other body fluids. There was power in knowledge, and it would seem he was about to get a payoff from his. "If she is so succulent, why hasn't one of your kind just devoured her before?"

"Erin Morgan is under the protection of the Vladarian Order."

A mortal under the protection of the damned? Very interesting. He wondered why, but didn't ask, didn't call attention to the oddity. Her blood would tell him what he wanted to know. This time he'd do the lab testing on Erin Morgan's blood himself.

For some reason, Erin meant power, and modern GPS tracking was going to put her right into the palm of his hand. His cell phone vibrated. Looking at the digital display, he inwardly smiled as he excused himself from the room a moment to take the call.

There was one thing he'd learned about evil over the past few years. Evil was, to coin a famous quote, "essentially stupid." His Elan blood might smell like trash to Shashur, but it gave him an edge over the Fallen.

Chapter Three

ERIN AWOKE FROM A DRUGGED SLEEP; every muscle of her body ached as if stretched beyond its limit to endure, and her head pounded as if a sledgehammer danced between her eyes. Awareness of other things besides pain came slowly. A sense of heat and the feel of stuffy air surrounded her. She was belted in, enclosed in a small place. But she didn't feel secure or comforted by the warmth and restraint. An odd feeling of danger tingled through her, awakening her mind, and her memory rushed back at her.

Her eyes sprang open to daylight streaming in though her cracked windshield. A fractured blue sky, a grassy field, and a naked man on the hood of her car filled her vision. She blinked twice, and when the vision didn't disappear, she promptly shut her eyes, searching for a reason for what she thought she had just seen.

There had to be a logical explanation for the fact that last night's nightmare had turned into pure fantasy. The silver werewolf and the black creature on the hood of her car had morphed into a dark-haired, naked Adonis.

"Mmmnn." The groan, deeply male and filled with pain, did not come from her.

Erin's eyes blinked open again. The man was still there, still naked, and now moving restlessly. She *had* hit something last night. Surely she hadn't hit *him*. Right?

There wasn't a sign that the silver wolf and the black creature had ever existed except, of course, her cracked windshield.

Had she been delusional last night?

Hell!

Even if she was delusional now, she couldn't just sit there. Snapping her seat belt loose, she opened the door, drinking in a breath of fresh mountain air, something she hadn't realized she'd missed by living in the city. As best as she could tell, she'd landed in a narrow green pasture near a sprawling lush oak, with a crisp mountain creek rushing along the right side. Several cows grazed in the distance, looking too normal to be part of her nightmare.

Her body moved like a rusty hinge as she slid her legs out of the car. Then, startled to see dried blood staining the front of her nurse's whites, she paused before she stood, her stomach clenching. It had to be her blood. She tentatively touched her face, feeling a crustiness on her left cheek, then a gash on her left temple that she hadn't even realized was there.

Behind her, ten feet up an embankment and past barbed-wire fencing and thick brush, sat State Road 44, the road she'd been on last night. She had a vague recollection of the thick fog, of missing a curve and plowing through bushes. Then the floating feeling of plunging downward, hitting hard, and bouncing over rough terrain until she came to an abrupt stop when the engine stalled. She'd sat shaken and alone in the middle of swirling mists, afraid to open her door or move at all. She remembered squeezing her eyes against the pounding pain in her head, thinking to rest for just a few moments before trying to find her way back to the road.

That was the last she could remember. The night had passed, and, judging by the height of the sun, most of the morning, too. She must have hit her head during the crash and passed out, for her moment's rest had stretched for hours.

The man groaned again, and she stood. Dizziness swamped her, and she grabbed the car door for balance. The world about her slowly came back into focus, an oddly bucolic contrast to the roller-coaster ride she'd been on and the naked man before her. She knew she had to have a mild concussion, because everything felt as if it just wasn't happening, as if she wasn't really there, but was dreaming it.

She moved hesitantly to the hood of her Tahoe, her gaze scanning the man's body for trauma as she fought for balance. She saw no apparent injuries. No blood. No bruising. No limbs twisted at an unnatural angle. He appeared almost too perfect.

Was he real or not? Either way, it wasn't good. If he wasn't real, then her mind had gone off the deep end. If he was real, then she'd hit him with her car last night—which meant he'd been walking naked in the dark, something only a person in trouble or mentally ill would do.

He lay on his stomach, one arm cradling his head, the other at his side. Longish, coal-black hair, with a shocking streak of silver at the crown, moved in the breeze.

She'd give her imagination a lot of credit, but was it really this good? She needed a Starbucks IV stat.

The man was broad shouldered and perfectly sculpted, his muscular back tapering to trim waist and hips, strong thighs, and long legs that hung off the edge of her car. The only oddity was the paleness of his skin. He didn't look as if he'd ever been out in the sun, which meant he had to be feeling the UV rays bombarding his backside.

She touched his shoulder, encountering burning hot skin backed by hard muscle. She wasn't imagining this, and the man was ill. Fevered. Concern gripped her. "Mister. Can you hear me?"

He groaned, but didn't answer. Moving closer, she slid her fingers into his hair, feeling the silkiness and the wild luxurious length of it as she searched his scalp for injury. Finding none, she pressed her palm to his burning brow. Never had she felt anyone so hot. "Hey," she said gently. "Can you hear me? You're ill."

Still no response. She had to turn him over. Hiking up her dress, she climbed onto the hood and grasped his shoulder and his hip to roll him her way, praying he wasn't badly wounded anywhere she'd yet to see. They were a long way from a hospital. When she pulled, he reared up, groaning sharply with pain and knocking her backward.

She tumbled to the ground, smacking her knee on the bumper hard enough to bring a sting of tears to her eyes. The man had moved faster than she had imagined possible. That sent a fissure of fear through her. She was out in the middle of nowhere. Alone.

Rolling to her feet, she crouched, prepared to spring up and run, but found herself nearly eye-level with impressive male anatomy that was starkly enhanced by black hair, hard muscled thighs, and washboard abs. He'd crossed his thick arms over a chest that rivaled Atlas for broadness and strength. She lifted her gaze higher.

He sat with his heels propped on her bumper, knees

bent and legs spread—not extra wide, but he sure wasn't trying to hide anything. Seeming thoroughly comfortable with his nakedness, he stared at her with bloodshot eyes the startling color of iridescent blue topaz.

She pressed her fingers to her head, searching through the throbbing mass of her mind as she studied his gaze. There was something familiar about his eyes, but she couldn't say what or from where, maybe one of those magazine ads where you just get a shot of part of a man's face that grabs you. She did know she'd never *met* him before. *That* would have been unforgettable.

Sweat beaded his flushed face, and she noticed that he held his left arm protectively against his chest. Dark stubble covered his chin, framing lips that had to have been fashioned by Eros—or Satan. He had the most erotically seductive mouth she'd ever seen, the only soft spot amid his warrior's features—chiseled nose, sharp cheeks, and brooding brow. His dark hair flowed past his shoulders, layered back from his face like the wings of a predator. He looked like a deadly warrior, with an odd gold-colored pagan amulet hanging on a chunky chain about his neck.

If she had hit him with her car, he hadn't suffered injury. She shook her head. No. If she'd hit him, there would be evidence of it on him and on her car besides the windshield. This just wasn't real. He resembled an actor she'd once seen in a mini-series on Attila the

Hun. This had to be a dream. A woman would have to be out of her mind to imagine waking up in a cow pasture with a naked man.

She managed a weak smile. "Hello, Attila the hunk," she said, her voice scratchy and unsure. What else could it be but a dream?

"You can see me?" the man asked in a deep voice. "You are mistaken. Attila the *Hun* died well over a millennium ago, and I bear no resemblance to that cursed scourge. I am Jared."

She narrowed her eyes, and a pang cut through her temple. That wasn't a very romantic, dreamlike response. At least, none that she could imagine fantasizing, which meant this was real. What did he mean, could she see him? How could she not?

Shaking her head, she wondered if she could just start over again. Last night's creature battle never happened. Yesterday's hell in the Sno-Med lab didn't exist. In just a moment, she would wake to her alarm clock in her apartment after the wildest dream/nightmare of her life. All she had to do was open her eyes, throw back her leopard-print spread, and flip on her Victorian feather lamp. Better yet, why not tuck her new hood ornament into bed with her?

"Jared what?" she asked, giving the dream option one last try. Hopefully the man would now speak in a Scottish accent, fulfilling her fantasy.

He stared at her another moment, scowled, then

looked around him as if she hadn't spoken. Too typically male to ever be a dream.

Erin set her hands on her hips, wishing that at least one thing in a million would go right. "If you won't tell me who you are, can you at least tell me how in the hell you ended up on my car? And where are your clothes?"

He flexed the fingers of his left hand as if to see how it worked. When he moved his left arm, he groaned and pulled it tighter against himself.

Erin winced at her own insensitivity and softened her voice as she touched his arm lightly. "Hey, you're hurt and fevered. Let me help."

"I'm damned," he said harshly; his eyes were stark and desolated.

He was delirious. "Jared," she said softly. "Let me see your wound. I'm a nurse—I can help." She moved closer to him. Oddly, she grew warmer inside, as if his nearness affected her. The heat, she told herself. She had to be feeling the heat of his fever.

"Nothing can cure a Tsara infection." Still, he unfolded his arm and shifted it to the side.

Erin moved his hair back and then sucked in a sharp breath at the sight of the deep burn that slashed his chest just above his left breast. Charred and angry, his wound oozed, looking as though someone had burned him badly only minutes ago.

"How in God's name did that happen?" she asked, forcing back a shudder.

"You say much to know so little," he said cryptically, then slid off the hood. From the sudden clenching of his arm and the deep furrowing of his brow as he tentatively gained his balance, she knew he was in great pain. Yet he stoically braced himself and straightened to his full height.

She stepped back, shocked. He towered over her five-foot-ten by a foot, a rare event.

Without glancing at her, he moved closer to the creek, staring up at the sky and clutching the amulet to his chest. "*Aragon!*" he screamed. "*Why!* You've betrayed me!"

His voice reverberated like thunder, and the marrow of her bones shook from the agony vibrating in it. Maybe she wasn't the one having a hallucination. Who was Aragon?

"Mister, uh, Jared. We need to get you to help."

His head bowed as if shamed. "There is no help."

He carried such an aura of authority about him that her heart sank, almost believing him, before she shook it off. She almost said "bullshit" to his doomed nonsense, but instinct told her she wouldn't be able to convince him he wasn't damned, and rather than get lost in a quagmire of verbal hopelessness she pulled her professional wits back into line.

"There is help," she said firmly. "First, you're going to sit in the car before you fall down. I hate to tell you, but if you faint, you'll lie where you fall, since I can't move you alone. And the cows will graze on whatever is exposed—which is everything, in case you haven't noticed."

He didn't move or react. He just stood there, staring up at the sky, pain etched deeply on his face.

Grumbling, she marched to him and slid her hand over his right wrist, touching the burning heat of his skin. She pressed her fingers to his radial pulse, measuring the pace of his racing heart. She had to get his fever down quickly and dress his wound.

He'd started at her touch and stared at her, confused.

"Please," she said softly. "Let me help you." She put her other hand on his arm.

His gaze moved to her hand, as if her touch bewildered him.

"This weakness of the flesh, this pain, is unknown to me," he said. "Why does it ease with your touch?"

A slight smile tugged at the corners of her mouth even as she puzzled over his odd phrasing. "Nurses always make things better. Come with me." She tugged on his wrist, and after a moment he followed her to the car. Opening the back door, she patted the seat. "Sit here, and I'll get my first aid kit." *And something to cover you with.*

Armed with a yellow towel, sports bra, med kit, and cool water from the creek, she joined Jared in the back seat, squeezing in to kneel on the floor at his side. He was so big there wasn't room for anything but that, or on him. Dousing her bra in the water, she placed the soft cotton on his forehead and flung the towel over his groin.

He stared at her as if he wasn't sure what she would do next. The blueness of his eyes struck a familiar cord inside her again, as if she should know him. She held up a tube of antibiotic ointment. "This is medicine. I'm going to put it on your burn. Then I will try and cool you down before we go look for help."

"There is no reason to care for me. The path to the Fallen cannot be changed."

"I have to help you," she said, refusing to respond to his delirious words of doom.

He gazed intently at her, as if trying to see her soul. The vulnerable sensations he evoked left her as disturbed as her encounter with Dr. Cinatas had, after she'd discovered the murders in his lab. She shivered, edging back a little from Jared before she realized it was the sheer power of his presence that got to her and not anything remotely to do with what had happened in the Sno-Med lab.

He brushed his finger along her cheek, his eyes widening with surprise. "I see you must. This ill is not of your doing, Elan, and you cannot change fate, but do as you will for now."

The man was delusional, more so than a high fever would account for. He wasn't in tune with the real world, which meant he could very well be mentally ill. There didn't seem to be another explanation. But he wasn't threatening her in any way, and he needed her help.

Still, her hands trembled as she worked, for her awareness of him, and the raw power of his appeal, grew as did her curiosity. He was a puzzle. She moved the amulet aside to apply more ointment and found that it was as hot as his fevered skin. Other than the unusual geometric design on it, she didn't see any identifying information. No engravings or symbology that she recognized to help her connect him to a national group or a club.

She kept glancing back at the amulet as she tended to him. It was unusual, just as were his speech and the circumstances of his appearance on the hood of her car. If this were fiction and not real life, she'd be tempted to wonder who Aragon was, and what a Tsara infection was. But right now he needed help, and she needed to do what she could to get him to it. Then she could get back to finding a way to expose Cinatas.

Chapter Four

JARED HAD KNOWN LITTLE but war as he'd searched for and guarded the Elan. He wasn't sure how to respond to the woman with him. He studied her curiously, realizing that over time he'd forgotten much of what he'd been told about the flesh and being mortal.

She had a tender touch, a caring to her nature that he admired, and he could sense her own pain and fear in her eyes. Did she know that he already hungered for her Elan blood? It has been the first thing he sensed upon awakening, before other sensations intruded.

He flexed his hand, disgusted by the limitation of his movements. This body was so different from his spirit form. He had had such fluidity of movement before that being in mortal flesh made him feel as if he were bound in chains—chains that seared his flesh with a burning heat and tormented his soul as the good within him fought against its inevitable death to the evil of the Tsara's poison.

He reached down to the yellow towel across his groin and frowned at the sensation of having something against his skin. She had covered him for some reason, though he'd not expressed a desire for that and would prefer to be uncovered.

"What does this mean?" she asked, touching his amulet.

"Everything and nothing. It's Logos's symbol. All those within the Guardian Forces wear it." To Jared the symbol represented everything he knew, everything he believed in, everything that was lost now. He had the prison of this mortal flesh for a time and then . . . damnation. Why had his brethren condemned him to hell?

And how long did he have before the poison consumed him? He didn't know exactly. A lot depended on the potency of the Tsara's poison. Pathos had been in the mortal world less than a week before he began hunting and feeding on the Elan. Soon after, he led the Vladarians on hunting trips, using his Blood Hunter skills for evil by adeptly finding the Elan for their feeding frenzies.

Few Blood Hunters had ever been bitten by a Tsara. Of the two Jared knew of—Pathos and another who had been able to redeem his soul with mortal love— but that was before the world had become so evil, and the Tsara's poison so vile.

The Elan studied him with soft golden eyes that seemed like liquid sunshine. Her skin and features were so perfectly formed, so soft and inviting, that she compelled touch. And the scent of her Elan blood was so sweet that she stirred hungers he'd never known before.

"Who are the Guardian Forces? Who is Logos?" she asked, touching his amulet again.

The question was almost as painful as the poison within him, for it was all that he was and could never be again. "All that is good, honest, and pure," he replied, gazing into her golden eyes again. In their depths he saw goodness and honesty and purity of spirit reflected. He'd always protected and defended the Elan, but had never given any thought to their spirits—only their purpose for Logos. The beauty in this Elan's eyes, her strength, her vulnerability, and her caring, tugged at something unfamiliar inside of him; something that stirred his spirit as well as his mortal body.

Before she began ministering to him, he'd noted the soul-biting edge of his pain lessened the closer they were together. When she touched him or he touched her, the pain disappeared completely, then raged back with a vengeance every time she stopped. So it wasn't that her touch healed him or eased the strength of the Tsara's poison spreading through him. He didn't understand it.

Her hands shook as she worked, and he slid his hand over hers. "Do I frighten you?"

"No," she said softly.

He sighed and brushed his fingers gently over her wrist. If she eased his pain with her touch, did that mean she was absorbing his pain into herself?

"Does touching me cause you pain?" He meant to release her, but the warm throb of her blood beneath his fingertips was too alluring to let go of just yet. He sucked in air through his teeth, gritting them against the surging desire in him to . . . taste her in a way that was different than his hunger for her blood. At least, he thought so, but he wasn't sure. The growing sensations and hungers confused him.

The Elan shook her head. "No. Now lie back and let me help."

He could see in her golden eyes that helping him was important to her. It wasn't the way of the warrior, and he shouldn't give in to the weakness of pain, but he grunted and closed his eyes, deciding to accept the ease she brought him for a moment more.

Erin shook her head. Why had he thought touching him would hurt her? What was he referring to when he spoke of the Guardian Forces and Logos? They sounded like names from a video or role-playing game; games she'd heard some people took so seriously they were attempting to live out them out in real life.

She kept looking for reason amid the confusion he

caused, searching for an explanation for him as well as her reaction to him. Her hands shook, not from fear, but because of the sensations touching him evoked. Telling herself the man was delusional did little to dampen his effect. A sensuality oozed with the heat pouring off him that no amount of sponging with water could cool.

Despite open doors, the car had become a humid, window-fogging sauna. Sandwiched between him and the rising, steamy sun, she felt seconds away from spontaneous combustion by the time she'd dressed his wound and sponged him down. Sweat trickled between her breasts and glued her white stockings to her skin, making everything that couldn't be politely reached itch. At least, that was the only explanation she accepted for how she felt in certain places. Anything else was unreasonable.

Her whole life was unreasonable.

She'd forced her ministrations to be quick and perfunctory, but the hard, chiseled planes of his body had put a dent in her professionalism. Dent? The way her pulse raced, he'd wrecked it.

She didn't understand the effect he had on her, nor her growing curiosity about him and the odd amulet he wore. The gold wasn't fourteen or more carat; it was too brass-bronze-like in color, with an odd opalescent sheen. Whatever the composition of the two-inch disk, it was a beautiful mixture of metals. But the jewels, randomly set amid an intricately woven star, were so small it made her question why the designer had ruined the perfection of the metal by using them. Who was he? Who was Logos? Who were the Shadowmen and the Guardian Forces?

Hell. She needed to get a grip. She had more important things to worry about, like a murdering doctor and her life. Inching away, she backed out of the car.

"MOOO."

Startled, she twisted toward the sound, and a cow butted her as if she were manna or momma. Yelping, she scrambled to sit on the edge of the seat, next to Jared's head, as she faced the cow and pushed the beast's wet muzzle away with her foot. It wasn't alone. Distorted by foggy patches on the windows were a dozen bleating monstrosities surrounding her navy Tahoe. Moos on a slo-mo warpath.

"I eat chicken and fish! Honest." Had she thought the cows a spot of normalcy in her surroundings?

The cow pressed harder against her shoe, its slimy, pinkish tongue swiping as it played king of the hill with her one-inch Dr. Scholl's. Where were her stilettos when she needed them?

With one foot still battling the cow in front of her, she twisted around to her left at a sound from behind her. A cud-chewing monster was licking Jared's feet. "Shoo!" she shouted. Leaning over him, she flung her hand out. The cow butted her foot again, and she lost her precarious balance, landing half on top of Jared, her nose to his chest and her breasts to his face.

He groaned, pressing a hot hand to her breast as he pushed upright, knocking her onto the floor. The cows bleated loudly. From her dazed position, she saw Jared narrow his eyes and growl, a feral, almost chilling wolflike sound from deep in his throat. Then he reclined on the seat and shut his eyes.

Erin sat up and stared at him in exasperation. They were under attack, and all he could manage to do was growl? "Some help you are," she muttered, looking to battle her bovine nemesis again. But they were gone.

The cows had retreated, running up the hill in a group as if the hunting forces of Wendy's, McDonald's, and Longhorn's were hot on their hooves. An eerie feeling crept over her that had nothing to do with the feel of his hand on her breast. She wanted to call the cows back, anything but be sitting next to a man who'd just . . . growled, and . . . what? Sent a herd of cows fleeing?

Coincidence. Something else had spooked them. She shivered and cautiously ran her gaze over Jared, assuring herself of his normalcy, then gave up. A six-foot-something hunk of power thighs, pumped pecs, and piercing blue eyes didn't walk by every day—and surely never posed as a naked hood ornament.

Okay, so, Attila the Hunk growled at cows. So what? Refusing to plant another foot outside her SUV until she'd left hostile bovine territory, she shut the door and crawled across the car. Jared's feet hung out the other side.

"Let's get you all the way inside," she told him, then winced. That just sounded so wrong.

He opened those too blue eyes. "They'll not return. Do not worry, Elan."

Elan? Odd name. The man really was ill, and the troubled, pained look in his eyes had deepened, making her want to brush his dark hair back from his fevered brow and soothe the tension clenching his jaw with her touch.

"Erin," she said softly. "My name is Erin Morgan. What is yours?"

"I am Jared."

"I know, but what is the rest? Your full name?"

"Rest?"

"Yes, Jared, what?"

"Jared . . ." He hesitated, then furrowed his brow, oddly. "Hunter."

Did he not know his name? Or did he not want *her* to know his real name? She drew a breath. "Well, Jared Hunter, help me get you inside the car."

He sat up in the seat, scooted back, and planted his muscled legs next to her, losing his yellow-towel coverage. Whoa. She snatched the towel back up, and he caught her hand with his. Her fingers tingled and trembled.

"I disturb you. Why?"

Heat stung her cheeks. As shallow and unprofessional as it sounded, he—*just say it without sugarcoating it*—attracted her?

Points for honesty on that understatement put her in the red. *Lust* would have come closer.

You don't know him from Adam.

Eve didn't know Adam either—at first.

First, hallucinations. Now, she was talking to and answering herself and developing rationalization issues. She needed to race to the nearest clinic, ditch him, and get on with the unraveling of her life—exposing Dr. Cinatas for a murderer and admitting to the world that she'd unknowingly been a pawn in his crime.

Jared released her hand and brushed her cheek with his fingertips. Then, staring into her eyes, he slid the pad of his thumb over her lips, flashing acute need across her nerves.

This was not happening. The injured, delusional stranger was not hitting on her, he was not pushing her hot buttons, and she was not responding to him.

She'd been seeing Ben & Jerry's exclusively for too damn long.

He brushed her lips again, and she gasped as little fissures of electric heat zinged to her breasts and below.

"Did I disturb you?" he asked, jerking his hand back.

The man was so potent that even his light touch was a heady aphrodisiac. The sensations he drew from her were stronger than anything she'd known, or at least could remember. It had been a while.

"No," she whispered. Now that he'd stopped touching her, she should move, scramble to the front seat and get out of range. But she didn't; she stared into his iridescent blue eyes as if mesmerized.

Jared couldn't stop himself from touching her mouth, fascinated by the new sensations of pleasure that replaced the pain in him. When he'd touched her lips, her golden eyes had changed, brightened and heated to the point that he'd felt the glory of the sun blaze in them. Powerful sensations spread to other places in his new, fleshly form, giving him his first taste of mortal desire.

The warmth of her breath upon his skin reminded him of sun-heated mists he'd traveled through as a Blood Hunter. The feel of clouds—such a simple thing he'd always known, yet never considered as pleasurable. Pleasure had been the sound of spirits singing in victory after a battle, not these urges to touch her, urges that seemed to be superseding his awareness and want of her Elan blood, almost drowning it out when he touched her or she touched him.

This pleasure made him want to touch her more, to explore the realm of desire he'd only heard of before, but had never experienced. When he'd pressed his hand against her a few moments ago, he'd felt such inviting softness that he wanted to bury himself within the comfort and ease she brought him. But that was not a warrior's way. A warrior didn't *need* another to face pain, discomfort, or battle. Softness weakened a warrior, and he needed to be strong to fight the Tsara poison long enough to assure he'd never take the path Pathos had gone.

Jared pulled his finger back, and pain stabbed at him, especially over his heart where the Tsara had bitten him, where his brethren had seared and sealed his fate. With the return of his pain, he could taste the heady sweetness of her Elan blood scenting the air—and his hunger sharpened. The idea of satisfying his lust for blood by consuming hers tore at everything good inside him. Everything he'd stood for since his inception in Eden was now threatened to be destroyed—by him.

He almost reached out and touched her again, to erase the awareness of her blood and ease his pain, but fisted his hand instead. It was wrong of him to use her for his own relief. That would make him no different than the Fallen.

He dropped his hand to his lap and sucked in air at the change in his fleshly form beneath the cloth. The burning pleasure that accompanied the brush of his hand against the hardened change in his flesh heightened his desire for her, made him want to touch her softness again. Touch every part of his mortal flesh to hers. Meld his body to hers. He groaned.

"You're in pain?" She pressed the palm of her hand to his brow. "You feel cooler, though."

Her voice, her touch, her care, enhanced his desire for her, urging such a strong need in him for more that he had to clench his hands to restrain himself. What name had she claimed for herself? "Erin. You mustn't touch me."

She drew her hand back. "Did I hurt you?"

"No," he rasped.

She immediately glanced down, as if she knew what was happening to him. Her eyes widened, and she jerked her gaze to his. A rosier hue flushed her cheeks, and he couldn't tell if his desire for her disturbed her or pleased her. It seemed to do both, which he didn't understand. Being in the mortal world was frustratingly different than anything he'd known as a spirit being.

"I think we need to get you help . . . uh . . . find a doctor or a clinic for you." She scrambled back from him, putting a cushioned barrier between them and the desire that had flared.

Jared leaned back in the seat and grimaced at the sharp edge of pain that grew stronger, the farther Erin withdrew from him. With that pain came a greater awareness of the sweet, heady scent of her blood and a dark hunger clamored inside of him. He gritted his teeth, pummeling the need with his warrior's steely will. Erin was safe for now, but he would have to leave—before he killed her. He didn't doubt that he would, for the hunger would grow as the Tsara's poison destroyed the good within him.

She was an Elan, and the Fallen fed upon the blood of the Elan.

He would soon walk with the Fallen.

Chapter Five

Erin SUCKED IN AIR and gripped the steering wheel. Her sensual awareness of Jared had been intensified by his obvious attraction to her. Even now that her brain waves were unscrambled and her knees had quit shaking, she still felt the punch. It had been unlike anything she'd ever felt before—one of those moments of attraction that she'd always thought to be pure fiction.

And it was. The sex-with-a-one-hell-of-a-tall-dark-stranger fantasy would never have any reality in her life. She was a slow kind of woman who really wanted to know a man well before she opened the bedroom door.

In her twenty-four years, she'd let one man all the way into the bedroom, so to speak. Others had gotten close to the bedroom door, even knocked and turned the handle a few times, but never all the way in. That one man had been an intern at the hospital where she'd done her clinical training. And a year later he'd waltzed out the bedroom door the minute his internship was up. He'd told her that he was breaking their engagement because *she* needed to have more experiences under her belt before she could really know what she wanted in life. She was also cluttering up his life with *reasons*; she never did anything just because she *wanted* to. Everything had to fit into her framework of what was right and wrong, and he wanted out of the box.

The next day he took a week-long cruise with two nurses in one cabin. After an angry, devastating week, she'd found a number of reasons why he wasn't necessary. Then she'd turned to Ben & Jerry's and hadn't found a reason to leave them yet.

Forget it. She needed to focus on what she had to do next. Get him to help, and move on. She turned the key, and the Tahoe cranked to life. The radio immediately blared, prompting her to wince and turn down the volume. Before she could, she caught the word Sno-Med, and her attention was riveted to the dashboard.

"Enrich your life with Sno-Med. We care. Come celebrate your Fourth of July Holiday at our Family Health Expo. Free health screening for the entire family. Free food. And free fun and games. This weekend only at the Appalachian Fair Grounds, located on State Road 44 just north of Powellsville."

That meant today and tomorrow. She shuddered. Just exactly what did Sno-Med extract from all of their free health screenings? She knew four people had paid in blood with their lives. Had they gone to a "free health screening" too? She had to find out as much as she could.

"What is it, Elan? What do you fear?"

Erin glanced in the rearview mirror, surprised that Jared, despite his own pain and injury, was so sensitive to her. She forced a grim smile. "Nothing. Just an ugly reminder of something very important that I have to do."

He didn't look satisfied with her answer, but didn't question her further.

Gunning the gas, she tugged her way out of the ruts her tires had dug in the soft earth and churned ahead. Everything appeared fractured through her cracked window, as if last night's events had skewed the world.

Several quick looks showed Jared sitting stiffly silent as she bumped along. His deep grimace was the only outward sign of the pain she knew he had to be in.

Squinting through the windshield, she located a log gate and made a beeline for it. As she shoved the Tahoe into park, she looked cautiously for signs of her bovine foes before opening her car door. "I'm going to unlock the gate," she told Jared, before slipping from the driver's seat.

With each step she took from the car, the fresh air

seemed to clear her head, making her roll her eyes at how attracted she'd been to Jared. Something about the guy had a way of scrambling a woman's internal GPS system, making her unsure of where in the hell she was and what she was doing—an effect she could ill afford right now. The sooner she found him help, the sooner she could figure out how to expose and bring down Dr. Cinatas.

The crude gate was simple enough. Unfortunately sturdy, too, a very thick log chained to a heavy post that could be opened two ways—either use a key on the padlock, or lift the log and chain over the post.

Erin glared at the sky. "Okay. If I can't have one thing go right, how about half of one instead? Can anyone hear me up there?"

Though she knew it was pointless, she tried to lift the log. It didn't move an inch. Digging into her pocket past yesterday's now-pulverized breakfast and lunch power bars, she pulled out from her kit of nursing essentials a pair of hemostats—tiny IV clamps with a fine point. Then, crouching down, she went to work on picking the padlock, pumping her mind with every Bond movie she'd seen.

Five minutes later she had visions of ramming through the gate with her SUV.

She felt Jared before she heard him. The heat pouring from him seeped all along her back and warmed her blood.

"What is it that you seek to do, Elan?"

She paused, turning to study him, his amulet, and his bandaged chest again, but still could not come up with a single plausible reason for his behavior and condition. Either she was becoming more lucid, or he was sounding more archaic, widening the gap between him and anything remotely normal.

He had remembered the yellow towel at least. He had it wrapped and tied about his waist like a hula skirt, with zero effect on his thought-scattering impact.

"Elan?"

"I'm trying to open the gate so that we can drive out of here."

He grunted. "I will do that." His cavemanlike tone implied that she should have asked him to take care of the problem long before.

Erin just rolled her eyes and stepped back. Once Mr. Macho found out how heavy—

With his good hand, Jared grasped the chain and lifted the log. He carried it across the road as if it were a bag of cotton candy.

She stared at him in shock.

He frowned at her. "Elan! Is this not what you wanted?"

"Yes." Erin stopped looking her "gift man" in his oh-so-sinful mouth and ran to the driver's seat. She jerked the Tahoe into drive, spinning her wheels against the incline for a moment before her car rumbled over the cattle grate and up to the road.

If she were in her right mind, she would just keep on going and put Jared and everything that happened last night and this morning literally out to pasture.

Instead, she stopped the car and got out to watch Jared reclose the gate. Though he handled the heavy log as if it weighed less than a pound, she could see the strain bulging the muscles of his arm, back, and legs. Who was this man?

She got out of the Tahoe and ushered him to the front passenger's seat.

"Buckle up." She slipped behind the steering wheel, belted herself, and popped the car into gear. The seatbelt alarm brought her to a stop. "You didn't buckle."

"How does one buckle, and why?"

"For safety. To help keep you alive if I crash." Where has this man been all of his life? Exasperated, Erin unbuckled and leaned across Jared, grabbing his seat belt.

He stayed her hand with his, and she met his stark blue gaze just inches from his face, able to see in minute detail all the rough nuances that made up the deadly whole—the silver starbursts in the center of his blue eyes, the contoured curve of his cheek, the sensual fullness of his mouth, and the sandpaper stubble of his beard, which already seemed longer than it had just a short time ago.

He took a deep breath, as if he were trying to inhale her. His nostrils flared, and his pupils dilated as his hand on hers tightened. He looked hungry. Very hungry.

"Keeping me alive may not be such a good thing," he said.

From the shadows filling his eyes, she knew that for some reason he meant it.

"Maybe for you," she said. "But not for me. I can't handle another death on my mind."

Jared released her hand and cupped her cheek in his palm.

"What is it?" His thumb brushed the underside of her bottom lip, stealing her breath. It was obvious that he found her more than desirable, as if he couldn't stop himself from touching her.

For a brief moment, she wished everything were different and the attraction simmering wouldn't have to be abandoned, would prove to be more than a dreamy mountain mist. As it was, they both had too many problems of their own.

"Nothing." Moving back, she pulled the seat belt across his chest and snapped him in, ignoring how the loss of his touch left a whispering regret inside her. He immediately shifted as if uncomfortable, and seemed to be glaring at the inside of her car. A quick glance assured her that the belt hit well below his burn, so she put her mind toward getting them out of there.

"Why these binds?" Jared said. "You've no freedom."

Erin glanced his way as she reached State Road 44, the road she'd taken the wild detour from last night. The road that the Appalachian Fair Grounds and the Sno-Med Family Health Expo was on, just a little bit north of where she was.

"Seat belts keep you safe," she told him.

After hesitating only a moment, she turned north toward Powellsville and the Appalachian Fair Grounds. It was also the way she'd come last night, and she wanted to see by daylight exactly where she'd been when everything had turned unreal. She could leave Jared in Powellsville in competent hands, and focus on Dr. Cinatas. Once she located a change of clothes, she could go to the Family Heath Expo and see a little of what Sno-Med was up to.

Somehow she also had to find a way to get into the Sno-Med Research and Development Center, which shouldn't be more than a hour's drive away in Arcadia, Tennessee.

Usually, the blood Dr. Cinatas used for the "cancer treatments" at the Sno-Med Clinic came via private jet from Arcadia. With free health expos, she had little doubt where he gleaned his blood donors from. Her big question was whether a trail of bodies lay behind the bags of blood. If there was, she'd find it.

"There is no freedom with these seat belts," Jared

declared. He shifted anxiously in the seat. "They harm you."

"Have you never been in a car before?" she asked as she reached the bend in the road where the creatures had hit her. She pulled to the shoulder for a good look and noticed a black Hummer parked on the opposite shoulder, just ahead. Two men, dressed in brand-new coveralls and shiny loaferlike shoes, were looking at something in the brush. They glanced up.

Erin's brain tingled first, and then her gut as a strange and frightening recognition struck her. She'd seen the men before, briefly, in New York, at the clinic Friday morning.

Somehow Cinatas or the king of Kassim's men had traced her.

"Oh, God." She slammed the gas pedal and death-gripped the steering wheel. Her tires spun. Gravel flew. And the back end of the Tahoe fishtailed as she hit the pavement like a rocketing stock car at Daytona.

The men, scrambling for their car, shot at her as she whizzed by. She saw their guns jerk and heard the pop of bullets hitting her car. They either missed or shot low, aiming for her tires, because no glass shattered.

She raced down the road, eyes searching for a turnoff. Nothing.

"We need to be free, Elan!"

"We need to go faster!" Erin pressed the gas to the floor as the Hummer rose in her rearview mirror like a stalking beast. The speed at which she flew through the mountain curves grew faster than she had the skill to maneuver. With minimal visibility through her cracked windshield, she skidded dangerously from one side of the road to the other. She was playing roulette with a head-on collision and had a gun at her back. Not good.

"We need to be free to hide, Elan, and that is something you cannot do when bound and trapped."

"What?" she asked, then groaned at the sight of another black Hummer, this one coming toward her, deliberately driving down the middle of the road, ready to play chicken or determined to make her into a Hummer sandwich.

"We must leave this vehicle, Elan." Jared voice grew louder, more urgent. "It is the only way to escape. Take the turn up ahead."

"The sign says it's a dead end. That means it goes nowhere."

"Trust me. We must."

"We can't. It's suicide." Nobody in their right mind would take a dead-end road while being chased by men with guns. It went totally against Erin's every instinct to abandon her protective, fast-moving car for her less-than-stellar ability to run. And at least the car's metal provided some protection from bullets.

"Do it. Trust me," Jared urged.

Erin swung as wide as she dared, jerking the wheel

to the right, instantly regretting her decision. She left the highway, missing the dead-end dirt road completely, and went airborne as the roadside gave way to a twenty-foot drop. They flew over part of a field, slamming into a faded Lucky Strike cigarette ad painted on the roof of a barn. The rotting wood did little to stop their momentum as they plowed into bales of hay. The seat belt burned a stripe across her neck, and she smashed into a suffocating air bag. A stale, powdery grit filtered into her mouth as the bag abraded her cheek and sent a sharper pain stabbing through her temple.

She had time to draw one breath before Jared jerked the air bag from her face as he ripped it from its anchor in the steering column, sending a deafening whoosh of air into her face. Blinking against her dry eyes, she registered the fact that they'd survived—for the moment. Her car sat at a precarious angle, as if the rear of it had broken through the floor of the loft.

It wouldn't take the men with guns long to reach them, and it would take even less time for her car to crash all the way through the barn loft, injuring them more. She unsnapped her seat belt but couldn't get her car door open. It was wedged tight against the loft's floor.

Jared ripped his belt from the seat, shredding material and scattering foam. The car rocked precariously. "We must hurry, Elan."

She tried looking for her purse while Jared shoved the passenger door open, but she couldn't find it and had to leave without it. Within a minute of the crash, he'd pulled her up through the dry, prickly hay and down from the loft. The emptiness of the stale, musty barn gave her the impression that it hadn't been used in years, which meant the likelihood of finding help close by wasn't very good.

Footsteps pounded the ground, and shouting voices reached her ears. "They're in the barn. Get the girl alive and eliminate whoever she is with."

At the barn doors, Erin groaned in dread. Woods skirted the edge of the field they faced, too far away for them to make it without being seen. Any second the men would come around the side of the barn, and Jared would be dead—and she'd be worse than dead. She searched for a place to hide, a weapon, anything to save them. "They'll shoot before we're halfway. We should have played chicken with the Hummer."

"Trust me, Elan," Jared said. He scooped her up, giving her no choice but to wrap her arm over his right shoulder as he ran.

"Are you crazy? Put me down. You're injured. We can move faster if—" She didn't get to finish her sentence. The speed he gained stole her breath and her ability to think. The world passed in a semi-blur. She was vaguely aware of the shouts of men, of their pursuit, and of shots fired. She was more aware of every breath and movement of the man holding her. His muscles strained beneath her touch; the silk of his hair flowed against her arm; and the heat of his skin seeped into hers. He flew faster than the wind, totally unhindered by any human limitations, a comforting and yet extremely disturbing thought considering she was disappearing into the forest, with him. She had nothing to protect herself with or to identify her, and she wondered just exactly where this whole wild escape was going to lead.

Jared rushed through the woods, weaving between branches and brush, breathing in the sweet scents of Elan blood, pine, earth, and the freedom of the air he'd always known as a spirit. The tension that had started clawing at him when the woman bound him in the car had increased the moment he'd sensed the predatory nature of the men across the road.

With no ability to control his movements or direction, he'd felt trapped within the mortal vehicle, and hadn't liked the feeling at all. With the Elan in his arms, taking away the pain of the Tsara's poison, he could think more clearly. Now he had power and choice on his side.

Jared ran as quickly and as far along the mountains as he could. He went deep into the forest where the odors of mortals dwindled to almost nothing beneath the scent of the creatures in the wild. He was meant to run in a place like this, free. It all felt so right.

But instead of keeping pace with the wind, as was his custom, his steps began to slow. A thundering roar filled his ears, no amount of air he breathed fed his need of it, and he could no longer hold the Elan in his arms. On an outcropping of rock where a spring trickled from the heart of the mortal ground, Jared came to a halt, shocked that he was unable to take another step. He eased to his knees and set the Elan down. Dark clouds kept encroaching on his vision, and he wavered, unable to accept the weakness stealing over him. Where was his strength? Why was he so weak?

"Elan, I must . . ."

"Rest, and you must call me Erin," she said, grabbing his arm, urging him to sit.

"Erin, then," he whispered.

She touched his cheek. "My God, are you burning with a higher fever or overheated from running? You should have put me down once we were in the woods. I tried to tell you, but it was like you never even heard me."

He hadn't. Something primal had taken him over in the forest. Even now in exhaustion, he still felt a strange urge inside to run free and wild. He drew in another deep breath and lay back upon the mortal ground.

She dipped her hand into the spring and placed her

palm on his brow, then repeated the motion, cooling his neck and cheeks as well. A droplet of water slid to his lips. He tasted the cool wetness with the tip of his tongue. It felt good.

He hadn't meant to allow more touching between them, hadn't meant to use her in that way, but the edge inside him needed her to soothe it. Her touch, her care, reached into him, and he felt a part of him grasp hold of that and pull it closer.

"You must be thirsty," she said softly. "Here." She brought more water to him with her cupped hand, and he drank, marveling at the new sensations of taste, and the feel and flavor of water. He could sense the earth and life and purity within it. Closing his eyes, he wondered again what the sweetness of her blood would taste like. Then he inwardly cringed, for to have that thought during this moment seemed like a clear gauge of how quickly the Tsara's poison was spreading inside him.

They'd escaped their mortal pursuers, but the greater danger lay within him. There was no way to stop his growing thirst for Elan's blood, and the only thing that helped him contain that need was her touch. Yet how could he accept that weakness in himself? He couldn't.

Chapter Six

Erin woke with a start. A quick glance at her watch told her she'd done more than doze just a few minutes. After Jared had closed his eyes to rest, she'd taken time to attend to a few personal matters in the bushes and refreshed herself with the cool spring water before resting herself. She felt almost human now, and a little safe. The forest cocooned them from the outside world, offering her a brief moment before having to sift through the implications of Dr. Cinatas's Hummer squad. That he'd found her so quickly was chilling.

Two hours had now passed since Jared had fallen into a fevered sleep, darkly mumbling about Aragon, being damned, and Elan blood. His dreams must have skirted nightmares. Just as her life was doing.

The sky mirrored his troubled thoughts, for gray clouds encroached on the brightness of the day, deepening the shadows beneath the canopy of trees covering them. Jared still felt overly hot to her, and she prayed the burn on his shoulder wasn't becoming infected. They needed a doctor and medicine for him. And given her state and headache, she needed one, too.

She'd always written off the tale of the Greek messenger who'd run from Marathon to Athens and then died as being impossible. But after what Jared had done, she could readily see it happening. Jared had done the impossible, right? Who was he?

She sat propped against a boulder, her back and legs and everything in between tinglingly numb, but she didn't want to move, didn't want to disturb the man who slept with his head cradled in her lap. She pressed her palm to his forehead, wishing there was more she could do for him than try to cool the heat of his fever.

She dipped her hand into the trickle of cool mountain water and bathed his face again, as before, feeling the sharp angles of his warriorlike features and the roughness of the stubble darkening his jaw. He was a raw, elemental male whose sensual features beckoned exploration.

Before she could give in to the temptation of touching his mouth to feel the chiseled softness of his full lips and the warmth of his breath, she directed her attention to smoothing the dark strands of hair back from his face. Somehow, her fingers found themselves threaded through its long silkiness and touching the streak of silver that stood in stark contrast to the raven's wing black. More than just a random chance of coloring, the silver seemed to mark him as being special, different. Her gaze, then her fingers, drifted to the amulet resting on his chest.

An odd twelve-point star had been stamped into the goldlike metal, and her fingers tingled as she touched it, as if energy was seeping into her from it. The sunlight filtering through the leaves of the full oaks and towering pines and poplars cast iridescent light over its surface. The metal was as different and unique as the man.

She'd always lived her life in an orderly way, always having to have a reason for anything she did, or she didn't do it. If there wasn't a purpose for an object in her life, she gave it away. Anything that happened had to have a cause and effect that made sense. Reason had ruled.

But there was no reason in murder. Erin shuddered, and Jared's eyes sprang open, as if her thoughts had gone directly to him. She pulled her fingers back from the amulet.

"What is wrong?" he asked, leaping up. He'd moved quickly, as if he shouldn't have been resting. After a sharp glance around, he set his probing gaze on her. "Why do these predators seek to harm you, and why do you fear them even now in this quiet place?"

He confused her. At times she got such a sense of strength and purpose and lucid intelligence from him that lay at odds with the moments of delusional behavior. She didn't know what to believe, but she did worry about him. He didn't need her problems, yet he had a right to know who had been gunning for him and why. He'd put himself at risk to help her.

She met his clear gaze. "I expected them to kill me on sight. To eliminate me before I had a chance to tell about the murders that I'm sure the doctor I work for committed. I can't tell you why they want me alive." She closed her eyes, reliving yesterday morning.

"You must tell me more, or I cannot help. Who is this enemy you battle?"

His fierce tone brought her eyes open to study him. He'd returned to the rock and now sat next to her. The masculine angles of his features had sharpened to a harsh edge, accentuating instantly his warrior-worthy alertness. She could easily see him wielding a sword in battle, fluid, graceful, powerful. Deadly.

"I work at Sno-Med, a clinic where Dr. Cinatas administers specialized blood transfusions to cancer patients. I was specifically hired to take care of the clinic's more affluent clients and worked odd hours. This weekend, I was to give four transfusions to Ashodan ben Shashur, the current king of Kassim. But things were different than before, and—"

"I don't understand. What do you mean by different?"

She dug her teeth into her lip. She'd been deliberately vague because she didn't have any real reason why every thing had seemed different from the moment she'd entered the clinic that morning. She just knew that it had. "It was my first day back to work after a week off to recover."

"Recover? Recover what?"

She gave Jared another assessing glance, wondering where his delusions were when she wanted them. He was asking things that were hard to explain.

"Trust me." He set his hand over hers. Its warmth, the alluring blue of his gaze, and the strength in them both touched her. She hadn't really told anyone yet. And the need to let it all out surged through her. She wanted to tell a stranger who wouldn't judge her, or even question her like her family or a friend might. They'd soon go their separate ways, and she'd move forward in her quest to expose Dr. Cinatas.

Still, her hand fisted beneath his. "Last week I nearly died from an allergic reaction, and it's been difficult getting back to normal ever since. My experience is hard to explain." She sucked in air and plunged on. "You see, I could see them resuscitating me from above, where I hovered in the cold shadows. Something powerful pulled at me, urging me toward a bright light, and as I drew closer, the light became hotter and . . . and . . . it was almost euphoric."

She glanced at him, looking for disbelief, but only found quiet acceptance in his gaze. "I didn't want to turn from the warm light, but a sharp pain ripped through me, and I was back on the stretcher being resuscitated, trying to breathe, trying to live."

"What happened after?" he asked, as if he already knew there was more to come.

"You're going to think this is strange, but ever since then I've gotten these strange feelings, a tingling in my scalp, my spine, a sinking feeling in my stomach. Feelings that make me act without a clear reason. Like leaving my apartment five minutes late because I sensed my mother would call, and she did, or calling the police because a stranger outside my apartment building gave me bad vibes. He ended up being on the FBI's wanted list."

Jared watched her intently. He didn't show a hint of surprise over what she'd said. A week ago, if she'd been listening to this story, she'd have come up with reasons for the experiences, like she'd only imagined what happened when she'd been resuscitated. She'd heard out-of-body stories before, and her mind conveniently filled in the blanks. Or that her mother had told her that she would call, and Erin had just forgotten it. Or that the man had acted strange, and that's why she'd called the police.

Jared didn't appear to be scrambling to rationalize what she'd told him. He seemed to be accepting her story wholeheartedly as the truth.

"That is how things were different?" he asked. "When you went into the clinic, you had strange feelings that were urging you to act?"

She nodded, feeling more and more of herself open to him. "I'd been on edge and tense all week. That worsened the minute I walked in the door. I brushed it off at first. But instead of settling down as I slipped into my routine, my discomfort grew. Then when I met the king of Kassim and prepped him for his blood transfusion, I sensed something very dark about the man, very wrong. The way he looked at me, as if I were the last meal on earth, unnerved me. I had to get away from him and clear my head. So when I needed more morphine than what I had in the syringe, I went downstairs to the pharmacy/lab to get another vial instead of calling for it to be sent up as I usually do. That's where I found the bodies and where Dr. Cinatas found me trying to call for help."

Everything flashed before her eyes.

Even before walking across the icy, off-limits lab, she knew they were dead, a man, a woman, and two teenage girls. As she felt for a nonexistent pulse, touching their icy, lifeless skin, her panicked breaths frosted in the air and her gut wrenched with dread. They'd been strapped to stretchers and drained of their blood. The bags still hung on the hooks above them, tagged for the Ashodan ben Shashur, the king of Kassim.

She turned from the bodies, her heart beating faster as her mind raced over what to do. Anger churned in her stomach. Grappling with the cold, hard evidence of four murdered people, she dug out her cell phone from her packed pockets, dialing 911.

"I wouldn't do that if I were you," Dr. Cinatas said, suddenly stepping to her side.

She bit back a scream at his sudden appearance and the assault his presence made on her new sensitivity.

Cinatas smiled smoothly, full of charm as usual, but this time she could see a darkness in him, as if the devil himself hid beneath his deep blue Armani. He glanced at the bodies behind her.

"Talking can be fatal, you know." Lashing out, he grabbed her, locking his surgical-gloved hand around her wrist like a vise. Snapping her hand down against the side of the counter, he sent her cell phone flying to the floor. Pain shot up her arm. He ground her phone into pieces beneath the heel of his Italian leather shoe. Then he bent her wrist painfully back, making her gasp. "You don't want to die, do you, Erin?"

Throat too constricted to speak, she shook her head, trying to think.

"Good. Don't ever think I won't kill you, because I will." His silver eyes glittered with amusement as he smiled gently, angelically. "And it would be such a waste to contact the authorities. No one will ever believe you," he whispered. "Have you thought of that, my little golden Erin?"

He slid a latex-sheathed nail up her arm, making her skin crawl. "The ramblings of a backwoods hick nurse against the word of a respected doctor with a miracle cure for cancer? You're smarter than that."

Erin jerked on her wrist, but he tightened his hold.

"What are you doing here? Why kill for blood?" she demanded.

"They didn't want to do what they were told to do. A shame, isn't it? Will you be a good girl and serve the Order, or will you die? Either way your blood will benefit me."

"Do what?" Erin asked, as she inched her other hand toward her pocket. "This?" she said, pulling a syringe of morphine from her pocket, aiming for his heart as she popped the cap off with her thumbnail. He feinted to the side. She shifted her direction, stabbing him at the juncture of his neck and shoulder and shoving the plunger home.

"You bitch," he yelled, grabbing for her, catching her hair.

She jerked against his hold, and he pulled harder. Tears sprang to her eyes. She kicked out, trying to hit his groin as she struggled, but only managing to strike his knee. The blow sent him off balance enough to let her break free.

Cinatas screamed, bringing one of the king of Kassim's guards dashing into the lab with his gun raised. Erin rounded a stretcher and rammed the guard in the groin just as he lifted the gun her way.

He fell forward, splattering the wall with bullets on his way down. Glass shattered. A computer screen exploded and wood splintered as bullets plowed into a desk, then ricocheted off the floor. Before the guard could recover, Erin ran. She hit the emergency exit with bullets pinging the steel door. Blaring alarms followed her dash into the throng of people moving on the street. Within minutes, *she reached her navy Tahoe, parked in a metered spot, and punched in her keyless entry code.*

"I left the city, but rather than running away and hiding, I'm determined to bring him down. I hoped that by going immediately to the Sno-Med Research and Development Center, I'd find out what he's up to. Cinatas said he'd killed them because they didn't do what they were told to do, so he has to have done something that others will die to keep from doing. And if he has murdered before, I hope I'll find proof to expose him." During the telling of the story, her fist had opened, and her palm was now pressed to his. He clasped her hand tightly.

"You must always trust your instincts, Erin. They have been heightened for a reason. And this predator may know you're near, but I promise, he won't reach you. Ever," Jared vowed. The passion in his voice was what miracles were made of, and it wrapped reassuringly around her. She could almost believe it possible that she could bring Cinatas down and still live.

Thunder rumbled deep and loud, jerking Erin from her thoughts. She shot her gaze toward the sky and gasped. A dark, angry storm was plowing at them with the speed and power of a freight train.

Jared leaped to his feet, pulling her up. "Come. We need shelter."

Before she could speak, the world exploded as a bolt of lightning ripped across the darkening sky and struck a sprawling oak tree ten feet away. The tree burst into flames, sparks of fire spewing up like a fireworks finale.

Erin felt as if she had taken a direct hit. Her breath caught, and her heart thumped hard, then raced. Goose bumps spread all over her body.

Jared pulled her in the opposite direction. Another bolt of lighting slammed into the ground even closer, this time to the right of them. The ground shook. Static electricity charged the air to an explosive level, lifting her hair and making her scalp tingle. She felt extremely strange, as if more was happening in the world around her than she could see.

"You'll not harm her!" Jared shouted as he led her to the left. A determined, deadly anger sharpened his voice.

With every step, the sky darkened. Black-green clouds roiled over the mountain, almost turning the day into night. She'd never seen such a ferocious storm, or one that advanced so quickly.

Wind whipped with a sharp bite, and heavy drops of rain fell with stinging force that paled against the following hail. The only thing saving them from being pummeled badly as she and Jared ran through the forest was the thick canopy of tree branches and leaves.

A loud roar of thunder shook the very marrow of Erin's blood. She cried out and slid to a halt. As Jared pulled her closer to him, she glanced up at the sky. Through the rain and ice she saw a battle between unbelievable nightmarish creatures, ghoulish dull gray shells of beings with twisted features brutally fighting ethereal warriors of golden light on glittering winged horses. The falling rain was the iridescent blood pouring from the wounded and dead of the golden light beings; the hail, pieces of their beings, shredded in the battle, pelting the ground. The ghoulish warriors evaporated into gray clouds when struck by the golden warriors.

She opened her mouth to speak, but couldn't utter a word.

"We must keep moving. It's not safe," Jared said, urging her forward. "There's a cave with warmth just ahead."

Erin pulled back and blinked, and the battling creatures disappeared, leaving only angry clouds, drenching rain, and punishing hail whipped by a roaring wind. Then a bolt of lightning cut across the sky, coming right at her.

"Erin!" Jared shouted.

She imagined it was like staring at a bullet about to hit her right between the eyes. Jared plowed into her, knocking her to the ground, covering her body with his body. The lightning zinged and struck the earth right next to them. She screamed as pain ripped through her, and she shuddered into a dark abyss.

Chapter Seven

RELIEVED TO ESCAPE the confines of Shashur's inflated ego for at least a few minutes, Cinatas cursed as he stepped from the white-gold Hummer limo into the miserable rain. He turned up his Burberry collar against the draft and adjusted the brim of his hat to see. Storms had delayed his flight from New York to the Tri-City Airport and grounded his helicopter, making the trip an exercise in torture.

Erin Morgan was turning into a thorn in his side, and his men were proving to be incompetent fools. They had so many Hummers and trucks parked on the side of the road that Cinatas had to walk a quarter mile upon the greasy filth of road to reach the gathered men. Carrying a red pocketbook, Manolo, his security chief, parted from the crowd and met him partway.

"Tell me, Manolo. If you see a horde of flies all in

one spot, do you pass by without a second look, or do you glance to find out if they're on a pile of shit or corpse?"

"Enough said, sir. Forgive me, I got caught up in trying to figure out what is wrong with every bloodhound we called in that I hadn't realized we'd gathered such a crowd." He held out the red purse. "Erin Morgan won't get far without this."

"Put it in the limo after we've spoken," Cinatas said, after a long stare. He barely restrained himself from wrapping the purse straps around Manolo's throat. Whether it was prized information or not, walking around with a handbag killed image. "What's wrong with the bloodhounds? I expected you'd have her by now. They can't have gotten far."

"We've two action teams scouting the woods, but haven't turned up any sign of them so far. By all reports, the man lit out of here at a fast clip, carrying the woman. I'm assuming she was injured in the crash. So he couldn't have gone far. We think they've found a cave to hole up in. But every damned hound that takes a whiff of the car goes whimpering into a corner and won't budge."

"Really," Cinatas said, thinking fast and going with his instinct. He glanced back, assuring himself that Shashur was still out of the way. "Send the hounds home. I don't want to call attention to the problem. Tell everyone the hounds couldn't pick up the trail."

The only time Cinatas had seen dogs behave like that was in Pathos's wake. Was it possible that another entity just as powerful as Pathos had appeared? Cinatas's pulse kicked up a notch at the pleasing possibility. "Where's her car? We need to eliminate it."

"Up in the hayloft of the barn. You'll need a crane to get it out. We're still not sure why the loft hasn't collapsed. Must be the oak beams supporting it."

"Remove the license plates. Clear everyone out and torch the barn. As far as the world is concerned, Erin Morgan has disappeared. Pull out all resources necessary, but I want them found before anyone else sees them. And I want them both alive."

"Consider it done. We've one other problem."

"What?"

"There's a dead man on the side of the road where Morgan's tracking device was knocked off."

"Does he have anything to do with her or us?"

"Not that we know."

"Then leave him where he can be easily found, and we'll see what develops. With a corpse to investigate, the locals aren't going to be too concerned about an old barn burning down." Disgusted but pleased, Cinatas returned to the limo. Careful not to contaminate the alabaster interior with his shoes, he shed them on the street. Then, making certain water droplets from his coat splattered Shashur, he ditched his coat and hat on the empty seat across from him.

"Well?" Shashur said.

"Nothing. Seems as if Erin Morgan has managed to escape again."

"Only until nightfall. The damned are so much more competent than you mortals."

Cinatas smiled, seeing in his mind's eye Shashur on his knees, begging for life. He could barely wait for the day.

A monkish chant—or was it more of a wolf's low cry?—called to Erin, luring her from the pleasure she sought to fly away to. She felt weird, warm in some places and oddly cold and wet in others. Part of her ached like a mega flu bug had taken a bite out of her hide—make that several chunks—and part of her felt too pleasant to be real. Her head throbbed with a vengeance again, and an all-over heaviness weighed upon her, as did a worrying sense that she needed to do something very important. Yet she couldn't move. She wasn't even sure she wanted to try. She'd seen the other-worldly light again. But this time it had been brighter, more beautiful, and so soothingly welcoming that she hadn't been aware of anything else.

"Erin." The deep voice vibrated through her, calling to her. "Erin."

She drew a breath and had the oddest sensation that she hadn't been breathing. Her heart squeezed painfully, then pounded as if it had beats to make up for. Her thoughts were like thick clouds—obscurely dense from a distance and disappearing into a wispy mist when she grasped for one.

"You've returned to me." Even though it was almost a whisper, the passion filling his voice shook her. "I'm forsaken, but not yet damned."

Jared! her mind shouted. Memory sent her eyes fluttering open to meet his intense gaze, his face mere inches from hers in a dimly lit place. He held her cradled in his arms, her head resting against his right shoulder as he leaned over her, his full mouth grim and his brow furrowed with deep concern. Although they were both soaked, heat radiated from him, warming her chilled body. He smelled of rain and the antiseptic that she'd applied to his burn before bandaging it.

The storm raged, but no rain fell on them, telling her he'd found shelter.

Her insides trembled and her nerves tingled, as if awakening from numbness to an oversensitized level of awareness. She groaned, immediately recalling the creatures battling in the heavens, the irridescent blood that had rained from the supernatural battle, the lightning, and then the pain.

This time, Jared had moved faster than lightning itself to save her from a direct hit. The agony that had ripped through her after the bolt hit the ground had to have been electricity. Too many weird things were happening, and more and more, Jared was a part of them in some strange way rather than an accidental encounter.

Throat dry and words slurring, she rasped her questions. "What happened? Who and what were those fighting creatures in the sky? Who are you? How did you move faster than lightning?"

His eyes widened in an expression that said, *You've seen something you shouldn't*, not *What in the hell are you talking about?*

Move over X-Files, *there's a new weird in town.* And she wasn't going to take it lying down. She tried to sit up, but dizziness washed over her as her head throbbed almost unbearably. She groaned.

"You're hurt."

"My head. This past week I've had headaches that even Ben & Jerry's triple raspberry fudge can't fix, nor any other flavor. Believe me, I have the pharmacy bill and the added pounds to prove it."

"Where?"

"Where what?" If he couldn't see where the added pounds were, she wasn't going to point them out.

"Where does your head hurt?"

"All over, but here is where I hurt the most." She touched her eyes, then her temples, careful to avoid the cut on her left one. The skin there was swollen and tender.

Jared brushed Erin's hands aside and placed his palms against her head, pressing as he closed his eyes to focus his being on hers. Her hair was damp, but still soft, as was her skin. And even though he held her in his arms, even though he knew he'd won against the darkness that had tried to steal her from this life, it wasn't enough. He wanted more than just to hold her. He wanted to know all of those things that his desire for her urged him to explore.

Inside, he felt as if he was still out in the storm, knowing she was about to be struck by a lightning bolt from Heldon's Fallen Army. His heart still thundered, and his stomach twisted and turned like a twig being battered by the wind. He'd been standing near her and had almost failed to protect her.

Was there a reason he'd been condemned instead of being executed? Why was it that he'd been the Blood Hunter to stop the Tsara from infecting her with Heldon's poison?

He almost wondered if Logos had some reason, some plan, in the events that had unfolded. No other mortal had ever seen him before, but Erin saw him in his Blood Hunter's cloak last night. Her horrified expression had distracted him in his fight with the Tsara. Meeting her golden gaze through the cracked windshield had been the first time he'd ever looked a mortal in the eye, and he'd been unprepared for the depth of her soul. That one look had cost him his own.

Was there one last task he was needed for? It seemed so. And protecting Erin for as long as he could was a part of that. As a Shadowman, he'd been bound within the spirit realm, as were all of the Guardian Forces, except a select few who walked the mortal ground to fight the Vladarians. Maybe Logos needed a Blood Hunter made mortal to be at Erin's side against the predator she faced.

Jared didn't believe for a moment that Aragon would be so foolish to chance a Blood Hunter's soul on a possibility of redemption. Not after what happened to Pathos. Not after what Pathos had done in his Blood Hunter's cloak to mortals before descending into Heldon's lair. The brutality of Pathos's werewolf attacks still haunted the mortal world today, though a thousand years had passed. And Pathos's leadership in the Vladarian Order had completely warped Logos's truth on Earth, bringing much darkness to the world.

Jared couldn't let that happen to him. Already the Tsara's poison grew stronger. Every breath he drew served as a growing reminder of the sweet purity of Erin's Elan blood and sharpened his need. He had never understood how Pathos had gone from protecting a being to tearing one apart in the twinkle of time. A part of him, still small but rapidly growing, now understood with a sickening clarity.

Holding Erin close to him helped ease that hunger, but also fed another. She never failed to cause changes to his fleshly form with her nearness. His desire to meld his mortal body to hers was growing faster, becoming stronger than his hunger for her blood.

He'd never bound his spirit with another, and as much as he wanted to experience a mortal melding with Erin, experience all that he'd never known and now craved, he couldn't afford it. Only unbound spirits made effective warriors, and he needed his warrior strength to fight the Tsara's poison as long as possible.

But how could he stay strong when her very nearness made him weak, made him crave intimacy? He closed his eyes and tried to call upon everything good that yet remained in his spirit to help her. He felt the throbbing ache in her head and eased it. He felt the exhaustion weighing heavily upon her body and strengthened her. He felt the fear and the worry in her spirit and sent his comfort around her. Then something else deep within her called to him, and he sent his mind deeper into her spirit. There he found a very lonely part of her that yearned for the passion of another. That yearning sent his blood surging, hardening his desire for her to an excruciating point.

In his mind he saw himself melding his lips to the tender fullness of her lips and delving into the passionate warmth of her mouth. He felt his hands exploring the soft curves of her feminine flesh, feasting upon the sensations of exploring her body with all of his. Then he saw himself driving all of his hard desire into the depths of her, totally melding his spirit to hers in a life-generating explosion of pleasure. He groaned deeply at the fire coursing through him. He opened his eyes and gazed into Erin's. She was staring at him, her golden eyes dark with desire. Her lips were parted as if waiting for his.

He groaned again, unable to deny himself just once the feel of her lips upon his. Sliding his hands from her temple to cup her cheeks in his palms, he bent his head toward hers and pressed his mouth to hers. Instead of leaning into him and opening to his caress as he knew she desperately wanted, she pushed against his chest.

"How did you do that?" she whispered. "How did you take away the pain? How did you warm me inside? It was as if you were there inside me, and we were . . ."

He sighed, dropping his hands, thankful that she'd called his warrior's spirit back from the ledge that would have only weakened him more. "Spirits made mortal have the strength and abilities that mortals have slowly lost over the ages."

Erin shook her head, trying to figure out what had just happened between her and this strange man. He'd taken away her pain like some miracle healer. She'd felt the energy of him inside her, as if by his touch he'd oozed part of himself into her mind . . . and further. She felt as if he'd made love to her, kissed her, touched her, buried himself so hot and deep inside her that even now she quivered from the experience.

Careful not to injure his bandaged shoulder, Erin pushed herself up from Jared's arms to crouch on the ground next to him, at eye level with him. For the first time, she was able to see that they were in a small cave, just deep enough to protect them from the storm and shallow enough to enable them to catch a little light from the fading day. A few feet away, water steadily dripped from a stalactite into a pool about the size of large mixing bowl before disappearing into the rock. After taking her surroundings in, she turned back to Jared for answers.

"Who and what are you, Jared Hunter? What happened out there in the storm? What just happened now?"

He leaned toward her and said, "You must seek cover when you see a storm brewing. You are in more danger than ever before during a storm."

"What do you mean more than before?"

"Your experiences with the spirit world when near death have weakened your protective aura. You are also in an area where spirit barrier has been thinned by centuries of worship from the ancients. That makes you especially vulnerable."

"Huh?" She got the danger part, but the rest? "In danger from what? Those creatures in the sky? No," she said, forcing herself up on rubbery legs to stand. "I did not just ask that. What I saw wasn't real. I had to have suffered a headache-induced hallucination." She threw her hands up and paced the short distance across the cave. "This whole day hasn't been real. Yesterday and last night did not happen. I am not in a cave right now with a miracle man talking about personal auras and spirit barriers." And she hadn't just had telepathic sex with him either.

Hell, the world had gone mad, and her scalp tingled with what seemed like a permanent itch.

She was vaguely beginning to identify with Alice in *Through the Looking Glass,* even down to the rabbit hole she was now in. Except she wasn't with a mad hatter or a racing rabbit; she had a tall, dark fantasy man wearing a yellow towel kilt that barely masked his continued interest in her, and who, if her thoughts could be trusted, was capable of making love via telepathic airwaves. In some ways she still felt as if he were inside her . . . her mind, that is. The rest of her felt as solid as Jell-O. Icy drops of water from the wet hem of her dress dripped down her legs, making her shudder. She desperately wanted a hot bath and a bed. Or better yet, she wanted to burrow back into his embrace, against his heat, and have that sensual experience she had to have imagined. She was certifiable to even have a thought like *that* at this moment. And Jared wasn't doing much to help her keep her balance either. She glared at him, wondering again what to think about him. He stood facing her, a pained expression on his face.

Jared clenched his fist as frustration built within him. Her scoffing sarcasm pained him in a way no warrior should ever feel vulnerable to. Something had changed between them since he searched her spirit and mind with his. He didn't feel it until she pulled away from him and stretched the bond that seemed to have fused between their spirits. He shook his head and rolled his shoulders, trying to shrug off the connection to her that pulled on him. It made a part of him want to run back into the forest just to feel the wind rushing upon his skin, while part of him wanted to deepen that bond.

Not only did his own reaction to this bond confuse him, but hers did as well. If she had wanted something so much inside of her, why had she pulled away from him? It wasn't as if she had to worry about her warrior's strength. It didn't make sense, and he couldn't decide if she feared herself or feared him. Whatever the cause, he knew it was essential to build a greater trust between them. It was too important. Not trusting him could cost her life.

Yet, how could he reach her? The urge to wrap his arms around her and hold her close to him was almost as overwhelming as his desire, but he sensed she would only pull away. He had to reach her another way. He wondered if telling her more about the spirit world he'd come from would help her to understand. Even though she kept rejecting the truth, she was still aware of it on some level.

Before he'd attacked the Tsara, he'd sensed something more potent about Erin's blood. The Elan were special, but Erin was even more so, though he didn't know why. She'd also seen the Fallen Army warring with the Shadowmen. That was something else that set her apart from others. Most mortals were blissfully ignorant of the horror in the spirit world that surrounded them—even the Elan didn't know. There were some mortals, Elan and others, who did sense the spirit world, and on very rare occasion got a glimpse of it. They never forgot what they saw, and often told others of it, too.

With Erin's personal protective aura compromised by her near-death experience, crossing the spirit barrier from the realm of the damned would be as easy as gliding through a cloud. And if that was the only danger she faced, the Blood Hunters would be there to protect her. But Erin's main danger was from the mortal predator, this doctor for whom she worked. A man who might be more than just a murderer in the mortal realm. Any time blood was involved, Jared immediately thought of the Vladarians, and this doctor had Jared wondering strongly if there was a connection.

Jared decided to be as truthful and direct as he

could. Honesty and acceptance were the pathway to trust. "You do not trust me, Erin. Why?"

Erin turned, walked to the edge of the cave, and faced the falling rain. "It isn't a matter of trust, Jared. It is a matter of reason."

He clenched his jaw at the sharpening of the pain inside him. He could not escape the fact that her nearness eased the effects of the Tsara's poison; the farther she moved away from him, the harder the Tsara's poison hit. But it would seem more than physical distance between them caused this to happen. An emotional distancing had the same effect. And this was new, as if the bond he'd forged by ministering to her had made this happen.

If he told her more of the spirit world, would she only withdrawal further? And how much should he—or could he—tell her about a world she could do little more than have nightmares over?

Stepping behind her, he set his hands on her shoulders and eased her against him. "Can you not see that I will do all within my power to protect you, Erin?"

Erin closed her eyes as Jared's heat and the hard contours of his body pressed against her back. She mentally pushed against the sensations stealing through her. He was in her mind, and she could feel his sensual caress deep within her.

He's delusional, a part of her shouted.

A deeper part of her shouted back, *He's laid his life*

on the line for you. And he is different in ways you can't explain. He healed you.

"Can't you see that?" he asked, more urgent that before.

"Yes," she whispered. "But—"

"No. There is only this. It is the most important."

He sounded like nothing else mattered, but it did.

She turned to him. "Who are you?"

He stared deeply at her, his gaze growing more and more desolate. "I don't know who I am anymore, Erin. I know what I am. I am damned, poisoned within my soul. Fallen."

That he'd reverted back to delusion brought stinging tears to her eyes. She set her hand on his shoulder, feeling the vibrancy of him as she tried earnestly to get him to understand. "Jared, we are all that in some ways. No one is perfect."

"You don't understand, Erin. I was a Blood Hunter. They are an elite band of the Shadowmen warriors, part of Logos's Guardian Forces. You saw a skirmish between the Guardian Forces and Heldon's Fallen Army during the storm."

Jared was even more delusional than she thought. More tears burned her eyes. She'd never felt as compelled to help anyone as much as she wanted to help Jared. "What does all that mean, Jared? What exactly does a Blood Hunter do?"

"There are things that feed upon Elan blood. A

Blood Hunter does whatever he can to stop that from happening."

Erin's heart squeezed painfully. How could she help him? She had to lead him away from his illness, show him that he didn't need to make up stories.

She forced a smile to her face. "Speaking of eating, I have some power bars, and I'm starving. Aren't you hungry?"

He inhaled deeply and looked at her, appearing suddenly ravenous. "Can't you see how important what I said is?" he asked. "Don't you want to know what feeds on Elan blood, Erin?"

Jared's tone and the intensity of want in his eyes sent a shiver running through Erin. She didn't suppose the nameless things he spoke of fed on oats and honey. But responding to his question would only feed his delusions, reinforcing thoughts that she felt compelled to pull him away from.

Why did he need such fantasies to bolster his importance? He was such a strong, dynamic man. What had happened to him, what had been done to him, to cripple him so? Did it have anything to do with the burn on his chest? To conquer the beast in his mind, maybe she would have to play the game a little until he realized he didn't need his delusions.

"Yes," she said. "I'm sorry. I do see that it is important. I just thought that you could tell me what I need to know while we eat."

He drew his finger down her cheek until its tip nestled on the pulse point of her neck. "No forgiveness needed. But you do have to understand there is more to the world than you know. Just as there is more to life than this small cave, there are greater realms outside the mortal world." His clear blue gaze searched hers with such reason that for the first time a tiny question burrowed into her mind.

What if he wasn't delusional?

She drew a deep breath and forced a note of bravado into her voice. "All right. Then in the greater realms you speak of, what things threaten me?"

After a moment, he broke her gaze, looking out at the darkness outside the cave. "There are creatures and beings who no longer own their souls. Heldon does. Chaotic evil is seeded deep within them. The higher ranks of his minions cross the spirit barrier protecting the mortal world. The demons, werebeasts, and vampires of the Vladarian Order are those who feed upon Elan blood within the mortal realm."

"Then I promise to watch very carefully for them. Now, I don't know about you, but I'm going to clean up and eat. I feel like I've been knocked down and dragged around in the mud and left to starve." Ignoring his shocked expression, Erin went to the dripping stalactite and rubbed her hands beneath its refreshing flow. Maybe it was the first time anyone had just accepted what he said, rather than arguing with him. At least, about the existence of vampires and werebeasts. She had no doubts that demons walked the earth. Cinatas was one of them.

After drinking some water from the fresh flow, she turned to Jared. He stood a few feet away, his scowl reminiscent of the earlier ferocity of the storm. She motioned to him. "Come join me. While we eat, you can tell me where you're from."

"From?"

"Yeah, like where you were born. And what your life was like growing up there."

"I was created in Eden."

"Where?"

"It is in the East."

"East of what?"

"Far east of here, in another land. Where are you from?" he asked.

Surely he didn't mean *the* Eden, as in the Garden of Eden. "Nowhere," she said. "Nowhere, Tennessee. It's about two hours south of here." That was where her parents still resided, but luckily, for the first time in their lives, they were somewhere besides Nowhere—a two-week cruise in the Mediterranean. She didn't have to worry about contacting them, or about Cinatas being able to harm them. Yet. But two weeks wasn't a lot of time to bring down Cinatas and the Sno-Med Corporation.

Jared stoically took her answer in stride, and this

time she was the one who gawked at him. He didn't laugh, and he didn't look at her as if she'd handed him a bunch of bull. Unless a person was from way back in her hometown hills, nobody she'd ever met had heard of Nowhere. She had a feeling she could have said heaven or hell, and he would have just nodded as if they weren't strange places to have been born.

He'd yet to move closer to her, so she motioned to him again. "Come on."

The heat from his body reached her before he did, sort of like lightning striking before the thunder blasts. She wished she had a thermometer or medicine, even the first aid kit so she could change his bandage again. Rain had soaked the gauze she'd applied earlier, but it was better to leave the wound alone than to expose it to more germs. Infections were a serious complication with burns. She pressed her palm to his cheek. "You still have a fever. Let's clean you up and eat. Then you can rest more."

Taking his hands, she guided them to the small pool of water, rubbing them with hers, feeling again the size and strength of him. She was by no means a petite woman, but he made her feel so. He had capable hands, gentle yet commanding hands . . . hot hands. Hands that made her tingle, hands that made her want to feel all that she'd imagined when he'd touched her and stolen the pain of her headache away.

A streak of dirt smeared his cheek, and she automatically dipped her fingers in the cool water, bathing the smudge away. Her gaze slid to the full sensual curve of his lips, thinking that it was very much in character with his hands, capable, gentle, yet commanding, hot. Eros, she decided, recalling her earlier question as to who had a hand in making this man. His mouth had been fashioned by Eros, not Satan. While Satan could tempt, only the god of love, lust, and the erotic could sculpt a mouth as beautiful as Jared's. She was close enough to see his pupils dilate and hear his quick indrawn breath just before he slid an arm around her back and pulled her flush against him. His heat instantly seeped into her, making her breasts swell and ache from the rush of hot desire. Her gaze shot to his. The fire of desire burning in his eyes disarmed her as much as the sudden passion of his embrace, and his lips claimed hers before she could think or react.

She leaned into him, pressing herself into his heat. The persuasive power of his lips claimed hers, and the hard press of his arousal against her demanded more. He made her want to strip naked and revel in the sultry sensuality of his hot . . . *feverish, Erin, feverish body,* her mind pointed out to her sharply. *Delusional and feverish. You're the nurse. You're the responsible one.*

Moaning at her total lapse of reason, she pulled back from him and dug a pulverized power bar from her pocket.

"Here, eat. Do you want oats and nuts or nuts and oats?" She held the wimpy bar up between their mouths, making a lousy barrier. Jared frowned, narrowing his eyes in such a way that she was sure the power bar was seconds away from becoming a *powder* bar.

"Eat," she said again, managing to shove the bar into his hand and slide from his embrace. "We're both so hungry that neither of us are in our right minds." In fact, she had to have lost hers completely, left it somewhere on this Oz-like odyssey that her life had become. "We better eat. I have a feeling we're both going to need every bit of strength we have."

Chapter Eight

JARED AND THE ELAN were in danger. Aragon felt it deep within him—danger not only from those mortals who were searching the woods for them, but from the craven creatures that walked the night, those that hid within its dark blanket and fed on the weak and unsuspecting. They hovered in the twilight, between heaven and hell, and sought to gain Heldon's favor by doing evil.

Jared hung on a precarious balance between the good in his spirit and the Tsara's poison, which grew stronger with every passing moment. The presence of any evil could tip that balance.

Aragon turned from where he watched the cave entrance to find that York, Navarre, and Sven had joined him on the mortal ground, each donning their Blood Hunter's cloak, melding into the wildness of the forest. Upon all fours, they mirrored the mortal world's creature that howled to the moon and walked the forest's floor. When the Blood Hunters walked upright, though, they gained the dexterity of mortals, skills most often needed to fight the damned.

"Has he not found this love that will save him yet?" York demanded, pawing the wet ground. "How long does such a thing take?"

"Jared was the fiercest warrior among us. He should have felled this foe in a day," Sven added, hunching low as he paced.

"Mortals are slow even when it comes to miracles. As difficult as it is, we have to remember that Jared is now mortal," Navarre said, seeking to soothe frustrations. "We also have to remember that Pathos, who was also a fierce warrior, failed to find this salvation."

"Jared won't fail," Sven muttered, though his words lacked conviction.

From what Aragon could sense of Jared's spirit, he might very well fail. There was a growing dark hunger for the Elan inside Jared, and Aragon had no idea how to help. Aragon growled in frustration, his obsidian coat bristling. "We would do well, brethren, to focus on how we can help Jared rather than talking. Night has fallen, and the moon's rising will only feed Jared's hunger. I also sense other forces in the forest besides the mortals I've been foiling today. There are more than just men hunting for Jared and the Elan."

"We are united and determined," said York, his Blood Hunter's eyes luminous in the dark. "We will not fail Jared. Heldon's army has been sent fleeing. The Shadowmen have secured a frontline across the entire Appalachia region for the Guardian Forces."

Aragon gritted his fanged jaws. "That can change in a moment, for there are reports of a massive gathering of forces in the Caribbean. Tonight, Jared and the Elan's real danger will come from those who have already crossed the spirit barrier to mortal ground. Those from the Vladarian Order are near."

"Pathos?" Navarre asked from where he hunkered upon a nearby rock.

"No, not yet," Aragon replied grimly, moving to pace closer to the cave. He hoped that someday Pathos would make a mistake crossing the spirit barrier, and put himself within a Blood Hunter's path. When that day came, Aragon planned to be that Blood Hunter. Though his duty was only to protect the Elan, to get Pathos, Aragon would chance Logos's righteous wrath. Pathos's powerful evil was a blemish upon all Blood Hunters, and one Aragon would wipe clean. As the leader of the Blood Hunters, he felt it was his duty. He owed it to his fellow brethren.

"What can we do?" Sven demanded.

"I don't know," Aragon snarled, then howled in frustration. Though Sven had made the initial choice to let Jared live, because he was the leader of the Blood Hunters Aragon had full responsibility for Jared's soul. He couldn't fail.

But Aragon's abilities were hampered in many ways. Spirits had limitations in the mortal realm. He stared into the cave from the darkness of the night, watching Jared and the Elan. All was not well within. "We have to find a way to call upon the goodness inside him during the dark hours."

The rain outside the cave's entrance had stopped long ago and night had fallen, but Jared couldn't seem to rest, as Erin did. She'd fallen asleep, and her head now rested against his right shoulder. Though his eyes were weary and kept drifting closed, odd feelings in his body continued to wake him. Sudden sharp, tight pains would shoot through the muscles in his arms and legs. And a deep urge would grip him, like a ravenous hunger. His mouth would water, and his teeth would ache. He had moments when he could smell more acutely than before, and see in the dark as if it were light. And then it would all go away.

He sat between Erin and the entrance to the cave, almost expecting that something would intrude, though it had been a quiet night, as if most creatures were still hiding from the fury of the storm that had rolled over the mountains—at least, those creatures who weren't seeking to do harm. *Those* were on the move. He could feel it. Sense it. Or was it something predatory inside himself he felt, like the sharpening hunger for the blood of the woman sleeping so blissfully ignorant at his side?

He inhaled through his gritted teeth, still smelling Erin's Elan blood. He slid his arm behind Erin and pulled her against him, realizing that giving in to his wrenching desire to touch her would dampen his urging for blood. It was the lesser evil. Even though intimacy weakened him as a warrior, that was better than letting the Tsara's poison spur his bloodlust.

He focused his mind on hers, and as he'd done earlier that day, he went in search for what lay hidden deep inside her. For just a brief moment, he wanted to feel a whispering of the passion that he knew lurked in her spirit.

"Erin?" Jared whispered over her senses like a caress. "Can you feel me? Can you feel my need for you?" He entered her dream, coming up behind her and pressing himself against her. Threading his fingers through the silk of her hair, he slid the thick tresses aside and pressed his lips against the nape of her neck. "Abandon your defenses. Come with me and explore what dreams may come for us both," he whispered, then brushed her skin lightly with the tip of his tongue.

Groaning, she leaned into him. He bared her back, kissed and caressed it, then stripped her dress down her shoulders and over her hips, leaving her in just her lace underwear. His hands slid up to cup the fullness of her breasts, molding her to his palms, then rolling her nipples to hard points.

He pulled her back against the heat of his body, kissing his way to her ear, whispering his need. "Trust me, Erin. Touch me. Let your mind go and feel the power of my desire."

Reaching up, Erin pressed her hands over his and let her head fall back against his shoulder. "Kiss me," she said softly, urging his lips to hers. She eased his hands down her stomach, beneath the lace of her underwear, and pressed his fingertips to the wet heat of her need. "Love me," she whispered.

Swinging her into his arms, Jared carried her to a golden cloud and laid her softly upon its airy warmth. The sun caressed them in warm waves, a sensual, heady drug that made her body melt beneath the demands of his. He kissed her lips, absorbing the very essence of her passion with the stroke of his tongue before moving lower to claim her breasts. He teased her, laving and nibbling until she cried out for him to fill her. He moved until he knelt between her legs, spreading them wide with his knees as he slid his hands to her hips and pulled the very wet heart of her desire to the hard thrust of his need.

A wolf howled, seemingly from just outside the cave, rousing Jared from his dream. The haunting howl was followed by three other long howls, each of them calling to something primal within him. They also made him yearn for what he would never be again, a Blood Hunter.

Jared could see Aragon so clearly in his mind, the very first time they'd met. They'd just been accepted from the ranks of the Shadowmen into the elite Blood Hunter brotherhood and assigned to the same watch. It was a millennium ago. Pathos, the legendary warrior they'd all admired and emulated for so long, had been bitten by a Tsara, and after a few short days in the mortal world, he'd began hunting the Elan with a ferocity never before seen. All Blood Hunters had taken his quick turn to the Fallen as a personal betrayal. If a spirit had been so good and brave and noble, then how could he become evil so quickly? Why had he not fought harder in the mortal realm and found his salvation through mortal love? It seemed to be an ill reflection upon the goodness of all Blood Hunters. Aragon had been more angry than most, for he'd been one of Pathos's greatest admirers. This anger had left Aragon distracted as he and Jared patrolled Stonehenge, an area where the spirit barrier was weak. There, Aragon swore that he'd caught Pathos's scent lingering in the mists near the mortal ground. Aragon had gone flying blindly amid the stones, determined to find and eliminate Pathos.

"Wait," Jared had called out to Aragon, sensing Heldon's underlings near.

"No. He's here. I know it."

"It's too dangerous. Besides, Pathos is now mortal. It is against Logos's order for any spiritual to hunt a mortal, no matter how foul. We must wait for Pathos to join Heldon's ranks and catch him before he crosses through the spirit barrier."

"I'm not willing to wait that long. He is an affront to all Blood Hunters and their honor."

"Then don't sacrifice your honor for him. Let Logos be his judge, not you. Come with me now." Jared dove to set his hand on Aragon's shoulder, to urge him to leave.

Suddenly a large band of Underlings rose up from the stones and attacked. Back to back, Jared and Aragon had fought until they could hardly lift their swords, but the Underlings kept coming, fighting ferociously.

"This is my fault. I led you astray. You go for help," Aragon said. "I'll delay them."

Jared knew that whoever stayed would be ripped to shreds. "No. We stay together and fight together. There is strength in unity. For us to separate would only help them defeat us." They'd stayed together and won, forging a bond that had carried them through a millennium of war. Until now. Now Aragon had left him to be shredded to pieces by a vile poison.

Something hot and bright intruded into his mind. He winced at the pain of it.

"Jared, my brother. Can you yet hear me? Is there still enough good within your spirit to answer?"

"Aragon?" Jared looked for his comrade but could not see him. *"Why did you not honor our pact?"*

"Jared. You must stay with the Elan. You must fight against the poison. Fight for your salvation within the mortal world. Watch your back, and remember that it was once possible to find redemption. Those from the Vladarian Order are near. Remember the ancients and the battle they waged on Earth."

The light disappeared.

"Aragon? Wait."

"Danger."

The searing pain in his mind stopped abruptly. Jared shuddered. The howling of the wolves outside changed to vicious growls.

Heart pounding, Jared turned to Erin, shaking her shoulder. "You must wake, Erin. We may have to flee."

"What?" Erin woke from her sensual dream, burning with need in places she'd ignored for far too long. She shook her head, trying to assimilate where she was. She had no doubt who she was with. She felt as if Jared was still inside her. The light was very dim inside the cave, and just a little brighter outside the entrance. "What is it, Jared?"

"There might be danger. You must wake."

She gasped, her breath catching in her throat as her

heart thudded. The gnarling and gnashing growls of ferocious beasts filled the night.

"Dear God. Wolves!" She rolled to her feet. Frantically, she spun around, trying to see through the darkness for any type of weapon. Her foot hit a rock, and she grabbed it. "Hurry, help me find more rocks."

"Wait here," Jared said.

"What!" Erin cried, whipping around. "Are you crazy? They'll kill you." But she spoke to air. Jared had already gone. She grabbed another rock and stumbled to the cave entrance.

The cloud-shrouded night let just enough moonlight through to see a few feet, but the forest remained a canopy of dark, hulking trees, and the area where she heard the wolves snarling was completely black. Erin moved just outside the cave as she looked for Jared, rocks ready to throw.

"Jared!" she said in a low, urgent tone. He didn't answer, but even she couldn't hear her own emphatic whisper above the battle. Suddenly, a deep chill hit her, and her skin crawled.

She wasn't alone.

Her new sixth sense shouted at her to turn to her right. Jerking around, she saw him, or *it*, less than two feet away from the entrance to the cave. So unnaturally white that his skin glowed ghastly in the dark, the man's grotesquely large mouth gaped much like the jaws of an attacking shark. Black-tinged foam spewed from his ice-pick teeth and down his chin. He reached for her.

Erin screamed and threw the rock as hard as she could right at his face. But the man-monster didn't even flinch, but kept coming. Howling from the dark shadows behind the monster, Erin saw what she thought was a huge glittering black wolf, or something wolflike, attack the creature.

Grabbed from behind, she screamed as heavy hands pulled her back. Heat and hard muscle pressed against her. Jared. He turned her away from the fighting wolf and creature.

"Come." He swung her into his arms again and ran.

"Oh, God." Erin shut her eyes, sure that any second they were going to smash into a tree head-on. She didn't know how long Jared ran, but it wasn't as long as it has been earlier that day. And this time, she never got the feeling that he'd left the bad guys in his dust. When he stopped, the air still snarled with menace. In the distance, gray light encroaching on the darkness signaled that dawn was near.

Through the gray shadows and mountain mists she barely had time to register that he'd halted in the center of huge white stone pillars in a forest clearing. The ground outside the ring of stones fell sharply away to a thick wall of surrounding trees, giving her the impression that they were on the crest of a mountain.

Jared's body had begun to shudder even before he

set her on her feet. His tremors worsened by the second.

"What's wrong?" she asked, grabbing his arm.

"Pain, poison," he gasped, then wrapped his arms around her and pulled her tightly against him. He howled, a bloodcurdling cry that made her bones shake and her soul tremble. Any lingering visages from her sensual dream of him evaporated like smoke.

The man was stark raving mad.

Chapter Nine

IT WASN'T UNTIL THE LAST reverberations of Jared's howl faded that Erin found the wherewithal to breathe. His body still shook terribly. Instead of pushing from his embrace, she clasped him tighter to her.

"Jared," she whispered. "Are you all right? What just happened?"

"Nothing, just . . . nothing. I am damned," he gasped. Wrenching from her, he stumbled out of the circle of pillars. "You're safe here until the sun reaches us. That is all that matters."

She drew three quick breaths, but still didn't have enough oxygen. "What was that thing by the cave?"

"A future minion of Heldon's," he rasped, sounding strange.

After studying him, assuring herself that he was all right, Erin shut her eyes and sucked in more air, bolstering herself for the real possibility that Jared was telling the truth.

"Which one?" she whispered. "Which one was he? You told me of those that feed on Elan blood. Which one was he?" She wanted to know—had to know because she never wanted to meet anything like that thing in the night again.

If all of this was as real as it seemed to her at this moment, then she had better figure things out fast before she ended up worse than dead. She had no doubt that meeting her end at the hands of a creature like that would be worse than death itself.

Jared sighed, a harsh sound of pain and despair. "I can't answer that question, Erin. There were a number of the damned surrounding us. Not all things are known to me, for I've not Logos's omniscience. What forms shape-shifters have within the icy fires of the realm of the Fallen are unknown. Those who cross through the spirit barrier can appear as mortal as you if they choose, but then they are as subject to the physical laws as you are. Only when they shape-shift do they appear as demons, vampires, or werebeasts. Then there are the Undead, the damned who've yet to descend and are waiting until Heldon decides to welcome them into his realm. It is my guess that is the creature you were battling."

Erin knew that somewhere between the thudding of her heart and the confusion in her mind she should say something, but she needed time to assimilate everything first. And not just the last hours before the growing dawn, but everything since her life had nose-dived into the bottomless pit of the unexplainable.

Her nagging little reason factor was trying to intrude, scrambling to explain away what had happened, but still coming up short. Forcing her eyes open, she was relieved to see that the sun had broken over the edge of the horizon. Light streamed through the ghostly thin mists, turning the white stone pillars to a pale gray with glittering specks. A sense of reverence and beauty seeped slowly into her, breathing a whisper of safety over her raw nerves.

Feeling steadier, she moved to Jared, setting her hand on his shoulder. He sighed loudly with relief, telling her that her touch comforted him greatly. Surprisingly, the ground wasn't covered with scattered leaves and withered pine needles as one would expect in the forest. Instead, cut grass and a colorful, lush flower bed ringed each of the pillars. Well-tended flower beds, signaling that civilization was near.

"Where are we, Jared?"

"With the ancients," he said, facing her in the light mists. "You are standing within the protection of their sacred worship stones. Though many ages have passed, prayers and praise still echo here."

"Someone else must come here as well," she said. "Look at the ground—the grass has been cut and the flowers beds weeded and watered. Someone goes to a lot of trouble to make a garden here on the mountain."

Jared walked, looking about, his movements slow and unsteady.

Erin watched him, concerned at how exhausted and in pain he looked. "It also means people are nearby, and a doctor or some sort of medical care. We can get antibiotics for you, bandages, and something to bring your fever down." And she could get a bath, food, and rest. That was as far as she was letting herself think for the moment. Soon, she'd have to face the big questions hovering over her—Jared, supernatural beings, and Dr. Cinatas . . .

If Cinatas had gone to the trouble to track her to Tennessee from Manhattan, then his Hummer squad would be combing the towns skirting the forest she and Jared had disappeared into. But they couldn't stay in the forest just to avoid Dr. Cinatas. Jared's trembling just a few minutes ago had left her very concerned. She almost wondered if he'd had some sort of light convulsions. She needed to get him medical attention as soon as possible, and she needed to do it while he was standing, because she wouldn't be able to carry him far. And she wouldn't be able to leave him if he fell, not with those wolves and the creature she'd seen.

She moved closer to Jared, needing to reassure herself that he was not worse. He could run like the wind and had unbelievable strength, but he seemed so weak after expending such energy.

Still trembling, Jared stared out at the forest, oozing such tension that she sharply studied the entire line of trees before she set her hand on his arm. "Jared . . . we must—hell, you're on fire." His temperature was raging higher than before. "We need to get you to help. Come on." She tugged on his arm, pulling him in the direction of a path leading away from the stones. She prayed that whoever kept this garden tended was at the other end of that trail.

Almost stumbling, Jared followed without saying a word, and his lack of response sent an even more urgent warning clawing through her. Ten feet through the trees, they reached a gravel road. She'd hoped for a house, but they'd reached a lonely mountain road with nothing but gravel to betray any civilization. Wrapping her arm around his burning back, Erin guided him downhill.

Jared shuddered violently as his battle with the Tsara's poison raged. Stepping into the sacred circle of the ancients had set his whole body on fire. The horrendous pain of it still burned in him; only the distance he gained from the sacred circle eased the agony and helped him to gather his awareness, but in its place came an overwhelming exhaustion that seemed to be sucking the very strength from his every muscle. It was another sickening reminder that he was fast becoming a warrior who could no longer fight with honor. Only Aragon's warning last night had helped Jared save Erin.

He shouldn't have had to be told that danger was so close, and he shouldn't have had to be reminded of the sanctuary the ancients' circle gave. He wasn't a warrior worthy of the duty of protecting anyone, much less a special Elan.

Jared knew that Heldon's attack had pushed Erin to the edge—he'd been aware of the dawning belief in her gaze. That she was reaching the point of believing and trusting in him would make his battle to protect her easier. With his judgment as flawed as last night proved it to be, she would need to know how to defend herself, for he knew he no longer walked the path of a warrior. He needed to leave her to protect her, to get as far from her as he could, but even then there weren't any guarantees that he wouldn't hunt her down the moment his mind became too poisoned to root out the evil from the good.

Cinatas smiled as the pure, clear light of dawn cut through the gray, cresting the tops of dark pines. He never missed a dawn; it was the only time the sun was worthy enough to behold, when its light was whiter and brighter and unpolluted by the haze of man's waste. It was orgasmic. Watching it over the mountains from his apartments above the Sno-Med R&D facility in Arcadia rivaled the sunrise over the water from his Manhattan penthouse.

Frustration and satisfaction warred equally within him. His men had yet to find Erin Morgan and her mysterious companion, but then neither had Shashur's *competent* damned. The damned's failing filled him with a giddiness he hadn't felt since he slit open his first patient and held God's power in his hands.

A knock at the door interrupted his musings and instantly put Cinatas in a sour mood. He walked the outer edges of the room to the door, careful to keep the shiny nap of his arctic white carpet free of footprints, and snapped open the door.

"There's freaking demons in those godforsaken hick hills." Manolo burst into the room, muddied and oozing tiny droplets of blood from scratches on his face. He'd strode halfway across the room, dripping on the white carpet, before Cinatas could stop him.

Cinatas stared at the mud, then looked with feigned dispassion at the next man who'd die in his service. "There's demons everywhere, Manolo. More so in the city than in Bambi's backyard."

"I'm not talking about normal shit here. The things we met up with were not human, and the wolves . . . were." He shuddered. "Do you understand what I'm saying here? I don't think Morgan and the man she was with will make it out alive."

Cinatas smiled. "That's not something I would bet my life on. Would you, Manolo?"

Manolo blinked, his swarthy complexion paling beneath the black stubble of his jaw and shaved head. He edged his way back to the door. "No."

"You've done as I asked? Every hole within a hundred-mile radius of the barn has got someone reporting to us?"

"Yes, sir," Manolo nodded, seeming to recall his place at last.

"Good. Why don't you pay a visit to the clinic downstairs and let them put my best salve on your cuts. Rest a minute before you tackle the Morgan problem again."

"Thank you, sir." Manolo turned to leave, bits of crusty mud flaking off with his every step, defiling the virgin purity and Cinatas shuddered at the crime.

After the man left, Cinatas went to the phone and requested his apartments be recarpeted immediately. Then he called the clinic downstairs and ordered Manolo to be assigned a subject number. Research was a beautiful thing.

As she walked along the gravel road, Erin told herself that once she got Jared to help, she'd think about everything that had happened. Then she'd come to a unrushed decision as to what she believed about him and about last night. Until then, she'd firmly push all of yesterday's events and emotions to the back of her mind, along with the remnants of her sensual dream about Jared. She had other things to think about, like not getting caught by Cinatas.

A glimpse of a black vehicle speeding toward them sent her pulse running with fear. It dipped out of sight before she could determine its make, leaving her with a growing Hummer phobia. She'd determined two winding curves back that if they encountered any car on the rutted gravel road, whether heaven-sent or not, that car would transport Jared to help. The only way it would pass by her without stopping would be over her dead body.

But the dread lurching inside her had her rethinking that foolish assertion.

Before she could utter a warning, Jared stumbled and fell to one knee, nearly pitching her down the grassy embankment skirting the road. She regained her balance, and he quickly climbed to his feet. Her warning about the approaching car died in her throat as a tar-black old-model pickup crested the hill ahead and beeped its horn as if the Super Bowl had just been won. The action, so far from the realm of stealth, took Erin by surprise and swayed her decision to flee. She stood and waited with Jared.

The pickup rolled to a stop, revealing a lone woman in the cab.

That it wasn't the Hummer-driving goons, and she didn't have to throw herself in the middle of the road to stop the pickup, Erin considered a major improvement in her recent run of unluck. At least, she did until the tinted window rolled down and she saw the woman—a silver-blond pixie with misty green eyes.

"Thank the Druids you've arrived," she sang as she looked at Jared from head to toe, eyes wide with wonder. Her gaze then drifted to Erin. "I've, um, been lookin' for ya for a bit now. I fancy the sacred stones, but mornings aren't my thing. If it weren't for me mother's angel's wings, I don't know how I'd've gotten through it." Shifting into park, she slipped from the truck, accompanied by the constant whispering tinkle from the gold bracelets at her wrists. With her Irish burr and dressed in a flowing, ankle-length emerald skirt and a form-fitting black lace corset over a silk blouse, she seemed a little too old-fashioned for the modern world.

"Well, come along. I'm in a rush. Today of all days," she said, shaking her head as if their timing was bad. "I've an important chat over the Net, and I forgot my bleedin' Blackberry at the office." She frowned. "From the looks of you both, we need to get you to a doctor first." The woman flowed like a sprite to the other side of the truck, opening the passenger-side door and motioning them in.

Neither Erin nor Jared moved.

The woman glanced at her watch and sighed. "Had a time of it, have you? Don't blame you a bit for being a wee cautious. I'd let you drive, but then Sam would have a go at me, and that would be none too pleasant. I've been borrowing his truck to meet you with because I knew the Mini just wouldn't do."

"Who are you? How did you know who . . ." Erin frowned. Had the woman indicated that she'd known they would be here?

She rolled her eyes. "Sorry, luv. I get in a rush and hash things up." She returned to the roadside and held out her hand. "I'm Emerald Linton." She bit her lip with pearly white teeth. "The truth might be a wee bit hard for you just yet, but my crystal predicted your arrival. Now, I don't know who you are, exactly when you'd come, or what your troubles would be. The Druids aren't so kind, but I did know you would come to the sacred stones during the sun's rise, and you would need help."

"And you came alone? To help strangers you didn't know?"

"Not a first. Dr. Batista and Sam wouldn't let me, but then they don't believe much in me angel's wings, and it's a long tale. You're needin' medical attention, and I've—"

"Got to go," Erin said. Since almost no matter what, she and Jared would accept a ride from the woman, rather than delay more, Erin stepped forward.

Jared set his hand on her shoulder. "Where are you going?"

"*We're* going. We both need medical help."

He met Erin's gaze for a long moment, then sighed.

"He's bleedin' real," Emerald said almost reverently, her gaze riveted on Jared. Then she shook her head.

"Why do mortals insist on trapping themselves?" Jared muttered, moving closer to the pickup. Erin slid into the truck, feeling a swamping wave of Jared's heat the moment he joined her. Was it her imagination, or were his movements slower than before?

When she tried to buckle him in, he stayed her hand, grasping the buckle from her. "I will hold the belt and not be bound as before."

The man was burning with fever, so Erin decided to argue safety later. He at least did get in the truck. She buckled her seat belt then glanced at Emerald in the driver's seat. She was so short she had to sit on the edge of the seat to reach the gas pedal.

Emerald adeptly made a three-point turn on the gravel road and spun rocks as she raced back the way she'd come. The curving road wound down the high mountain; bright pines, lush oaks, and fluttering poplars stood tall and proud, solid markers of passing time. Patches of morning mists filled ravines, appearing like magical lakes where fairies and sprites might play in secret.

Beside her, Jared oozed tension. The man did not like close quarters. She set her hand on his, giving him a reassuring squeeze. He glanced toward her and seemed to relax a little, as if comforted. She moved a little closer to him, so that her shoulder and arm brushed his. Then she turned her attention to her surroundings, looking for dangers that might be lurking in the shadows.

Erin kept scanning for a road splitting off the graveled one they were on, but she didn't see any. Nor were there any buildings or fences, nothing but the road to show civilization existed at all. She and Jared would have had a very long walk. "Where are we? I mean, what mountain are we on?"

"Spirit Wind Mountain, where only the breath of spirits is allowed to dwell."

Erin recognized the name, having heard as a child that only ghosts lived on the mountain. There were many stories whispered throughout Appalachia of people meeting specters, both enlightening and horrifying, on the mountain. Local Native Americans used to make their spirit walks through the shadows of the dead at the crest of the mountain centuries ago.

She shivered, wondering if there wasn't a great more truth to walking through the shadows of the dead that she'd ever known. She'd definitely felt *something* within the sacred stones, and she still couldn't explain the gruesome creature she'd encountered outside the cave. Unless . . .

"So, it's true," Erin said softly, seeing no signs of habitation all along the lonely gravel road. "No one lives on the mountain."

"Only the souls of those who have died and are needin' a dwellin' place between heaven and hell." Emerald sounded as if she knew the souls of which she spoke, and Erin didn't pursue the subject.

At the bottom of the mountain they turned right onto a paved road. Immediately, signs of man's intrusion into nature began shaping the land. Small and large homes were carved into roadside niches and finger-wide valleys. Old weathered barns with faded ads straggled amid tractors and farming paraphernalia. Orchards, mainly apple with a few cherries, skirted the postage-stamp fields of blossoming crops. The sprawling habitation soon gave way to close-knit houses stacked by the road, eventually interspersed with a business or two as Emerald descended into a wide valley between mountains where a small town had nestled itself.

"What did you say the doctor's name was?" Erin asked after few minutes. She felt both relieved and strange to be out of the woods. Well, at least literally. In every other way, she, and possibly Jared, were still in the thick of trouble. Erin hoped that she could call one of her credit card companies, claim her purse as lost, and get enough help to at least pay for the doctor, medicine, and lodging.

"Dr. Batista. She's tops. It just takes her a wee bit longer to believe in what she can't prove."

That was something Erin could well relate to and felt lost without. Just as she opened her mouth to ask what town lay before them—something she should have done before getting into the truck—they passed a city limits sign that made her scalp tingle.

Welcome to Twilight, Tennessee.
Where everything is possible.

Chapter Ten

Too stunned to comment on the town's name, Erin focused on absorbing the place. One sign announced the combined elementary, middle, and high school, inviting parents to support the town's Twilight Knights in their summer football fundraiser. The three-building setup mirrored Erin's school experience.

Emerald slowed her speed to the requisite twenty, then came to a stop at a red light, which seemed to mark the hub of Twilight's metropolitan offerings. It was a town of ones; a Laundromat, a library, a gas station, a bank, a fast food and ice cream parlor called Burger Queen's Delight, a dollar store, one tiny church each for three different denominations, and an office complex, of which Emerald pulled into the parking lot and put the pickup into park.

The signs above two of the doors jumped out at Erin. One read "A. Batista, MD. Internal Medicine," and the other said "Psychic Readings for Seekers of Truth and Light," under which there was the name "Dr. Emerald Linton." The woman at her side.

"You're a doctor, too?" Erin asked.

"Clinical psychologist, luv." Emerald glanced at her watch. "And I've just enough time to see the look on Dr. Batista's face before chat time with my clients." She opened the door and slipped gracefully out before Erin could ask how psychology and psychic readings meshed.

Jared had already bailed from the truck and stood scanning the area with an alertness she'd missed seeing in him since the sunrise. Erin scooted out, feeling as if she'd made a thousand-year journey in the last forty-eight hours, and the ride wasn't over yet.

She and Jared followed Emerald into Dr. Batista's office. He had to stoop to fit though the doorway, and immediately looked uncomfortable at being inside.

The furniture, inexpensive chairs of muted colors and chrome-framed tables, was completely generic and seemed temporary or rented. Only the degrees and official certificates, a prestigious slew of them, hung on the wall, but they were framed in ordinary dime-store black metal, which made Erin immediately suspicious.

A quick glance at the woman's qualifications induced more questions than it allayed. Erin wondered why the doctor was in a small town and not working for a major cardiac hospital, with her surgical training.

No pictures or posters hung on the stark white walls, nothing to indicate more about the doctor.

"Time to stop foostering around, luv. I've work for ya now. They're here," Emerald called loudly through the open door leading to the inner rooms of the office.

"Emerald? Hold on." The answering call was followed by clipped steps, and a woman with intriguing dark eyes appeared. She lifted eyebrows, crinkling her classic Latin beauty with skepticism and a healthy dose of surprise as her gaze zeroed in on Jared's yellow towel. She wore a white lab coat with a stethoscope hanging from its pocket, and her thick wavy hair was pulled into a severe knot, as if she had to contain everything tightly.

"They're finally here," Emerald said. "Found them trudging along on Spirit Wind Mountain."

"Em, just because they were on Spirit Mountain at dawn doesn't mean—"

"They need your help, and I'm late for my chat. Naked without my Backberry, on today of all days," Emerald interjected. She ducked out the door, waving, her bracelets tinkling like a magical chime. "I'm just next door, luvs," she called just as the door shut.

"Well," the doctor said, inhaling as if surfacing from underwater. There seemed to be deep shadows in her dark eyes now, or they had been there before and Erin had missed them. "Who are you really, and what can I do for you?"

"I'm Erin, and this is Jared." Erin nodded at the degrees on the wall. "Not to be rude, but why is someone with your training here, practicing in a small town?"

Dr. Batista lifted a dark brown. "Few people read those. Look, my reasons for being in Twilight have nothing to do with my competency as a doctor. You both look as if you need help."

Erin didn't exactly like the doctor's evasive answer, but she'd have to accept it for the moment. "Jared needs his burn examined. He has a fever, and I'm worried about the possibility of infection. Then I'll need to borrow your phone, too. I'm sure my credit card company has a fund set up for preferred customers who have emergencies. I'll be able to pay you—"

Dr. Batista waved her hand, crisply motioning for Erin and Jared to follow her. "Don't worry. You can send me a check when you get home later. You've a nasty gash on your temple as well. Any nausea or dizziness? How were you hurt on . . . the mountain?"

Erin followed, uneasy. The hard part had arrived. How much of what had happened to her could she explain? Would it only thrust her and Jared into more danger if she did tell someone about Dr. Cinatas without proof? Jared kept close behind her. "I've had some dizziness, but no nausea to speak of. I, uh, bumped my head when my car ran off the road."

"When?" Dr. Batista asked, motioning Erin into a treatment room. "I'll put you across the hall in there, Jared." She nodded her head that way.

"No," Jared said firmly. "Erin stays with me."

Erin sent Jared a reassuring glance. "I'll be fine. It's just across the hall."

"No. We cannot fully trust her," he said.

Erin's breath caught in her throat. Did Jared know or sense something she didn't? He'd known that danger was imminent in the cave.

Dr. Batista studied Jared a moment before replying. "I assure you that my medical qualifications are unblemished. Both of you can have a seat in here and let me take a quick look. If you're still uncomfortable, I can either have the local sheriff vouch for me, or Emerald can take you over to Arcadia, where she takes her daughter. There's a brand-new clinic with several doctors on staff. Perhaps you can find what—"

"No," Erin said sharply. Even if the new medical clinic in Arcadia had nothing to do with the Sno-Med facility, Erin wasn't going near Arcadia until she was ready to go after Cinatas. "Sorry. It's not you." She slipped her hand into Jared's, detecting that his fever had cooled some but was still significantly high. "He's a little confused. We'll just stay together. We're fine with seeing you."

"He's first, then." Dr. Batista crossed the treatment room and replaced the paper on the examining table.

Her expression clearly questioned who they were and where they had come from.

"Help Erin first," Jared said as he urged Erin toward the doctor, then crossed his arms as if he'd brook no argument.

"Looks like you're up. Lie back and let me have a look at you." Dr. Batista patted the table.

Erin complied, glaring at Jared. "He's the one who needed treating."

"Relax," Dr. Batista said as she adjusted the exam light after checking Erin's pupils, reflexes. "Now how did you say this happened?"

"I, um, ran off the road and bumped my head."

"When?"

"Uh, last night," Erin said, scrambling to think. It just sounded too suspicious to say that she'd hit her head the night before last and was just now seeking attention.

Dr. Batista paused as if she knew she was being lied to, but then didn't question Erin further. After finishing, she forced a smile. "I've put a butterfly bandage on the gash to help the wound heal without scarring. The dizziness may be from a very mild concussion, so I suggest you rest for the next few days and don't drive. You can remove the bandage the day after tomorrow. Do you need anything for a headache?"

Erin noted with some surprise that she'd been relatively pain-free since Jared's little "healing" in the cave.

"No. I've had migraines recently that I use Relpax for at home, but I'm fine right now."

"Take Ibuprofen for anything minor. I've a few samples of the other I can give you, too." She glanced at Jared. "Were you burned in the car accident this morning?"

Hell, Erin thought, she should have planned out a plausible story for Jared's injury ahead of time, too. "No," she said. "He hurt himself a day or so ago."

"How?"

"Welding. It was an accident," Erin finally replied, biting back a groan. She was a terrible liar. From Dr. Batista's expression she knew it, too.

"I'll be right back with the meds. Then we'll take a look at your friend's burn."

The doctor's tone had cooled a number of degrees, and Erin winced as the woman left the room. She sprang up and, motioning to Jared, tiptoed from the treatment room. Four steps let her hear Dr. Batista in another room speaking. "Emerald is in over her head now. You better get here ASAP . . . I'll explain then. Can't now."

Hearing the phone hit the cradle, Erin backpedaled to the treatment room, dragging Jared with her.

"What is it, Erin? Do you wish to leave here?"

Jared's flushed skin and pain-filled gaze settled Erin's quandary. Dr. Batista had called someone, but she hadn't mentioned either Erin or Jared. She'd only spoken of Emerald. Hopefully they could get Jared seen and leave before that person arrived.

Erin shook her head. "No. Not until we get help and medicine for you. Then we'll go."

Dr. Batista entered just as soon as Jared sat on the treatment table. Her manner was as it had been before, crisp and professional, but the suspicion was there, in her eyes and in her voice. "All ready, then." She handed Erin unopened boxes of the medicines, then moved to a metal warming cabinet and pulled out hospital-issue gowns and blankets. She pushed a gown at Erin. "Why don't you clean up while I check his injury?"

Erin grasped the toasty gown. Besides Jared's care, it was the most comfortable thing she'd felt since she'd left her apartment for work a lifetime ago. Even a paper-towel scrub would feel like heaven, but she handed the soft cotton back with a strong twinge of regret. After finally getting Jared into helping hands, she found she couldn't walk away. Something bound them together that was as inexplicable as the events in the cave and the man himself. She couldn't leave him. She feared she might be starting to believe he really was a spirit being—and that meant he needed her protection, and they needed to hurry. "No. I'd rather wait until I can take a shower."

Dr. Batista sighed, and Erin saw concern as well. "At least take a warm blanket." She held one out, and Erin slipped it around her shoulders.

The doctor set the gown down and moved to Jared. "Now, let's have a look at you."

Jared clenched his jaw and fisted his hand as Erin sat in the chair across the room. The more time he spent in this fleshly form, the more he hated everything to do with it, the weaknesses growing inside him, the wearying pain knotting his every muscle.

They were wasting time here, but Erin had thought it extremely important, and he didn't have a solid plan as to what they should do.

What happened to him at the sacred stones had nearly undone him. He had millennia of experience with the spirit world's war. He'd fought against every kind of dark minion of the Fallen, from Underlings to demons to Tsaras and worse, and had never reached the depths of agony and exhaustion that wrenched through him at the Sacred Stones.

If Erin had been attacked at that moment, Jared would not have been able to save her. He was too weakened.

The dark-haired woman who'd seen to Erin's injury approached him with an unmistakable wariness that puzzled him and made him wonder how he caused such fear in others. Erin had feared him as well.

She'd placed a basin of water next to him and, after pulling on thin gloves, reached for the bandage Erin had put on his shoulder.

He caught the dark-haired woman's wrist before she

touched him. Her gaze snapped to his; she was more frightened than Erin at his touch. He released her quickly. "Do not fear me. What you seek to do is unnecessary. Nothing can be done to help."

Erin moaned. "Please, Jared. Let her help."

He shrugged. "Do as you will." What was it about these mortals? Their need to care ran deeply and as strong as his determination to duty.

He winced as she pulled up the tape. With Erin across the room, the pain throbbing around his Tsara wound bit deeper into his mind.

"You've a high fever," the doctor said as she touched his bandage, concern shadowing her fear. She hurriedly removed the bandage, then looked puzzled. "Your burn has healed nicely. No need to cover it anymore. I'm more worried about your fever. How long have you had one?"

Jared noted that her touch held none of the pain-easing power of Erin's.

"What do you mean, healed?" Erin crossed the room quickly, golden eyes wide with confusion.

"How did he burn himself?" Sounding suspicious, the dark-haired woman narrowed her gaze at Erin. "It appears as if he was branded with something that had etchings on it. Do you want to tell me what is going on here?"

Moving to the woman's side, Erin gasped as she looked at his chest. She shook her head and placed her fingertips over the scar, instantly easing his discomfort, enabling him to draw a free breath.

"It's not possible," she whispered. "It just isn't possible." Her gold eyes searched his eyes; confusion warred with fear in their clear depths. "Your burn . . . how . . . how have you healed like this?"

She snatched her hand away, more fearful than ever before.

Pain pierced him, wrenching his stomach and knotting in his chest until he could barely breathe. Erin's fear twisted inside him.

No! He was stronger than that. He could take the pain. This weakness was only because the Sacred Stones had drained his strength. Still, he needed her. "Erin, don't fear me," he gasped.

She shook her head, pulling farther away. "What are you, Jared? How can you heal like that?"

He exhaled through gritted teeth and clutched his fist to his chest. With the pain came a hungering need to taste her Elan blood. It, too, was sharper than ever. He had to touch her, he had to ease himself, or he would sink his teeth into her soft flesh.

He shut his eyes against the fear in hers and tried to draw from all that he knew was good and true, but faltered. All he could think about was satisfying his desire for her blood. The empowering glory of it, the heady intoxication of—

"Jared?" Erin whispered.

He felt her hand cover the fist he'd pressed to his heart, and the pain ebbed back. He trembled.

"Lie back," Erin urged. "And let the doctor take your temperature." He complied, letting go of everything but Erin's hand as he shut his eyes and focused on the ease her touch brought. The doctor urged something into his mouth and under his tongue. He concentrated on breathing, on letting Erin's touch help him fight the Tsara's poison for what little time he had left.

He was no longer a warrior. He could not stand alone. He needed her.

Erin couldn't believe what her own eyes saw. The charred and oozing skin from yesterday morning was now smooth, pink scar tissue, as if weeks had passed rather than a mere day. And the doctor was right. Now that the burn had healed, it could be readily seen as the branding from something with strange markings on it.

Her hand in Jared's trembled with the strain of her emotions. There was something else difficult to believe as well. Whatever caused the deep agony that gripped him, her touch had the power to help him. Just as he'd eased her migraine in the cave, she had some strange sort of power to do the same for him.

She tightened her hold on his hand, and he opened his eyes, his gaze riveting to hers. The blueness of his eyes and his need pierced though her, wrapped tightly around her. Though it seemed impossible, she knew they were connected in a way she could not explain.

The digital thermometer beeped. Dr. Batista looked at it, gasped, then shook her head. "This machine is broken. I'll be right back." She set the thermometer aside, and Erin blinked at the flashing red numbers. *One hundred and fifteen degrees.*

Erin had a strange feeling that there was nothing wrong with the machine. That the reason Jared's temperature was so high was because he wasn't a normal man.

"Annette!" a man shouted from outside of the room. "Do you want to tell me what's going on? I just spoke to Em, and she bit my head off! I don't need this right now. Slater has a dead man on Forty-four and a burned-out car over in Winder, and the Rangers have hikers fleeing trails, screaming zombies have invaded."

Jared rolled from the examining table, fluidly moving into what Erin could only describe as a fight-ready stance. He pulled her behind him.

Straining to see over Jared's shoulder, Erin found Dr. Batista standing in the middle of the doorway with her back to them. "We're in here, Sam." She groaned before adding, "Anybody tell you that you've got the stealth of a jackass? Why did you speak to Em?" Turning, she shook her head apologetically. "I called the sheriff," she said, meeting Erin's gaze directly. "Emerald believes you two are beings she's supposed to help from the spirit world, and we all know that isn't true."

Chapter Eleven

DR. BATISTA DIDN'T EVEN turn back to face the sheriff as he descended into the room. Close-cropped black hair and a military bearing told Erin this lawman didn't give either himself or anyone else an inch. There was a harshness to his appearance that made him as rugged and dark-looking as a mountain at midnight.

The doctor kept her puzzled gaze on Jared, looking like she wanted to put the thermometer in his mouth but had thought better of it at the moment. "Sam," she said, "meet Jared and Erin. This is Sheriff Sheridan."

"Mind telling me what this is about?" Sam drawled, his voice deceptively more relaxed than the keen edge of his gaze.

The doctor's office door open and slammed. "Nett! Bleedin' hell! What the divil did you ring him for?" Emerald steamed into the room, green eyes flashing.

Dr. Batista sucked in air. "Because this has gone far enough. You're not just scouring ancient stones for a spirit to help. You've picked up a practically naked man and a battered woman and brought them here all by yourself."

"You've bleedin' mucked up the day. I doona need Sam a breathin' down my neck." Emerald's burr thickened with her irritation.

Dr. Batista shook her head. "You don't understand, damn it. Anything could have happened to you. Anything . . ." Her voice trailed to a whisper.

Emerald sighed. "Luv, I'm not Stef. And we don't know anythin' yet about where she's disappeared to, so let's not be assumin' the worst yet."

"Em, I can't believe like you. Not after six months. People don't just disappear. My sister didn't just disappear. Not without something bad happening."

"No," Emerald said.

"Yes," interjected the sheriff. "You picked up strangers off the side of the road and told nobody what you were doing. Something could have happened to you today."

Emerald shot a glance of apology toward Erin, then settled a fiery glare on the sheriff. "Samuel T. Sheridan! I'll not have you insultin'—"

"No, you listen. You should have called me or Annette on the phone we gave you and informed us where you were and that you were picking up hitchhikers. I'd have been there in minutes." The sheriff punctuated his words with a fierce scowl. "Whether you like it or not, Annette is right. And you could have been *dead* wrong!" Then the lawman narrowed his steely gaze at Jared. "Who are you, and where are you from?"

"Jared Hunter, from Eden," Jared said, his arms folded over his chest and his broad shoulders resolute.

Erin groaned.

"Eden where?" the sheriff asked.

"In the east—" Jared said.

"East of here," Erin added, angling herself from behind Jared to stand at his side. "I'm Erin Morgan. Jared is from the Lake Eden area, near Black Mountain, North Carolina. We . . . we've had everything stolen. His clothes and wallet, my purse. Everything."

"Where? When?" the sheriff demanded.

"Nowhere," Erin said, blurting out the first thing that came to her mind. "My parents live in Nowhere, and we went to visit them. It's about two hours—"

"I know where Nowhere is," the sheriff said impatiently. "How and when were your things stolen? You've reported it, of course."

"No." Erin swallowed a huge lump in her throat. Just how deep was she going to dig her own grave? "I was too embarrassed to make a report. We'd stopped at a lake to . . . um . . . swim and didn't lock the car. When we got back to it, our stuff was gone. We were on our way to Lake Eden to fix that problem." Since this was the Fourth of July weekend, Erin figured it would take the sheriff a day or so to expose her lie.

"Where is your car, then?" the sheriff pressed.

"We ran off the road last night and . . . got lost in the woods looking for help, then found the stones on the mountain."

"So your car is on Spirit Wind Mountain?"

Erin rubbed her temple with her fingertips and sucked in air. The lies were getting more and more complicated. And she was beginning to feel dizzy. Why not just tell the truth about everything that had happened since she found the bodies in the lab? Then what? They'll contact Cinatas. How could they not? And she didn't have proof . . . yet. She wasn't ready for anyone to call Cinatas. "Yes, it may be. Off the road in a ravine."

"Color, make, model? License plate number?"

"Two thousand four navy Tahoe," Erin said, rattling off her New York license plate number and her driver's license number. "I'll have to look at a map after I rest and try and figure out where we lost it."

The sheriff let a long pause hang in the air, then eyed Jared again. "You don't say much."

"There are more important things to attend to than your questions," Jared replied.

Erin thought smoke would rise from the sheriff. Even from across the room, she saw his angry flush and the agitated tic in his jaw. "What is your driver's license number?"

"He doesn't drive, and he lives with me in New York," Erin said.

The sheriff's glare hardened. "Then why were you going back to Lake Eden?"

She'd hung herself in her lies, and everybody knew it. How long could he arrest her and Jared for suspicious behavior?

Bravely inserting her petite self between them and the sheriff, Emerald planted her hands on her hips. "Enough of it now. They've done no harm. I'll take them to get clean and to rest, and anythin' else you're wantin' to know can wait."

"What?" the sheriff asked, incredulous. "You aren't taking them anywhere. And especially not to your place. You don't know anything about them."

Emerald sighed softly. "I'ma knowin' who they are, Sam. Been expectin' them for a long time. That's why I had Silver Moon built. It's for them to stay in. And I'ma knowin' them better than anyone who's a rented it while I've waited."

Erin's scalp tingled. A woman had built a place just to house people from the spirit world her crystal had told her to help?

"Good God, woman!" the sheriff exploded. "For someone so smart, you can be so clueless. These people aren't otherworldly beings. You heard it yourself.

They are from New York, and—" He glared at Jared. "Lake Eden or New York. I don't give a shit what your crystal ball says."

Though it went completely against Erin's interest, she was beginning to agree with Sam.

"That's going too far, Sam," Dr. Batista interjected.

The sheriff raked his hand through his crew cut. "You can't have it both ways, Annette. Do you believe Em or not?"

"That's not at issue here. I'm worried about her safety, no matter where these two people are from. Don't attack her crystal."

"If you're speakin' to me, then be doin' it to me, thank you," Emerald said, affecting a determined resolve. "I'll not be abandoning what I came across the sea to do. So unless you're arrestin' without cause, they'll be staying at Silver Moon."

The sheriff continued to glare at Emerald, and she at him. The air between them crackled with frustration and sizzled with something too passionately volatile to touch.

"If they don't check out, they're mine." He riveted his hard gaze back at Erin and Jared. "I better find you when I come looking, because I can guarantee you don't want me to have to hunt for you . . . for any reason."

Erin gritted her teeth. Unless she'd heard wrong, the law had just told them not to leave town.

His departure left a ringing silence that Emerald broke first. "I'll be remembering this, Nett."

Dr. Batista sighed. "If you thought I was in danger, you'd do the same." She turned her dark gaze to study Jared. "First, we need to work on your fever before anything else." She patted the examination table. "Sit here for me." After popping the thermometer in Jared's mouth, she said, "How long have you had it?"

"Since yesterday," Erin said, turning her mind to what had to be done next, which was get what they came for and then decide if they were going to stick around for the sheriff or not. She had a feeling that having him hunt for her would be much worse than facing him when he didn't turn up any record of a Jared Hunter in Lake Eden.

The thermometer beeped, Dr. Batista glanced at the readout and gave a puzzled frown. After changing the sterile tip, she stuck the thermometer in her mouth. "It's working," she mumbled when it beeped. Changing the tip, she took Jared's temperature again.

"One hundred and fifteen," she declared. "What's wrong with this thing?"

Emerald clapped her hands together, creating a light tinkling that oddly made Erin think of fairy or angel wings. Emerald drew a seemingly satisfied breath before speaking. "Nothing's wrong. It's pairfect! He's pairfect. What greater proof are ya needin' to see before you'll believe? No mortal man can be that hot."

She winked at Jared. "Temperature wise, luv. Not to be cheeky, but I couldn't resist."

"Em," said Dr. Batista, closing her eyes in exasperation. "Be serious. An elevated temperature doesn't prove a thing other than this man has an abnormal medical condition."

Two days ago, Erin would have said the same thing. It was a perfectly logical answer, grounded in reason. And the fact that Erin didn't think of it, but had immediately considered that Jared was who he claimed to be, showed her just how far she'd strayed. Between last night and this morning, she'd come to the realization that Jared Hunter was very different and could very well be the spirit being he claimed he was. She also couldn't turn away from him. He needed her, and she had to do whatever she had to do to keep them together until she figured out why he was here.

"Time will tell, luv. My bet is that *is* his normal temperature. For now I need to cozy them into Silver Moon before the dragon returns."

Despite the gravity of her situation and Emerald's too-accurate-to-ignore crystal declarations, Erin found herself warming to Emerald. *Dragon* so accurately pegged the fire-breathing sheriff.

"Come over to my office a moment and let me get the keys to my Mini and lock up." Emerald motioned for Erin and Jared to follow in her tinkling wake. Erin slipped her hand in Jared's and urged him off the examination table.

"Wait," Dr. Batista said. "You're not going without me." She picked up the two boxes of sample medication Erin had left in the chair. "I'll put a bag of medicine together and meet you at your car."

"You don't have to do this," Emerald said. "I'll be safe."

Dr. Batista studied Jared, then Erin felt her scrutiny as well. "Maybe so, but I'll feel better if I do."

"You can drive my Mini then, and I'll take them in the pickup. I don't rightly think he'd fit," she said, eyeing Jared. "That way I'll have both cars at the cottage and I can run you back to town after."

When they exited to the breezeway between the offices, Jared breathed deeply and flexed his shoulders, reaffirming Erin's feeling that being indoors made him uncomfortable. When they reached Emerald's office, Erin didn't follow her inside, but stood in the open doorway with Jared behind her. "We'll wait here for you."

"I'll be only a sec," Emerald said and dashed through the open door across the room. Her office had the same setup as Dr. Batista's, but instead of generic rented furniture, a world of color, texture, and miniature art filled the room, making it almost a tiny forest of the unusual, the unique, and the beautiful. Nothing at all what Erin imagined a psychic's place or a psychologist's office to be, but then she was thinking of gypsy palm readers and ghostly séances.

"I'm ready," Emerald said, hurrying to the door.

"So how do psychology and psychic readings go together?" Erin asked.

"Not very well on occasion. But a gal has got to do what a gal has got to do to help how she can. I don't have my license to practice here in the States yet, and even if I did, I don't rightly think Twilight's ready for Dr. Em's brand of therapy just yet." She held up her Blackberry. "I keep me patients in Dublin happy and do what readin's I can. You're a needin' to have one done, but today Megan wants to go with Bethy to the fair, and I can't be letting her go alone."

Erin worried her bottom lip. "You've done more than enough for us already." She honestly felt as if she'd intruded far too much upon the woman's goodwill. Erin also felt the biting sting of her dishonesty. "If you could lend me just enough money to buy a few supplies at the dollar store and then take us to a hotel, we will be fine for the night."

Emerald shook her head. "Luv, I'ma supposed to be helpin' you now," she said and then sighed. "The nearest inns are a bit of a way in Arcadia. And"—she bit her lip anxiously—"I've already bought everthin' you'll need. If the clothes aren't the right size, the online store will overnight what you need and credit me for the ones I've purchased. I know it's a stretch, but ya just need to be relaxin' now, because there's more troubled times ahead."

"I'll repay you for all of this," Erin said softly, touched by the woman's generosity. "But how did you know we were coming? How did you know so much about us?

"No need to repay me, luv. By the time we work through everythin,' we're going to be more than beholden to each other. As for how I knew so much, I've been seein' you in my crystal for a very long time."

Dr. Batista arrived, giving Erin no time to question Emerald's cryptic words. How had she seen them in a crystal, and why would they all be beholden to one another? What were they going to work through?

The four them left the walkway for the parking lot. Erin scanned the area, looking for a black Hummer, a dragon sheriff, or anything else that struck her as out of place. A rusted Dumpster filled with cardboard boxes from the dollar store stood at the far end, and a huge Salvation Army bin with precariously stacked plastic bags peeking from a broken hinged door was next to it. Beyond lay a small grassy field where two hound dogs barked from the back of a faded blue truck lumbering through it. Everything appeared to be just as normal as it could possibly be, but it wasn't.

Erin, Emerald, and Jared sat in the pickup as before, and Dr. Batista followed in a cheery Mini

Cooper, looking like a bright Pop-Tart on the road next to the chunky truck.

Erin had expected Emerald's residence to be a short distance from Twilight's main crossroads. Instead, they headed west from the traffic light and after a number of miles they cut off the main road and started climbing up the mountainside. The road wound along a rushing creek and forested dropoffs through sharp switchbacks before Emerald pulled into a dirt driveway. Then, after passing a modest home that looked like a gingerbread house, they went farther up the mountainside until the road gave way to a clearing. A woodsy, comfortable-looking cabin hung onto the side of the mountain. It had a huge deck with a hammock and the most breathtaking view of mist-shrouded mountain peaks that Erin had ever seen.

Emerald put the truck in park. "We're here. This is Silver Moon."

Erin gasped with the wonder of it and heard Jared emit a sigh of relief as he barreled from the car and started walking around, enjoying the free space and open fresh air.

"I'll show you around a bit, and when Megan and I get back from the fair, I'll have you over for dinner tonight."

"Fair?" Erin asked. "Are you going to the health expo at the fairgrounds?"

Emerald's eyes widened as she glanced at Jared, then

back to Erin. "Does the expo have to do with why you both are here?"

"I, uh, nothing. I heard the advertisement on the radio and was curious about it."

"You're an awful liar, Erin," Emerald said with a warm smile. "Just tell me to mind my bleedin' business if I ask too much. Megan and I have angel wings protectin' us, but if there's a reason my daughter shouldn't go, I'd like to know now."

"All I can say is that you should enjoy the food and the games, but don't participate in any of their free health screening."

Emerald sighed. "Not quite trustin' me yet. Doona blame ya. Why don't you settle in, and after Megan gets home from school in a few hours, I'll give you a ring and see if there's more you want to tell me about the health expo." Silver bells tinkled, and Emerald dug her Blackberry out of her purse. She groaned as she looked at the message. "This one's going to take a bit. Let's hurry."

Erin nodded and quickly followed Emerald through the cabin. Half of her mind was on Emerald's tremendous generosity. The other half was on Dr. Cinatas and the health expo. From what Erin knew of Dr. Cinatas, a mountain fair would be well below his radar—too dirty for his taste. Erin wondered if she should chance going to the fair. She would have to leave Jared alone for a short while, but just being able to see what the Sno-Med Corporation was up to in the community would be worth the trip. She knew she wouldn't learn anything to help her expose Cinatas, but seeing how Sno-Med operated in the area couldn't hurt. And she might make a contact with someone familiar with the inside of the research center, which would be a big plus on her side. First, she'd get Jared settled and then see what she could do.

"How do you get a shower, and why do I need it so badly?" Jared frowned, looking at the shower stall the same way he'd scrutinized the truck.

Cooling Jared's temperature with a shower was a top priority. But Emerald's question in the clinic had Erin wondering if the bag of medication Dr. Batista had given them was necessary. What if Jared's temperature was just naturally more elevated? She decided to wait a little while longer before medicating him.

Emerald had known Jared would have trouble with small spaces. He didn't like confinement of any kind. Jared had stayed outside on the deck, scouting out the area in all directions, as Emerald showed Erin where everything was in the cabin. Throughout the two-bedroom mountain home were little touches of the magical miniature art Emerald had in her office. Oak-paneled walls, a stone fireplace, wood floors, dark green furnishings, wide windows, and cathedral ceilings made the cabin seem in harmony with the surrounding forest.

Erin had never had a "space" problem before Jared joined her in the cabin after Emerald and Dr. Batista left. His prowling back and forth across the great room ratcheted tension up Erin's spine and made her tingle strangely inside. There was no mistaking the potent male hunger in his gaze, one that she was finding harder and harder to ignore. And her sensual dream about him wouldn't rest; it kept awakening little tingles of erotic curiosity that shouted to be heard. She also couldn't ignore the truth of who he was; his strength, his ability to heal both her and himself, and the fact that she had *seen* a creature from the dregs of the damned made a very convincing argument.

She was alone with a man who wasn't delusional, or crazy, but a warrior from the spirit realm. It was time to accept that or continue scrambling for reasons to explain the unexplainable, and quite frankly, she was exhausted.

She had other dire things to think about, such as Dr. Cinatas, her life, and what to do next, but all of those could wait until she and Jared had bathed, eaten something, and rested.

Moving over to the tiled shower, which was larger than the postage-stamp space she expected, she turned on the double heads, setting the temperature, and turned to Jared.

"I take a shower every day, and I'm desperate to get one now. A shower will get you clean, refresh you, and in your case, help reduce your elevated temperature." She adjusted the etched glass door to give him as much privacy as possible.

A soft robe hung on the hook next to an extra-large, fluffy towel. Everything was ready. Now she just needed him naked.

Drawing a stiff breath, she looked at him. "To shower, you remove your clothing, then you get under the water and clean yourself from head to toe. Use shampoo for your hair and soap for everything else," she said, pointing to each of the bottles as she spoke.

"Another cleansing ritual," he said, shaking his head in confusion. "It seems mortals waste much time covering, uncovering, and cleansing themselves." Jared began untying the yellow towel.

"Believe me, it's necessary," Erin said, backing her way out, deliberately avoiding looking at him as he dropped the yellow towel. Unfortunately, her gaze collided with his image in the elongated mirror on the opposite wall. She should have shut her eyes, but didn't. She had her fill of looking him over from toes to chest. Twice.

Realization that Jared was making no move to enter the shower dawned slowly.

"You can get in whenever you are ready," she told him. "The hot water won't last forever."

"I'm waiting for you," he said.

She gaped at him. "What?"

He frowned. "Did you not say you were desperate for a shower?"

"Yes, but . . . men and women don't shower together. Well, I mean they do, but only if they are intimate."

He moved closer to her, and she snapped her gaze from the mirror to his. He slid a finger to her cheek, his touch gentle, hot, and potent enough to send fiery rushes of desire through her. "We are intimate," he said softly. "If you knew my thoughts you'd realize that."

She inhaled and shook her head. She was very much afraid that his thoughts were exactly like those that had filled her dream of him. He was from another place, and it was her responsibility to help him understand her world. "Intimacy comes with time, with emotions, caring, desire, and love. You must have those things to make intimacy possible."

"Explain." He trailed his fingers to the pounding pulse in her neck, then moved lower, pressing his palm to her heart. Desire exploded tiny pieces of pleasure everywhere inside her. "I feel the rush of your blood and the power of your want," he said.

"Feelings are more than desire. It is a need to be part of the other person, to give to them."

"Do we not share in those things now? Does my touch give you pleasure?"

How could she deny the simple truth of his words? How could she accept them either? As thrilling as her sensual dream of him had been, it did not have any basis in reality, right? "I don't know," she whispered.

"Can you not see the truth, feel the truth? I can," he said softly. He stepped into the shower, his arousal leaving no question that he was ready for anything.

Erin sank to the commode lid. She didn't have the legs to walk the miles she needed to run.

Jared stood beneath the warm water, feeling comfort and pleasure slide all over him. Surprised, he gasped as the water sluiced down his skin and hit the erection Erin always managed to swell in him. The sensation made him ache to hold Erin, to press himself closer to her. That thought made his erection throb to a painful point. Closing his eyes, he groaned, desperate to control these human reactions of pleasure and pain. He exhaled sharply.

"Is the water too hot? Are you in pain?" she asked.

Opening his eyes, he found Erin standing outside the stream of water, her hand reaching for him. He leaned her way and wrapped his arm around her, pulling her against him and holding her close beneath the water.

Chapter Twelve

"Jared!" Erin cried, sounding almost frightened as she stiffened in his arms.

"Stand with me a moment. Help me ease this pain."

He felt her exhale, heard her troubled sigh, and knew the moment she gave in to his need. She pressed her cheek to his heart and wrapped her arms around him. He closed his eyes and pulled her tighter, wanting to feel everything about her. He wanted her naked, but sensed her caution. He could wait . . . a few moments, at least.

He stood beneath the warm water, absorbing the deep scent of her, the shape of her supple softness pressed against him, and the excitement surging inside them both. He knew the thud of her heart, the rush of her pulse, and the growing heat of her blood. He also sensed her confusion and realized that he was the cause of it. He eased his hold on her, and she stepped back.

"How do you bathe yourself?" he asked, wanting to comfort and ease her. Perhaps the bathing ritual would soothe her.

Water turned her hair darker, sleeker. Long, spiked lashes framed eyes the color of sunlit starbursts. She stared at him intently a moment, then sighed and reached for one of the bottles she'd pointed to earlier. "I'll show you," she said softly.

He wanted more, to be touching her, soothing and enjoying her. Having her bathe him wasn't exactly what he had in mind, but . . . he could accept it for now. Then he could bathe her.

Putting a small amount of liquid in each of her hands, she looked up at him. "Keep your eyes shut while there is soap in your hair," she said, slowly sliding her fingers into his hair. He smiled at her and closed his eyes to enjoy her touch, her smell, her nearness.

Erin was sure she was now totally certifiable. Though she'd already stripped off her shoes and stockings and trashed them, she still wore her ruined uniform and now stood in a shower with a naked man—uh, naked spirit being from Eden?

She barely knew the man, but she was totally sunk by his plea to help him. The need in his iridescent blue eyes and the sinful pleasure of his lips—a mouth made for seducing anything that breathed—had pulled her beneath the spray with him as much as his hands.

There was one thing she kept forgetting, though— to breathe in between her dizzying moments of total brain meltdown. The man was drowning her in sensations, and she grabbed onto the erotic lifeline he'd thrown her: showing him how to bathe.

Massaging the shampoo through his velvety black hair and its lone silver streak was an exotic exploration. The silk of it, the length of it, the feel of it made her even hungrier to know every nuance of him. The dark strands, rinsed free of the suds, fell well past his broad shoulders. Picking up the soap, she breathed its fresh tangy smell of highland lavender and set to work on the supple planes of his face, the dip bisecting his chin, and the tickling softness of his shadowed beard.

She memorized the feel of his full, lush mouth, the curve of his cheeks, and the determined angles of his nose and brow. Then she moved lower to the cords of his neck and the hard contours of his chest, feeling him, his heat, his hot smoothness. She covered every inch of him all the way to his waist.

She didn't linger in any one place; she kept her movements fluid. She knew at this point she could instruct Jared on how to finish bathing himself. He might not know the specifics of her world, but he caught on fast, and she had more than an inkling that his intelligence and knowledge were phenomenal, which meant she was being suckered. She also knew she wasn't going to stop until she'd touched every inch of him. She'd get him out of her system, and then she could go back to the eroticism of a quart of Ben & Jerry's.

She moved behind him, her hands roaming down his back in long strokes, her palms sliding over his firm buttocks, feeling his powerful muscles quiver at her gentle touch. Then she reached around to his arousal, almost feeling as if his intense heat burned her sensitized nerves when she slid her hands over his shaft.

He groaned and clenched his hands into fists. She quickly directed her touch to the thickness of his thighs and the sculpted perfection of his calves. When she finished, he rinsed. She stood watching, almost regretting that the task was done.

"That's how you shower," she said to Jared's back. "Now all you have to do is step out, dry off, and put on the robe that's on the hook." There were two robes there, one for each of them.

Jared turned to face her. "No, Erin. Now that I know how *you* like to be bathed, I will bathe you. And just so you know, I much prefer your cleansing ritual to any I've known before." He brushed her wet cheek with the pad of his thumb.

"Me?" she squeaked. Then it dawned on her that he

hadn't been asking her *how* to bathe in general, but what she liked. Her cheeks burned even as her stomach clenched at the idea of Jared doing to her what she'd just done to him.

"Your cleansing ritual, Erin. I must see if I have this right while everything is fresh in my mind." He pulled impatiently on the sleeves of her dress. "How do these clothes come off?"

Erin moved his hand to the zipper of her dress and showed him how to tug it down, exposing the front clasp of her lacy white bra. Apparently he liked what he saw, because he yanked the zipper down the rest of the way and pulled the dress off her shoulders like a kid at a gift-opening frenzy. Her dress fell to the tile floor, and she sucked in air, standing in lacy underwear beneath the tantalizing spray of warm water and the burning interest of Jared's fiery gaze. It was almost like her dream.

He pushed the straps of her bra from her arms, freeing her breasts. She slid her arms from the binding elastic as he tugged the bra down to her waist before exploring the full contours of her breasts, running his hands over her in sensual circles. "Why do you keep such beauty hidden and bound so tightly? How do you breathe like that?"

Before she could answer, he knelt and pulled down her underwear in one swift move. Heart racing, she stepped free and unclasped her bra with trembling fingers. He ran his hands up her legs and over the curve of her bottom, kneading her gently before brushing his hand over the curls of her sex. He pressed his fingers against her sensitive folds, making her groan as the burning heat of him set her even more on fire.

He stood, sending a rush of anticipation through her. The fullness of his erection pressed hard and hot between them as he pulled her into his arms. His deep groan of satisfaction sent her shaky pulse into an erratic flight.

But he didn't kiss her, he didn't tease her breasts into aching points of need, he didn't slide his hot fingers between the lips of her sex to fan her desire, or thrust his erection into her wet heat.

He stepped back and picked up the shampoo.

Erin's mouth had gone so dry she couldn't speak, though water sluiced everywhere and steam filled the air with a heavy mist.

He put an overlarge amount in both his hands and dropped the bottle. She didn't have the mental capability at the moment to tell him he had too much soap. His hands were on her, and she couldn't think. She stood frozen in place as Jared wove his fingers into her hair and covered every inch of her head with his firm but gentle touch. So much lather bubbled up that it poured off her head, covering them both. She stuck her head beneath the spray. He ran his fingers through her hair again, and more lather appeared.

Erin stuck her face under the water spray, scrubbing her hair again and managing to oust the last of the shampoo. Then she looked at Jared, blinking at him through the water.

He smiled and picked up the soap. Following her earlier example his hot soapy hands slid over her breasts and to her neck, where he stroked and cleaned all of the soft contours of her throat and nape, then moved his way down to her shoulders and arms. The strength of his hands turned his simple caress into a body-melting massage that she gave herself completely over to.

Jared slid his hands over Erin's soft body, enjoying his exploration of every dip and curve. She'd shut her golden eyes, so he couldn't see what she was thinking or feeling about his touching her, but he could feel the race of her pulse beneath her delicate skin, and hear the catch in her breath as he filled his hands with her lush breasts. Her nipples changed beneath the press of his palms, hardening to little points; when he rubbed over them, she moaned. The fashioning of her female to his male was so beautifully different that just the sight of her naked flesh had his desire clamoring so loudly that it took every fiber of his will to resist seeking pleasure.

As he explored her, his sensitive fingers felt the tiny little responses that her body had to his touch. He knew just where to caress to make her pulse rush. He knew just where to press to make her breath catch. He knew just where to slide his finger to make her stomach clench with a need that surely had to match his. He ran his fingers up the inside of her legs to slip into the burning folds of her sex, relishing the texture of her soft golden curls and the smooth heat of her need. She groaned so deeply when he found a tiny little spot of firm flesh hidden there that he surged to his feet, unable to hold back a moment more.

"Erin," he said, his voice rough with his want as he swung her up into his arms.

She opened her eyes. He expected to see burning desire within the golden depths of her eyes. And he wasn't disappointed, but something else lurked there, too.

"Wait," she said. "We must talk." She shook her head as if waking from a dream. She wiggled for him to set her down. "We'll talk while we eat," she said. "I'm starving. Last night's power bar has long since deserted me." Her voice quavered as if she found it hard to speak.

When he didn't move, she pressed her fingertips to his lips. "I'm sorry," she said softly.

Jared inhaled deeply as he reined in his want of her. The force of his effort made his breath rasp and his body shake. The moment of claiming Erin as his slipped between his fingers like the mists of a cloud.

Erin's stomach clenched with need, and with a pang of regret that she hadn't been able to just seize the moment. Jared's sensuality demanded that a woman explore his east, his west, and his forbidden south with her hands and tongue, but she curled her hand into a fist and pressed her lips closed.

No matter how right sex felt at the moment, there were too many unanswered questions and too many important reasons to keep them from indulging. And she'd remember them all the moment her brain decided to function. They both needed a distraction, and she'd never met a man yet who didn't like to eat. And she really was very hungry for . . . food.

He reluctantly set her on her feet. She turned off the shower and stepped from the steam to the bath mat, grabbing them each a towel. After handing Jared his, she dried off and wrapped herself in the thick terrycloth robe.

Jared had dried and stood waiting for her. Naked. She handed him his robe off the hook. He frowned at it, then at the one she'd put on. "I like you unclothed. There is so much more freedom and beauty that way. Why do you cover yourself?"

"Because you're supposed to," Erin said, searching for the right words. "Everyone can't go around naked."

"Do you find yourself shameful? Do you find me shameful?" he asked.

Erin snapped her gaze to his. "No. It is our custom to be clothed. It is considered wrong to go unclothed unless . . ."

"What?"

"Unless a man and a woman are being intimate with each other, and that is something that comes with time, as trust and acceptance and love are built between two people." She could tell that her answer upset him in some way, but decided that the sooner they ate and set their minds on something besides their attraction, the better off both of them would be. "I'll be in the kitchen," she said, exiting the bathroom and hurrying down the hall. On her way, she fingered her hair into place, wondering if her cat-dragged look would improve the appearance of her black eye and bandaged temple. To be honest, Jared made her feel so good, so beautiful, that she'd truly forgotten the fact that she was just a banged-up ordinary girl. He made her want things that were completely unreasonable and impractical, like making love and running around naked instead of facing reality and being responsible.

Once she reached the kitchen, she set about fixing them a snack. Jared showed up minus the robe, but had wrapped a blue towel around his waist. He leaned against the door jamb, arms folded across his chest as he watched her. She had little doubt that she was the meal he wanted. He had no interest in the food she put on the tray.

Keep busy, keep him distracted, Erin told herself. Unfortunately, his probing blue gaze kept searing holes through her resolve. When he moved up behind her and drew in a long, sexy-as-hell breath of air, as if he found her scent intoxicating, she knew she was sinking faster than her mind could bail her out. Feeling him press up against her was just like her dream in the cave, and made the kitchen just too small a place to be. Desperate, she gathered the gourmet cheese spread, canned peaches, and juice and led the way to the TV in the great room. He shadowed her every step. Sitting on the sofa, she placed her tray of goodies on the coffee table and went to work.

Jared stood next to the sofa and kept his gaze on Erin, absorbing her nervous movements as she spread all the food on the table. Since he'd let his mind accept that he needed her to help him protect her, the pain inside him had eased back from its raw edge, and his awareness had returned to a familiar sharpness.

Sunlight reached through the window glass, showering her with a golden light, making him want to touch her glory. His hand still throbbed from the feel of her softness, and his body ached to know more of the pleasure she made pulse in his blood, stronger than any poison from the damned. His mouth watered from the strength of the scents assaulting him.

As a Blood Hunter, he'd only known the scents of good, evil, and the blood of the Elan. What he detected now was different from anything he'd ever known, and his reaction unlike anything he'd ever experienced. She evoked hungers inside him, cravings that were consuming him.

"Join me," Erin said, patting the place beside her. Drawing a deeply satisfying breath of her scent, he settled onto the seat, feeling as if he'd sunk into the softness of a cloud.

Smiling, she handed him an object. "This is a remote control. It works the satellite TV over there, which is a way to see almost anything that is happening in the world. The catch is, you're only seeing what certain powers want you to see, but it is better than nothing."

She guided his finger on the remote and pushed his finger down. The wall in front of them erupted in a mortal battle of weapons and death. He stood quickly, his blood throbbing to act until he quickly realized that what he saw wasn't real and sat back down.

"Push this button up or down, and you'll see different things," she said. "I'll be right back. I forgot napkins."

He clicked the button to find a group of mortals arguing over matters that had no worldly significance and dismissed them, moving on. He did that two more times before finding something of interest—a man and a woman in each other's arms, kissing deeply. His insides clenched, and the vivid feel of Erin's fingers upon him rushed over him.

"We've just met, but I feel as if I've known you forever."

"Hurry, we have very little time." The man kissed the woman again. She moaned, and they grabbed at each other's clothes, scrambling to take them off. Jared shook his head. Their life would be simpler if they dispensed with clothing, period. The man moved his lips from the woman's mouth to other places along the woman's neck and shoulders, using his tongue and teeth upon her skin. Pushing the woman onto her back, the man spread her legs wide and kissed the darkened flesh there before he moved against her and thrust his erection into her flesh. He heard Erin returning, smelled the clean scent of her before she even entered the room.

"Oh, hell," Erin said.

After a surprised moment, he realized the images of the man melding to the woman disturbed her.

"I do not believe Heldon's realm has such pleasures, but then spiritual beings do not concern themselves with the physical aspects of the mortal realm. There are more important matters," Jared said, gliding his gaze down her body, wanting to see, feel, and make her cry out as loudly with pleasure as the woman on the screen.

She pulled the remote control from his fingers and turned off the images. "Snack is ready," she said, shoving a plate and fork at him before she sat next to him.

He took her offerings, frowning at her as he sensed her unease. "You are afraid of the satellite?"

He found it odd that she hadn't reacted strongly to the death battle, but had to the man and woman.

"No," she said. Using a fork to spear food, she put it in her mouth. She chewed and swallowed. "Eat."

He found the supple movements of her mouth and lips fascinating and focused on them. "Then you were afraid of the man and the woman?" he asked.

"No. Eat."

"They were intimate?"

"Yes. Eat."

"Do you fear being intimate?"

"No. Eat."

"Do you fear me?"

"No. Eat."

"Then I don't understand."

She took her fork with food on it and put it to his mouth. "Eat," she demanded.

Frowning at her, he opened his mouth, and she put the food in. Instantly, a sweet pleasure filled his mouth. He moaned. "What food is that?"

"Peaches."

He took his own fork, stabbed a peach, and brought it to Erin's mouth. "Peaches are better than oats."

She frowned. "Jared—"

"Eat," he said, pushing the peach into her open mouth. He sensed that she battled with want just as he did. He sensed she wanted to be intimate with him, but wouldn't allow herself to be, and that disturbed him. He leaned toward her, parting his lips, ready for his peach.

Her frown deepened, but she fed him more peach. "It is customary for each person to feed themselves," she said. "People only feed each other occasionally."

"When they are being intimate?" He gave her another peach, watching the sweetness of it glisten upon her lips.

She blinked at him. "Well, yes."

He smiled and set his plate on the table. "Good," he said, feeling a rumble of pleasure inside. Moving deftly, he pressed his mouth to hers and opened his lips to taste the juice of the peach and an essence his keen senses had now defined as Erin.

She stiffened a moment, her golden eyes widening with surprise. Then she melted to him, softening her mouth to his. He leaned closer to her, pressing her back against the sofa, and sent his tongue searching for more of her.

Desire once again surged within him, making his heart race and eradicating any lingering Tsara pain for the moment. As he licked the traces of peach from her lips, her tongue met his, sliding gently against it. He matched her movements, increasing them as his want of her burgeoned. He shifted his mouth from hers to touch and taste the softness of her skin along her cheek. He slid his hand to her sides, pulling her closer to the ache of his erection. Her robe bunched between them, and he tugged it open until his hand made contact with her skin.

She groaned. Her fingers threaded into his hair, and she arched her back. Leaning back slightly, he spread her robe completely open and gazed at her breasts and naked womanly body. He drew a deep breath, this time detecting the scent of her sex and her desire. Her want of him was stronger than his awareness of anything else, and nothing was sweeter to his soul than that small reprieve.

"Jared," she whispered.

"Erin. Beautiful," Jared said, lowering his head. He closed his mouth over her, and the very tip of her breast changed to a hard nub as he brushed his tongue against her. She moaned, and he flicked his tongue over that tip until she cried out, arching to him.

Her pleasure sent a bolt of pleasure through him so sharply that his hips jerked, bringing his erection hard against her leg and loosening the towel at his waist.

He snatched the towel away and covered her body with the heat of his gaze before he set his lips and tongue to tasting her again. He moved to the flat planes of her stomach and the soft, golden curls of her aroused sex, brushing his lips and tongue and teeth all along the softness of her skin until her heart hammered and breast quivered with every breath. Then he spread her legs wide and set his mouth there, thrusting his tongue into the sweetness, exploring the glorious taste of her.

Erin closed her eyes and let her head fall back into the soft leather as each stroke of Jared's tongue shot shards of pleasure right to her center. Between her own heated desire and his hot touch, she felt every degree of his hundred-and-fifteen temperature. Lava had replaced her blood and lit her afire. It was like being personally kissed by the midday sun and made her feel utterly decadent, as if she wanted to luxuriate naked in his warmth forever. The thought of having his heat inside her sent her erogenous zones into a frenzied chaos of sensation, and she came apart. Her orgasm erupted through her like a volcanic explosion of such magnitude that her world was forever altered. She cried out from the glory of it.

Jared rose up to thrust his erection against the soft, wet heat of her sex, pressing himself against her and sliding up the slick folds. She arched to him, sliding tighter along the side of his erection, and the need and pleasure that had been building within him exploded, consuming his entire being in a shuddering pleasure that sent his spirit soaring to a place he'd never been before.

Chapter Thirteen

Erin knew this shouldn't have happened. She should be protecting Jared from an involvement that wouldn't help either of them at the moment, but she hadn't stopped, hadn't wanted to stop, and honestly didn't know if she could have stopped. Everything inside her had been caught up in feeling and knowing the power of his passion.

And though they technically hadn't had intercourse, a sexual bond had been forged between them—one that she was sure they were both going to regret.

She pulled him to her, her racing heart slowing as reality stole away the euphoric magic of Jared's touch. His long hair was a dark curtain around them, closing out the world that she wished had never existed. All she wanted to know was the feel of him, the touch of him. To luxuriate in the supple velvetiness of his hard warrior body.

He leaned back from her, an intense question shadowing the iridescent blue of his eyes.

"You find great pleasure with me, yet I feel turmoil. Why?"

How did he know so much of what she felt?

Erin glanced at Jared's amulet, hanging between them. She touched the smoothness of the metal and once again felt its heat as her fingers tingled. She eased the edges of her robe closed and searched for the last threads of reason, dangling somewhere in her mind. "Yes, there is great pleasure with you, but I am torn inside because I don't know you. I know hardly anything about you. We haven't had time to—"

"Time?" he said, easing to her side so that he lay next to her on the couch. "Time is irrelevant to the spirit. I've heard millennia can pass before one spirit learns to soar with another. You do know me. You know all that matters. You know my spirit, for yours soars with mine, embraces mine. I felt it." He set his palm over her heart.

"You felt passion, desire, sexual arousal. That's all different than knowing what love really is. That only comes with time. You have to be patient, and when you understand all of this more, you will know I'm right. And you're wrong. I don't know you. I believe you are who you say, a Blood Hunter, a spirit being made mortal, but what does all of that mean now?" She placed her palm against his amulet, feeling the heat of it.

She must have hit a nerve, because Jared pulled his hand from her breast and climbed off the couch. She sat up, belted her robe. He paced the great room naked, and she held out the blue towel he'd had on.

He frowned at it.

"Please," she said. "I can't think with you naked."

"I think very well when you are naked. Perhaps your thinking isn't necessary at the moment."

Erin stood, marched to Jared, and wrapped the towel around his waist. From the look of him, she knew just what he thought of her naked. "Believe me, if I don't get to think, then nothing will ever happen. I want you to tell me everything about you, even what you told me before. This time I will hear you."

"What did you hear before?"

"My own thoughts."

He spoke, and this time she listened to what he had to say about his service as a Shadowman warrior in the Guardian Forces. His elite band of warriors, known as Blood Hunters, protect humans with Elan blood. She understood that the center of the forces for good was Logos, and a spiritual battle was waged against the evil Army of the Fallen, led by Heldon.

Erin shuddered. "I'm assuming from what you've said that not all humans have Elan blood."

"That is correct. You do, and you must understand what that means."

Erin drew a breath, looked at her hands, seeing

nothing different about herself, feeling nothing different about herself than anyone else she had ever met or known. The only thing she felt that set her apart was the growing sixth sense she'd experienced this past week. "Did my nearly dying make me an Elan?"

"You didn't become Elan, Erin. At least, I don't believe that to be true. It was my duty to protect the Elan, not to define the Elan. What makes you special is in your blood, and that powers your spirit, or your spirit determined your blood. Either way, you were born an Elan."

"That would mean my parents are and my ancestors were Elan as well."

"No."

"Why?"

"Only Logos knows. His mysteries are as deep and varied as the universe. You need to understand that you are in danger because of it."

"You said there are evil creatures who feed on Elan blood. Why?"

Jared seemed to hesitate a moment, inhaling deeply as if what he had to say was very difficult. "Those who cross through the spirit barrier to prey upon the spirits and bodies of mortals are the evil creatures that I speak of. There is great power in the blood of the Elan. The demons, werebeasts, and vampires of the Vladarian Order not only crave that power, but need that power in order to exist in the mortal realm and spread Heldon's evil to create hell within the mortal world." He turned and walked to a wide window to stare out at the thin mists rolling across the tops of the mountain peaks.

"Where are these creatures? How will I know them? How can I protect myself from them?"

"You'll know. I'll make sure you know. And I am here to protect you for a time," he said softly.

Erin knew there were more questions she should ask, and would think later to ask, but his last words snatched her attention. She riveted her gaze on Jared.

"What do you mean, for a time?" He looked so alone, silhouetted against the mountain peaks and mists outside the window, that she went to him and set her hands on his broad shoulders.

He stiffened at first. Then, when she pressed her cheek to his back, he sighed and relaxed into her embrace.

"I am damned, poisoned by a Tsara, one of Heldon's spiritual assassins. I can no longer serve the Guardian Forces. I can no longer walk with my Blood Hunter brethren. I will walk as a mortal for a time, and then I will no longer be."

The words hit Erin in her chest, right about her heart, and left her struggling against burning tears. She didn't want to believe what he said was true. His life couldn't be that fleeting. Yet she'd chosen to accept that he was a spirit being, so how could she not believe this, too? She moved to face him, needing to know more. His gaze was shadowed, his mouth grim.

"What do you mean, you will no longer be?"

He pressed his palm to her face and brushed his thumb against her cheek. "I can't answer that because I don't know yet myself."

He leaned down and kissed her then, lightly, reverently. She wrapped her arms around him, holding him so tight she was sure neither of them could breathe. "It's not going to happen," she whispered. "I won't let it happen."

He didn't say anything, but she knew he didn't believe her, any more than she had believed him before. The storm of events swirling around her life thickened to a dark cloud. It wrapped around her, strangling her with its force, and she was very much afraid Jared was irrevocably bound with her. She buried her face into the heat of his neck and placed one hand over his heart, making a silent vow. She didn't understand what or how, or anything else, but when the time came, he would be safe, too.

A jarring sound brought Jared to full alert, letting him know that danger didn't lurk, but something extremely annoying was intruding on their quiet rest. Erin slept in his arms, as golden and promising as a gentle sunrise. He didn't want to let her go, but the annoying sound would not cease.

Easing from beneath her, he followed the short, blaring notes, gritting his teeth against the unharmonious clatter. He found the offending object in the kitchen. Since glaring at it produced no results, he pushed it with his hand. It slid, hit the wall, and fell apart. The noise ceased. He thought he'd harmed the thing until he heard the woman Emerald. "Hello . . . are you there?"

"Yes," Jared said, scowling at the thing.

"Everthin' all right, luv? You sound a bit distant. Are you holding the phone?"

Jared picked up the phone and held it dangling in front of his face. "Yes."

"Erin and I spoke of the Sno-Med fair. We're going, and—"

"Include me," Jared said, his irritation switching from the phone to the conversation. Had Erin planned to go fight this enemy alone?

"Well, I hadn't thought . . . are you sure you're up to the trip?"

"Yes."

"In a jiffy, then."

"What is a jiffy?" Jared asked, but all he got for his trouble was a loud continuous blare that stopped after a few moments. *If you wish to dial a number, please hang up and try again.*

"Jared?" Erin came stumbling into the room. "Who called?

"What's a jiffy?" he asked.

"Depends on what kind of jiffy."

"Emerald is in a jiffy. Why didn't you tell me about the Sno-Med fair? Were you going to fight this predator alone? If you go, then I go, Erin."

"Whoa. Wait a minute. Emerald was on the phone?" Erin picked up the now silent offender and put it to her ear. "Hello?" She put the thing back together. "What did she say?"

"I just told you. We're all going to the fair, and she is in a jiffy." Curious, he picked up the phone and examined it, hearing the noise again. "Show me," he told Erin.

Erin blinked at Jared, realizing what his problem had been. "I'm sorry. I didn't think about you needing to learn a few things about the world you're in." She didn't exactly know how it had worked out, that she and Jared were going to the Sno-Med event, but she wasn't going to let the opportunity slip from her hand. Even if Dr. Cinatas had people looking for her, they wouldn't necessarily be able to recognize Jared. They couldn't have gotten more than a glimpse of him. It was herself she'd have to come up with a disguise for, but she'd worry about that shortly.

She showed Jared how to use the phone by calling Emerald back on the number posted by the phone. "She'll be *here* in a jiffy. That means fast. And we have to put on clothes quick, and we don't even know that they fit." She grabbed his arm and dragged him back toward the bedroom. They'd barely managed to slide into slacks, shirts, and tennis shoes before Emerald arrived. The only thing that didn't fit of the very generous and tasteful clothes Emerald had supplied were the bras. Erin opted to go without.

"Mum, he's a real giant," whispered a girl of about ten—who had to be Emerald's daughter—as Jared ducked through the doorway to join them on the porch. There was no mistaking their kinship. Megan was Emerald in miniature, silver-blond and petite, only Megan had an endearing exuberance and wonder shining in her misty green eyes.

"Not a real giant, poppet. They're much bigger. But he's a *real* guest at Silver Moon."

Megan's eyes grew impossibly wider, making Erin wonder what that meant. Then she introduced herself, holding out her hand. "I'm Megan, and I'm so glad you're finally here. Mum can stop grumbling, and I won't have to go to Bethy's so early every day now."

Smiling, Erin clasped the girl's hand, and Jared did the same, seemingly bemused by the girl's charm.

Emerald rolled her eyes, her cheeks flushing. "It wasn't that terrible."

"True," Megan said. "An ogre would be worse." Then she ducked off the porch laughing, a sound akin to tiny silver bells. Though she spoke everyday words, there was a melodic quality to the child's voice that seemed almost magical. "Let's hurry. Bethy's already going to be there before us. I don't know why we had to do a second reading today before going."

"Had to be sure, poppet. You're too precious. Climb into the back seat and buckle up." Emerald directed her gaze to Erin and then to Jared. "The two of you are looking better. Not as shook, but still a bit like the divil hashed you and you could use more rest. This must be important, then? Part of the reason why you have come to me, perhaps?"

Erin lowered her gaze, not wanting to reveal what she wasn't ready to tell. "Let's just say I want to look around at what Sno-Med is doing in the community."

Emerald sighed. "We'll chat later, then."

"We'll see." In the face of Emerald's open generosity, Erin knew her caution seemed like a slap, but at this point Erin didn't have a choice. They piled into the pickup, but before they could leave, a light tinkling of silver bells sounded.

"Hold a sec, luvs," Emerald said as she fished a BlackBerry from her purse. She frowned at it a few moments, then typed in a quick message. "There," she said. "Page forty-two should get them there for now. And I'll have to speak with them in the mornin'." She put the truck into gear, and before Erin could ask what Emerald meant, Megan began talking excitedly about her day at school, and the moment passed. The conversation flowed amid the twists and turns of the day as they wound along the mountain road.

With each mile closer to the fairgrounds, Erin was vividly aware of Jared's nearness in the seat next to her and his growing tension. She knew he didn't like tight spaces, and the long drive had to be getting to him. Not having looked at a map, she hadn't realized how far Jared had run across the mountains between yesterday and this morning.

But there was something more that she sensed under the surface. Something she couldn't put her finger on, and she wasn't even sure if it was her own anxiety about venturing out into public with Cinatas close by, or if her sixth sense was telling her there was more going on with Jared than what she knew.

Once they reached the fair and Emerald parked amid the hundreds of others out for a free Sunday afternoon on Sno-Med's dime, Erin's worry eased some. The concealing crowds and normalcy of the activities made it seem as if everything was right with the world—at least, on the surface. A banjo-driven band played lively bluegrass music that danced in the mountain air and sent even the stiffest of feet to tapping. People milled about the open-air big-top tent centered in the middle of a wide, grassy glen. Printed on a huge banner across the top of the tent was Sno-Med's emblem and motto, "Enrich your life with Sno-Med. Let us care for you." Hobolike clowns mingled, some on stilts, others sporting dozens of colorful balloons with Sno-Med's big emblem blazoned on them. Children ran about, laughing and playing little ring-toss games, and across the field small amusement rides were whirling with fun.

Everything looked so normal it made Erin cringe inside. Was she the only one who knew that something wicked lay beneath the surface of their lives? At least no Hummers or limos were in sight.

"Do we do this together or separately?" Emerald asked.

Erin met the woman's gaze with honesty. "If I am seen by certain people, it would be better if you weren't seen with me."

"Mum! I see Bethy! Come on." Megan ran up and tugged on Emerald's hand. "I'm coming," she said. Glancing at Jared and then back at Erin, she said, "You're not alone in this, but no one can help unless you let them." She turned and left with Megan, and Erin began to doubt her own caution.

"Erin, why have you come here amid so many whom you cannot trust?" Jared asked, sliding his hand to her back and edging her closer to his side as they walked into the crowd.

"I want to see what Sno-Med is up to." A clown handed her a balloon, and Erin slipped the bright blue ribbon between her fingers, feeling the balloon dance as she walked.

"They are either deliberately for Heldon's cause or ignorantly so," he said.

"What do you mean?"

He pointed to the emblem on the balloon, a pinwheel of four blue triangles with their points toward the center but not touching in any way. "The equilateral triangles here are pulled apart, separated, representing disharmony and chaos in each of the four corners of the universe."

Erin narrowed her eyes and shook her head a little. "All I see is an abstract snowflake for Sno-Med. Cinatas is big on white. The clinic looks like a winter wonderland, his limo is white, and everyone who works for him has to wear white."

Jared shrugged. "All is not seen at first, Erin. You'll learn."

They wandered into the tent. Spread out between free ice cream booths, free cotton candy, free cider, and free food were stations for blood pressure readings, glaucoma testing, bone density, diabetes screening—the usual tests for a health expo. But there were more tests for blood than anything else, from blood analysis to blood donations to stations encouraging everyone to know their blood type.

Was it a free med screening like this that led those four people in the Manhattan clinic to their death? Seeing the lines of people waiting enthusiastically made Erin's stomach twist, and she had the strongest urge to gather all of the children in her arms and run like hell. Jared must have picked up on her anxiety, for his hand tightened against her back.

A grandmotherly lady with elegant silver hair and warm hazel eyes handed Erin two forms to fill out. Jared must not have seemed very approachable, because she took one upward glance at him and backed away. Looking over the form, Erin realized there was very little Sno-Med would not know about every single person lined up before the day was through. Just as she was about to turn away, feeling as hemmed in by the large tent as Jared did by a car, she saw Dr. Batista manning the blood analysis booth. The doctor smiled at the woman from whom she was drawing a tube of blood.

Erin's first instinct was to hurry away before Dr. Batista saw her, but on second thought Erin decided to speak to the doctor and went to the booth.

Finishing with her patient, Dr. Batista looked up at their approach, and her eyes widened with surprise, then grew suspicious. "You're both looking better, but I'm surprised to see you here." Her statement was more of a question.

Erin shrugged. "I've heard of Sno-Med. I didn't realize you worked for them."

"I don't. But I do volunteer work for the community. I like to stay busy." She shrugged. "The stalwart woman in charge of organizing this huge event called for trained personnel to help. It's such a great thing to do for a community."

Erin bit back her reply. "You've done this often, then?"

Dr. Batista's eyes suddenly darkened, and her hand on the counter fisted. "No. This is the first I've been here to help. But my sister used to tell me about the expo. Sno-Med has one every six months." She glanced at Jared. "Sam's right. You don't say much at all." She didn't give Jared a chance to respond before directing a question at Erin. "Is Em here?"

"Yes. She and Megan are with Bethy and her mother." Erin wanted to ask more about Dr. Batista's sister, but the time and the place were wrong. Learning that the doctor's sister had worked for Sno-Med and was missing made Erin want to ask more than just a few questions.

The doctor nodded and leaned closer. "Why are you here? At Em's? Where are you from?"

"I told you this morning," Erin said. "And don't worry about your friend. She'll be repaid."

Dr. Batista shook her head. "I'm not worried about money. By accepting her help, you're letting her believe you are someone you are not."

"I understand," Erin said.

"No, I don't think you do, or you wouldn't be so cruel. I'll see you tonight. Em's invited everyone to eat at her house." Looking very unhappy at the prospect,

Dr. Batista turned away and welcomed the person handing her their information form.

"Let's go have an ice cream." Erin directed Jared to the line where several girls were playing Jacob's ladder with yarn. Two wore blue rubber sports bands with the Sno-Med emblem on it that read, "I'm a Sno-Med pro." One wore a white band. She'd seen white sports bands like it before, on the wrists of the two young *dead* women in the lab at the Sno-Med Clinic Friday morning. Her stomach churned as she wondered if those bracelets had read, "I'm a Sno-Med pro."

"Nice bracelets," Erin said. "What do I have to do to get one?"

The girls, not more than six years old, looked up, all bright smiles. "You have to be brave and have your blood tested," said the curly redhead with bright blue eyes. She held up the blue band proudly, then whispered, "Tierney is special. That's why she got a white one."

"You weren't supposed to tell anybody!" the little girl with the white bracelet cried, her soft brown eyes filling with tears. "I'll get in trouble."

"Don't worry," said Erin. "I didn't hear anything. Did you, Jared?" Erin glanced at Jared. His gaze was transfixed on the girl with the white bracelet. Erin had to tug on his arm to get his attention.

Meanwhile the little girl with the white bracelet backed away from them. "Bad man," she whispered.

"Bad man." Then she turned and ran, crying for her mother. Several people looked up in concern but went back to their fun when a woman ran up and wrapped the little girl in her arms. After a moment the woman set her gaze on Erin and Jared and came marching their way.

"What happened? What did you do to scare Tierney?" the mother demanded, a high, angry note ringing in her voice. The little girl had her face buried against her mother's neck.

"I'm sorry," Erin said. "I just asked the girls how to get a bracelet like theirs."

"I upset Tierney," said the curly redhead. "I tolded something that was a secret."

The mother's tense expression relaxed. "That's all right, Junie." She glanced at Jared, her expression guarded, then smiled at the other girls. "Why don't you two come with me and we'll get ice cream, okay?"

The girls nodded, following the woman.

"She has Elan blood, Erin," Jared whispered.

"What?"

"The child with the white bracelet has Elan blood. We must go outside. I need to leave here," he said, taking her hand and urging her from the tent.

Erin followed Jared out of the tent, feeling extremely queasy inside. Tierney had Elan blood and had been given a white bracelet, the murdered women in the lab had worn something similar, and Erin had this Elan blood and had been singled out by Dr. Cinatas for special patients . . . all of these pieces had millions of questions raging through Erin's mind. She was afraid she'd have to tell more than she wanted known to get the answers she wanted to these questions.

She also wondered if Jared was telling her everything. She now had no doubt that his appearance in her life was in some way connected to Dr. Cinatas and Sno-Med. It could be just as simple as he said it was. She had Elan blood, and he protected the Elan.

As she passed the happy, excited people who didn't have a clue that they might be selling their lives for a free lunch, she kept looking at their wrists. Many people wore blue bracelets, some wore none, but she didn't see another white one.

Jared led Erin from the tent, desperate to break free of the deafening noise inside. There were so many people, so many voices, so much sound hounding him. His head pounded from the punishing wave of the noise. When he'd caught the scent of Elan blood other than Erin's while they were speaking to Dr. Batista, his hunger for its taste had cut like a knife through his heart. An innocent child with sunny hair and tearful blue eyes had looked at him as if he were the worst of the damned. Her fear ate at him. He was a protector, a warrior who fought to preserve all that was good and true. That was being stripped away from him one excruciating piece at a time, leaving him raw, bleeding, and consumed with a dark hunger.

He clenched his fists, bit down on his tongue hard enough to taste his own blood, and strangled whatever it was inside him that fought to break loose. He felt his body grow extremely hot, and he trembled as he moved forward, weakened by the battle. Reaching the outside mountain air, he breathed deeply and pulled Erin into his arms, drawing from her the ease only she brought, ease that tamed the beast inside of him. The deafening noise piercing his mind ebbed away.

"Jared, what is it? Let me help."

He pulled her closer with a shaky arm. "There is no help, Erin." Self-disgust ate at him. Children often knew what adults had become too inured to sense. The child knew that the Tsara's evil lurked inside him, and it was only a matter of time before that evil consumed him.

Chapter Fourteen

JARED SAT IN THE GREAT ROOM of the cabin, watching the evening shadows creep across the soft blue of the mountain-sloped horizon. Ever since leaving the fair, he'd felt a growing tension within him, as if some force greater than his will was seething to be free from his iron control, and he didn't want Erin to know. The darkness in him needed to stay hidden. So he didn't reach for her, didn't try to kiss her, and a distance that was more than space sprang up between them. He knew it was his fault. He couldn't explain what was happening inside him; he felt it was wrong, but he couldn't stop it.

She'd tried to fill the tense void by showing him many things within the cabin and how they worked. The ringing of the phone brought a sigh of relief from her that had chastened his heart. He was supposed to be protecting her—easing her burdens, not adding to them.

Erin answered the phone in the kitchen, and Emerald's distinctive voice filtered through to Jared's ears. "I've made a stew and bread pudding for afters. And a bit of a warnin' to ya. The dragon is here. So I can run the lot by if you don't want to face him, or you can come here for a bite. Would that do?"

"Yes," Erin said. "We'll be more than glad to come there." She hung up the phone and returned to the great room.

"Jared, we're—"

"I heard," he said softly.

"Your hearing is that sensitive?" she asked, sitting next to him, her gold eyes wide with wonder and a softness that was a gentle as her touch.

"Yes." He inhaled deeply, drinking in every nuance of her scent. Something was different about him tonight. He could sense more, smell better, and hear more acutely than he remembered since coming to the mortal world. "The noise within the tent was too loud to bear."

"I didn't know. Do you want to stay here and rest while I go eat? I have questions I'm hoping to find answers to. I want to know if Emerald, the sheriff, or Dr. Batista have any other connection to Sno-Med than what we've seen so far, and I want to know exactly how Emerald knew we were coming to the Sacred Stones."

"No. We will stay together." He, too, had questions. The sheriff showed up to take them to Emerald's.

His harsh manner scraped Jared's nerves as much as the tight space in the pickup, making Jared even more uncomfortable. He couldn't figure out why he felt such unease, or why it was growing with the shadows.

It worsened when he neared the cottage. The little house was set so low and deep beneath the boughs of thick trees that Jared felt an oppressive weight settle on his shoulders. He immediately missed the open freedom of the mountain crest where the cabin sat.

The sheriff clamped a hand on Jared's shoulder at the door to the cottage. Jared shrugged it off sharply, turning to face the man who stood just half a foot shorter. Whether the man thought he was protecting those he cared about or not, Jared wasn't going to give the guy any more room than he had to. Jared barely had room to breathe himself. "Have you got something to say?" Jared demanded.

Erin touched Jared's arm lightly, trying to soothe him, and Jared drew a breath, feeling a deep urge to run through the woods until this tension inside him eased.

The sheriff kept his gaze on Jared as he spoke to Erin. "So far you've checked out, Morgan, but I'm waiting for more to come tomorrow. Then we're going to locate your car on Spirit Wind Mountain, and we'll see about you staying in Twilight at all. Em insists on your being here tonight. I don't like it, and I'm not going to pretend to like it. Say or do anything to upset her, her daughter Megan, or Annette, and your accommodations will get bars faster than you can blink."

The sheriff shoved open the door. "Have you got a problem with that, Em or Annette?"

Emerald and Dr. Batista stood just inside the doorway, eavesdropping.

"You're too serious, Sam." Emerald smiled, motioning them in with a wave of her arm. "Watch yourself now. My humble digs are a wee bit small."

Jared had to duck low, and once inside he felt the full force of a strong magic, something much greater than the enchantment at Silver Moon. His gaze shot immediately to Emerald and studied her as she welcomed Erin into her home as well. When they finished, he caught Erin's hand and urged her to his side. Magic this strong was not to be trusted very far. Logos never aligned himself with magic, for though magic wasn't evil in itself, through the ages Heldon had become very adept in twisting the power of the mortal ground to his destructive purposes.

Erin tightened her grip on Jared's hand as she glanced about Emerald's home, wondering what bothered him. She could feel him winding tighter and tighter, like a spring ready to burst, and she didn't know how to help him. He seemed to be withdrawing from her, yet needing to keep her close as well.

Given how their first hours in the cabin this morning had gone, she'd thought they'd crossed barriers that had made them closer than she'd ever been to another. She still felt that way inside, but Jared's actions were telling her he didn't. Old hurt tried to well up in her, but she firmly stamped on it. She had to believe that when he was ready, he'd tell her what had upset him. It had to do with the Sno-Med fair and their discoveries there. That's when he'd started to change.

"We're all set to eat. Megan has the table ready, so I hope you're hungry."

"Very," Erin said, forcing a smile. Before falling asleep on the couch, she and Jared had finished eating the peaches, cheese, and crackers that she'd fixed for a snack after their shared shower. But that snack was long gone, and she was very hungry.

Emerald's home was the *Better Homes and Gardens* version of magical comfort. The rooms, though small, were filled with a treasure trove of diminutive art. Cabinets burst with figures of ethereal fairies and graceful, winged angels no larger than Erin's thumb. The walls, though painted in dark tones of burgundy, green, and blue, sparkled with light as if dusted with glitter.

The heavenly smells of beef stew and fresh bread made for a mouthwatering invitation that everyone accepted despite their reservations. The savory stew and buttery bread bridged a gap the initial lack of conversation had left. Compliments went to Emerald and Megan for the delicious dinner. Erin noted that Jared watched what others did before acting himself. For a man just introduced to the physical world, he functioned remarkably well and learned fast.

"What is happening with Sheriff Slater, Sam? You said earlier that he had trouble his way." Dr. Batista spoke as she lightly buttered a piece of bread. She'd changed from her lab coat to an attractive outfit of brown pants and shirt that matched the soft lights in her eyes, but she'd kept her hair tightly knotted and her shoulders stiff. "I didn't catch wind of it at the health expo today. Usually if something is up, everybody is talking about it."

The sheriff followed his spoonful of stew with a sip of water before answering the doctor. "I think Slater is trying to keep the situation quiet until he can figure it out. It's a puzzle that is only getting worse." He glanced at Megan, who listened intently to his every word as only ten-year-olds who think they're all grown up can. "I'll have to tell you the details later," he said, making Megan frown before he continued. "But the man they found on the side of the road came up with a print match in the computer. Unfortunately, there's an obvious glitch in the system."

"What?" Dr. Batista bit into her bread.

"According to his fingerprints, the man was on death row for a number of years and had been executed in South Carolina two years ago."

"Away with ya, Sam Sheridan," Emerald exclaimed,

brows rising. "The body of a man who's already dead."

"Mum, will you be doing a readin' of it?" Megan asked, her green eyes wide with interest.

"No. You know readin's are special now. Can't be doin' them on everythin'."

Sam rolled his eyes. "So your crystal ball can identify dead men now?"

"Sam." Dr. Batista glared at him.

"I've wrangled with fiercer dragons, Nett." Emerald set her cool gaze on the sheriff. "I don't know what my crystal will reveal or won't reveal. The Druids are rarely kind in the secrets they give up, but I could tell ya somethin' if I were of a mind to."

Dr. Batista nodded. "It'd be better than the report they got today. Sometimes I think the system is useless. They've yet to determine whose prints were on Stef's—" Her voice broke.

Dr. Batista had mentioned her sister's connection to Sno-Med at the fair, and something bad had happened. "I'm sorry. You spoke of your sister earlier as if something is wrong. I can't help but ask what."

Dr. Batista took a deep breath. "She disappeared six months ago."

"How? From where?" Erin asked.

Emerald sighed. "I found her backpack at the Sacred Stones."

Dr. Batista softly said, "Stef was to meet a group of her Sno-Med coworkers at the Sacred Stones Saturday morning to go hiking. She'd called me Friday and left a message on my cell to call her back that night. She said she had something important to ask me, and she sounded more concerned than usual about it, but not especially upset. There was an emergency at the hospital. I'd been in surgery for hours, and when I got her message, I didn't call. It was late, and I was tired. She didn't answer my call in the morning. Several hours later, I received a call from Emerald."

Erin shifted her gaze to Emerald's. "You worked for Sno-Med?"

"Mother Mary. Whatever gave you that idea . . . ah, the hikin' with the coworkers. No. I'd gone to the stones at dawn lookin' for you two and found the backpack. Stef's information was inside, along with Annette's as an emergency contact."

It took Erin a second to absorb this new fact. "You were out looking for Jared and me six months ago?"

"It's a story," Emerald said.

The phone rang, and Jared started. Erin set her hand over his, remembering his sensitivity to sound.

"It's Bethy ringing," Megan said as she jumped up and ran to the phone. She picked up the receiver, totally assured that she knew who was calling. "Bethy!" She listened to what Bethy had to say, then squealed with delight. "Hold on." She pressed the receiver to her chest, eyes shining. "Mum, can I go to Bethy's tonight? She just got Fairy's Fantasy X, and her mum's said we can have a marathon until we best the Dark Lord. Can I? Sarah, Susan, Barb, Mel, Beanie, Mish, and Carrie are all going to be there. It might take us days!"

Erin recognized the newest game craze for the younger set of videomaniacs, where a force of tiny fairies managed to defeat all foes in their quest to save the world.

Emerald sighed. "It's Sunday. We've not done your readin' for tomorrow yet. You can't be goin' tonight."

"But Mum!" Megan's eyes grew mistier with tears. "It's just Bethy's! Please. We did two for today. Can't it wait a day or two—"

"Meggie—"

"Just once, please. Can't I be like everyone else just once, Mum? Please."

Emerald inhaled as if she was facing a foe she didn't know how to fight. "Tomorrow, then. Ya need to come home tomorrow night for your readin'. I'll delay no longer."

"Yes," Megan squealed into the phone. "Mum will run me by in a jiffy."

"After we've finished," Emerald cautioned.

Megan dashed back to the table, kissed her mother's cheek happily, and sat to finish her meal. She bubbled with so much excitement that Erin thought she'd float to the ceiling before it was over with. Emerald seemed distracted for the rest of the meal and through the afters, which turned out to be dessert.

Jared commented on the sweet bread pudding. It was the only thing he'd said since speaking to Emerald when they first arrived. "Peaches," he said. "Peaches would be good with this."

The heat of his thumb caressing the inside of her wrist told Erin he hadn't made an idle comment. Her pulse raced back through the memory of him and peaches and juicy kisses.

Dr. Batista gave Jared a puzzled look that soon turned to compassion. "Peaches are good, Jared," she said, as one might to a small child. "You like peaches? I like peaches too."

Emerald sputtered her coffee and shook her head. "Nett, both you and Sam are goin' to be eatin' a load of crow."

Erin frowned, then realized Dr. Batista had come to the conclusion that Jared was mentally handicapped. And from the look in the sheriff's eyes, he was reaching the same conclusion.

Hell, Erin thought, deciding not to disabuse them of the notion. Having them think Jared was impaired would go a long way to avoid having to explain anything. The silver-bell sound that Erin was beginning to associate with Emerald's Blackberry tinkled, and Emerald quickly rose up to attend to it.

"I'll get my stuff ready to go to Bethy's," Megan said, jumping up and dashing away with a big smile on her face.

Sam shook his head as he spoke to Dr. Batista. "Em's so married to her Blackberry that she can't have a life of her own."

Dr. Batista glared at him. "You wouldn't be saying that if I'd gotten a call for emergency surgery."

"That's different."

"No. It's not."

"What good can she do? Tell them to go to page sixty-nine now?"

"You are impossible. Have you ever even read her book? Do you even know what is on that page?"

"I don't have to," Sam grumbled.

"What book?" Erin asked.

"*Sexual Synergy,*" Dr. Batista said. "Emerald is a sex therapist known as Dr. Em in Dublin."

"An online sex therapist," Sam said. "I bet her clients e-mail her from bed. Gives a whole new meaning to 'you've got—' "

"Don't you dare say it." Dr. Batista groaned.

"Male," said the sheriff.

Emerald returned, and the meal soon ended on a more congenial note than it had begun. The sheriff returned Erin and Jared to the cabin with an "I'll see you in the morning" good-bye.

Erin stood for a moment next to Jared, looking at the soft fingers of moonlight bathing the cabin in a silvery glow. It appeared almost mystical amid the dark shadowy trees and black edge of the rugged earth. The humid air was fragrant with the sweet scent of honeysuckle, bringing childhood memories of plucking the nectar from the hearts of the delicate blooms. More fireflies than Erin had ever seen at one time flickered like a carpet of fairy dust about them, blanketing the area in beauty, and quietly reminding Erin that Twilight was different than other places. Just the fact that Emerald, Dr. Batista, and Jared had all ended up there told her that, even if her sixth sense hadn't.

The sound of a wolf howling cut through the magic of the night and made Erin shiver.

"Hurry," Jared said, taking her arm and urging her into the cabin. Once inside, she turned to find him stripping his clothes off in the doorway.

"Jared, we need to talk. We can't let what almost happened happen."

He stood naked in the doorway, powerful and hungry. He breathed deeply, his nostrils flaring. His eyes glittered an eerie blue in the moon's silver light.

He walked to her, sending her heart fleeing places her feet didn't have the sense to run to. Her breath caught, her lips parted, and her insides clenched, already heated with the memory of the pleasure he alone had branded upon her.

He shoved the clothes into her arms. "I have to run," he said harshly. "Lock the doors, and whatever you do, do not leave the cabin." He turned and ran into the dark of the night.

Chapter Fifteen

"YOU DON'T LOOK AS IF you are feeling well, Manolo," Cinatas said holding up a bottle of Chateau Petrus merlot to the intense surgical light he kept next to his seat while dining. He examined everything for impurities. Manolo stood subserviently in the doorway, his body shivering from fever, which Cinatas knew would become very painful shortly. Marburg virus, or as Cinatas liked to call it, Marvel virus, for it miraculously wiped any nuisance from his life within a week's time, purged the host of all impurities before his very painful death.

Almost as painfully as his dinner was progressing, Cinatas thought. Shashur had decided to join him, and the tedious affair was becoming a pissing contest. One that Shashur couldn't even dream of winning.

Cinatas smiled at the secret progress he'd made in locating Morgan and her not quite mortal friend. Erin had to be traveling with someone not of this world; nothing else could explain Morgan's ability to evade capture.

Shashur reached over and snatched the bottle from Cinatas. "If you're going to fraternize with your idiots, I'm at least going to have a drink." He sank his dentally altered fangs into the cork and twisted it free of the bottle.

Cinatas shuddered at the violence of the act. His manicured nails cracked to the quick as he dug them into the arm of his Louis XIV chair, carved by André-Charles Boulle himself. Shards of pain ripped up Cinatas's arm, and he silently vowed that Shashur would fall subject to the same hemorrhagic fever as Manolo. It would be interesting to see what its purging effects would do for the damned.

"I'm fine, sir," Manolo said, answering Cinatas's query. "Reports are that Sheriff Sheridan ran a check on Erin Morgan today. She's in Twilight. We've ears in his office and a man on his tail. We should know at any minute where Morgan and—"

"You've got a team ready to act, right? Then keep up the excellent work," Cinatas hissed though his pain, interrupting Manolo before he could say anything more about the man with Morgan.

Manolo disappeared, and Shashur drained his wineglass, then poured another. "You've no cause to feel smug," he said. "The damned found them on that godforsaken spirit-ridden mountain. It was an easy deduction to know they'd surface in the nearest town."

"Of course," Cinatas said. "I'm sure incompetence had nothing to do with your inability to secure Morgan. What can the damned do when a few Blood Hunters from the spirit world bare their teeth?"

Shashur stood, shoving his chair back from the table. "I'm bringing your insolence and this whole incident up for review before the Vladarian Order. Pathos found you, and he can replace you."

Cinatas only smiled. Shashur would be dead before that meeting in three weeks.

Jared ran out of the cabin with the Tsara bite burning as if he were being branded anew. The poison in him roiled, scraping the insides of his chest like a beast clawing to be free. When he'd exited the sheriff's vehicle just minutes ago, something had told him to run as far from Erin as he could. Whether it was the full light of the moon shining on him, pulling the evil in him to the surface, or if the sudden release from the magic of Emerald's cottage caused an eruption of evil, the bloodlust had reared its head.

He escaped into the forest, moving like the wind across the mountain terrain. The scent of earth mingled with the fertile green of the leaves and the decay of yesterday's life. Wildlife skulked. He could smell the fear of those hiding, and the hungry power of those lurking for smaller prey. He could also sense their awareness of him, and with growing satisfaction, their fear of him. No other predator could match his prowess.

Too late, he realized the mistake of running into the wild and giving free rein to the poison. The deeper he delved into the recesses of the forest, into the primal heart of savage rule, the darker the night became, and the more his soul fed upon the feral air. His vision sharpened, his hearing heightened, his incisors cut into his lip, and he savored the taste of even his own blood.

He howled as his blood pumped through his veins so forcefully that every fiber within him throbbed painfully at the pressure. He gasped for air, his body trembling, shivering. He ran harder, forcing himself to the very edge of his abilities. His mind was consumed with the need to give in to the darkness and taste her Elan blood. He ran until his lungs could stand no more, and when he came to a stop beneath the light of the moon, he stared in horror at his body.

His Blood Hunter's cloak had appeared, but the pure silver of it was gone, faded to a dirty gray-white, a ghastly, twisted caricature of his once sleek coat. He was no longer pure and true of heart.

Within him grew a hunger for any blood to temporarily stave his overwhelming desire for Elan blood. As he crossed over a ridge, the scent of roasting meat on a campfire curled up from the valley. The laughter of mortals grated in his ears even as the scent of humans and of blood filled him with a lust he had to satisfy. He howled as he hurled himself toward them, his primordial cry sending creatures fleeing from their hollows, obliterating all instincts but flight.

The wolf's ravenous howl, carried by an evil, icy wind, ripped through the Blood Hunters gathered on the mountainside. Silver moonlight bathed their glittering cloaks that bristled with horror at the torment of one who could no longer be called their own, but whom they couldn't turn their back upon. The blood-lust in the wolf's howl ripped at Aragon's soul.

"His pain is mine," Aragon said harshly. "I chose wrongly, and he's suffering a slow death that no warrior should ever face."

Sven paced. "You're giving up too soon. His soul isn't damned yet. He hasn't given in to his lust for Elan blood."

"He's close," Aragon whispered, lowering his head. "The Tsara poison is too potent for him to ever redeem himself."

"You may be right," Navarre said angrily. "Other forces are working against Jared as well. The presence of the Vladarian Order and this search for Jared by both mortals and the damned is a grave concern. We have to consider that Pathos is trying to get Jared, to force Jared to join the Vladarians."

Aragon raised his head. "The damned are searching as we speak, and Jared is running wild—he can't even hear me above his bloodlust."

"Then we run with him," Sven said, stepping forward.

"I will run as well," said York. "We'll surround Jared and slay any demon who tries to capture him."

Navarre paused. "The plan has merit."

Aragon wanted to tear the world apart with his pain. He'd already risked too much on the possibility of Jared's salvation, and as leader of the Blood Hunters, he didn't dare risk more. The consequences within the mortal world could be devastating if Jared were to become as Pathos. Having another Blood Hunter in the Vladarian Order as strong or stronger than Pathos would likely bring hell to reign upon the mortal ground. "Let us find Jared and then we'll see." The dawn was too far away for Jared to survive the forces of evil, and Aragon knew he would have to be strong enough to kill Jared this time. A human scream echoed through the forest as the Blood Hunters ran, telling them that they might be too late.

After Jared left, Erin churned, at odds with herself and him. His behavior had been strange. He'd abruptly left, and she felt the void. The television held no interest for her, so she went to the computer, thinking she'd check her personal e-mail; her parents were going to try and let her know how they were by e-mail.

She froze with her finger on the enter button. When she'd come to work for Cinatas, she'd been astounded at the employee benefits, insurance, discounts on living accommodations and cellular phones, free Internet through the Sno-Med system, and worldwide travel opportunities. When the job offer had been passed to her through her nursing supervisor at the hospital, Erin decided it was time to see more of the world. The Sno-Med Corporation, touted as the leader of bioscience, had been generous to a fault with its benefits. She'd overlooked it those months ago, but she couldn't ignore it now.

If she logged in, Sno-Med could trace her IP address. She hit the delete button, then decided to Google Dr. Anthony Cinatas and the Sno-Med clinic. Avoiding the corporation's official sites, she looked for anything associated with his name, the clinic, and the name of every patient she recalled helping treat.

She found noteworthy American Medical Association articles on his studies on blood proteins, international interviews, and articles about Dr. Cinatas's life. She was surprised to learn that he'd been considered as a Frankenstein early in his career because of his radical ideas about using large quantities of treated blood to cure disease. He'd had an accident ten years ago. His car had gone off a bridge in icy waters, and he'd nearly drowned but been revived. After that his career sky-rocketed, and he was now touted as a hero for his fight to preserve the sanctity of life.

Articles about the Sno-Med Research and Development Center in Arcadia, near the very place his car had gone off the bridge, heralded Dr. Cinatas as the economic savior of the town. Grabbing a pen and paper, Erin started jotting down notes.

Then she made a list of the men she'd given blood transfusions to over the past few months and the basic facts about them that she could gather off the computer. There were eleven, twelve if she counted Shashur's—all rich, influential, and from different areas of the world.

But nowhere in any of the material did she find a reference to the word Elan, or special blood. And she also looked for anything that would label blood as being white or pure. She did find articles about Dr. Batista's sister Stefanie Batista, who'd simply vanished from the Sacred Stones on Spirit Wind Mountain. Or had she? What if she'd discovered something she shouldn't have in the lab? Could she have met the same fate as the four other people in Manhattan?

She stared at the page, wondering if there were more people in and around Dr. Cinatas's world that had "disappeared."

The howling of a wolf outside startled her.

Her scalped tingled, and the hair on the back of her neck rose, just as it had when she'd walked into the Sno-Med clinic Friday morning.

Jared was out there alone, and her sixth sense told her something was wrong. She glanced at the time on the computer screen. Hours had passed since he'd left.

Worry itched its way through her. What if he was in trouble? What if the wolves they'd seen last night were after him? What if he needed her?

Rising, she left the bedroom where the computer was housed and went to the front door. She started to unlock it and to call for Jared, but remembered Jared's words. *Lock the doors, and whatever you do, do not leave the cabin.*

What did he know that she didn't know?

His behavior all day had been different, as if he'd known there was something wrong. What if those creatures from last night were back? What if Jared had left to protect her? It was the only explanation that she could see that fit. He'd practically glued himself to her side for almost forty-eight hours, and then he'd suddenly left.

Whether she wanted to admit it or not, she felt the yawning void of his absence with every part of her.

Glancing at the window, she could only see black outside. But the sensation that something was out there, that something predatory was watching her, suddenly screamed at her. She killed the lights and moved to the kitchen, looking for a knife, anything to hold in her hand that would be useful to protect herself.

Had Cinatas found her? Was he out there?

Knife in hand, she tiptoed from the kitchen, listening intently to every sound, listening so hard that when a bloodcurdling howl cut through the night, she jumped. Chilling fear stabbed right through her.

Something hit the door hard less than ten feet from where she stood.

"You were right, Aragon," Sven yelled from where they stood on the mountainside, not far from Jared. "I failed in my duty, and now many are paying for my misdeed."

"We *all* chose. And I am the leader," Aragon shouted, his spirit sickened at the violence of Jared's craze. "The Tsara's poison is stronger than ever before. I thought there would be more time." Aragon gritted his teeth in frustration. "He's tasted mortal blood and is determined to reach Elan blood. I must end it."

"Jared hasn't taken a soul yet," Navarre said, placing his hand on Aragon's shoulder. "He is not wholly damned yet."

Aragon shook off Navarre's hold. "Are you asking me to wait until that happens, damning us all?"

Navarre stepped back, shaking his head.

Aragon didn't ask for unity from them as he swirled from his Blood Hunter's cloak to his human form and held up his sword. He could tell, read it in their eyes, that the brethren were no longer one. He wasn't fit to lead.

"Give him another day," York shouted.

Aragon turned his back and ran after Jared. The wind whirled with the force of his blade. Thunder crashed through the heavens at his war cry, and a bright blue bolt of lightning cut across the sky. He landed onto the mortal ground next to Jared.

Jared turned. The feral gleam lighting his eyes stabbed a fissure of pain deep into Aragon's gut. Aragon lifted his sword, remembering all that had passed between them. The battles they had fought side by side in. The time when Jared had spent the last of his strength to bring Aragon from certain death.

Instead of issuing the killing blow, Aragon flung his sword aside and returned to his Blood Hunter's cloak. He tackled Jared with his bare claws. Jared's first full blow knocked Aragon back twenty feet, slamming him into the hard wood of a thick tree trunk. The combined strength of mortal and Fallen shocked Aragon. The oak cracked and splintered in half. Dazed, Aragon stumbled for balance, determined to keep Jared away from mortals. Dawn wasn't too far away—if they managed not to kill each other, maybe one more day might make the difference.

Chapter Sixteen

JARED ARCHED BACK in pain as reason and the morning light stabbed his conscience like bolts of lightning. He sucked in gulps of dewy air scented with blood and sweat, hissing at the agony. He opened his eyes to find that he stood in a wide circle of destruction. Churned ground and twisted and broken trees surrounded him, as if a tornado had touched down there and nowhere else.

He smelled his own blood and, with heart-stopping realization, that of a mortal. He could smell it on him. Not Elan blood, but just as damning. Nauseated, he spat until the point of being ill, but had nothing within him but dry heaves.

Horrific images of people, blood, a campfire, a storm, and a black wolf flashed painfully at him, all too vague in detail to be anything more than a cloudy blur.

Erin. He had to see her. Finding a cold mountain stream, he stepped into the foot-deep water, which hissed and bubbled at contact with the heat of his body. He went to the center and lay down, letting the water rush over him. He bathed himself three times and still didn't feel clean, though no traces of blood remained. Had he killed someone? He searched his mind but couldn't remember anything but a red haze. If he had killed, wouldn't he know it?

The darkness was in his soul, and nothing could save him now, but he had to save Erin. And the only way to do that would be to determine if the mortals they were with, Emerald, Sam, and Dr. Batista, had the resources and the will to help Erin. He'd given Erin's story about the doctor she worked for a lot of thought, and finding the little girl with Elan blood at the fair had verified his suspicions. Dr. Cinatas was likely connected to the Vladarian Order.

Rising, he went looking for Erin. He had nothing but darkness and despair to offer her. He was damned. The cabin was locked tight, and Erin didn't answer his knock. He decided to let her have a few more minutes of innocent sleep before burdening her doorstep. He went to the hammock on the deck and watched the sun crest the mists covering the mountain peaks.

He longed for Erin. He wanted to take her into his arms and hold her close, as he'd done yesterday, but he couldn't, for deep in his soul, he knew what he wanted with her could never be. He had to leave her before he killed her. He had to destroy himself before he joined the forces of the damned.

The bright lights of the lab were blinding, burning her eyes. All she could see was a blur of white ceiling and white walls. Erin tried to move and couldn't. Pain punctured her chest. Her hands, feet, and head were tied to a stretcher. Squinting, she looked down at her arms and saw blood-filled tubes running from her limbs to the side of the stretcher. She forced herself to writhe against the leather bindings, knowing that every movement she made pumped more of her blood from her body into the blood bags labeled for the king of Kassim. But she didn't have a choice; she couldn't just lie there and watch her life end a drop at a time as her blood was drained from her.

Cinatas appeared, his suave smile and gleaming silver eyes cold and dead. "Did you really think that you could run from me, Erin? Did you think that you could bring me down?" He shook his head. "Tisk, tisk. You're a fool for even trying, and now you'll die a fool's death."

She struggled against the bindings.

"You've no more second chances, Erin. You're dead. Life is over. I win."

Erin woke from her nightmare and sat up, screaming. The vision of watching her blood being drained had seemed so real that she ran her hands over her body just to assure herself it wasn't. She sat on the couch in the cabin where she'd fallen asleep waiting for Jared to return. The storm had lashed the night for hours. On the coffee table in front of her lay the knife.

Erin had decided the slam against the door had been the wind blowing a tree limb against it.

How long had she slept? Rising, she hurried to the kitchen, then nearly groaned at the clock's digital reading. Six in the morning.

What if he'd tried to get in, and she hadn't heard him? She ran to the front door and unlatched the locks.

"Jared!" she called into the shadows and swirling mists, still hovering despite the dawn. She moved to the edge of the porch, calling again, and the sensation that something lurked just beyond the mist grew. She went down the steps, thinking she heard a groan, but before she reached the ground, she caught sight of the hammock on the cabin's deck. There was no mistaking Jared's long, dark hair or the naked contours of his six-ten power punch. Moving closer, she saw with growing dread the bleeding cuts and scratches covering his body. He writhed in the hammock as if he were in pain.

She ran to him and set her hand on his shoulder. Twigs and leaves were tangled in his long hair, and heat poured from him. Erin was sure he had to be hotter than ever before. Had she been wrong about him needing the medicine Dr. Batista had left? "Jared?"

He groaned. "Erin?" His voice sounded ragged.

She sighed in relief. "What happened to you? You're hurt again."

"I'll heal," he said in a tone of voice she'd never heard him use before. It held such self-disgust that it almost made her take a step back from him.

"Come on," she said, urging him up. "Let's get you cleaned up. Were you having a nightmare? You looked as if you were in a lot of pain."

"It is no less than I deserve," he said starkly, easing away from her touch. His body trembled as if hit with a stronger wave of pain. The stubble darkening his face made him look dangerous, and the clear iridescent blue of his eyes had dulled to a muddy gray.

"Jared?" She reached for him, and he stepped away from her touch, leaving her no choice but to close her hand tightly, making her feel as if her own heart lay painfully in her fist.

"I can shower myself," he said, and walked away.

Erin followed slowly. Just before she shut and locked the cabin door, she wondered what Jared had gone through during the night. What had brought him to such a desolate edge that she had a fear even she couldn't reach him?

She had to try. She could hear him in the shower as

she paced back and forth at the door. As she listened to his groans of pain, she couldn't stand it any longer. He needed her now, whether he admitted it or not, and she needed to go to him. Her sixth sense told her that later might just be too late.

She opened the bathroom door and stepped into the steam swirling through the room. Undressing, she went to the shower door and drew a deep breath before joining him. She had a feeling she was in over her head, and she wasn't sure if either of them would survive.

That only forty-eight hours had passed was almost inconceivable. Oddly, she wondered if the true measure of time travel wasn't in fast-forwarding a clock, but in fast-forwarding the human experience to the point normal barriers no longer existed.

Jared was no stranger, and her emotions were far beyond what she had ever imagined they could be. She slid open the shower door, and Jared turned to face her.

"Erin, you mustn't. You don't understand."

"No. I don't." She set her hand over his heart, over the scar branding his chest. The scratches on his body had already healed. "But I know you need me. I must help. I cannot leave you, Jared. Please, let me." The last came as a whisper that she was sure the fearful pounding of her heart had drowned out. "Please."

She leaned up to press her lips to his.

Jared groaned as Erin's lips met his, as the ease of her touch gripped him. She was too trusting, and that trust would lead to her death. He knew it, but he didn't have strength to tell her that now. He met her kiss with a punishing kiss of his own, one that devoured the softness of her mouth. He angled his lips to hers and thrust his tongue deeply inside.

Moaning, she met his angry challenge with a passion he couldn't turn from.

He growled deep in his throat and pulled her to him, dragging her against the hard heat of his erection.

Erin had time to draw one clear breath before Jared backed her to the steamy shower wall. His hands were everywhere upon her, slick and hot, like liquid sunshine. He knew just where to stroke to leave her gasping for more. He cupped her breasts, burning them, molding them to his mouth as he claimed each of her nipples, making them dance to the erotic beat of his lashing tongue.

She arched into his touch, moaning again as his fingers slid over her stomach and the curves of her hips to the aching need of her sex. Waves of hot desire rippled though her, jolting her hips to the rhythm of his touch as he eased his fingers between her legs to the hot pulse of her center.

She opened her eyes to the heated need of his.

He smiled and knelt down. As she watched, he parted the lips of her sex and closed his mouth over the excited nub of her arousal. Her legs trembled, and she grasped his shoulders and held on as he laved her, lapping her sex, driving her to the very edge of an orgasm.

She gasped and moaned, helpless but to rest her back against the heated wall and arch her sex to the pleasure of his touch. Water pelted her sensitized breasts, driving her pleasure higher. Then he stood.

"Jared, come inside me." She wrapped her hand around the thick heat of his erection, easing her palm along the hard velvet softness of his sex. "I want you to be a part of me."

He picked her up in his arms and opened the shower door. Leaving the water running, he stepped from the shower, moving into the bedroom. She wrapped her arms around his neck, kissing him hard. Water spiked his dark lashes, making the blue of his eyes starkly beautiful. The grayness and the shadows of pain in his eyes had disappeared, but she knew they still lurked. Rivulets dripped down his face and along the lush curve of his mouth. She licked the droplets from his lips, running her tongue across the corner of his mouth, so thirsty for everything he could give her.

She'd been in the desert too long.

He groaned, turning to kiss her. His tongue thrust and searched deeply, as if he wanted to reach her soul. He lowered her legs to the floor, wrapping his arms around her buttocks, pulling her sex tight against the hard press of his erection. The hot length of him slid between her legs, along the wet heat of her sex.

"I want to be inside of you, but you don't know—" His deep voice vibrated the very heart of her.

"No. Later. Let me love you. Let me make you feel everything there is," she said, kissing him deeply. Stepping back, she took his hand and led him to the bed, urging him to lie down. Joining him, she traced her fingers over the angles of his face and chest, exploring every nuance of him that had drawn her gaze from the moment she'd seen him.

He gasped as she followed the erotic trail of dark hair bisecting his stomach to gently grasp the silky heat of his erection. When she brought her lips to his pulsing need and covered him with a kiss, he threw his head back against the bed, arched his spine, and groaned deep.

He reached for her, and she went to him, kissing his mouth as she slid over him until she straddled his erection. Then she guided him inside her. Having the hot fullness of him deep inside brought her desire surging like a stormy tide. She eased up and slid down, stroking him with waves of pleasure. She wanted to take him on a slow, magical journey to heaven, wanted his first lovemaking to be all that any man could ever fantasize.

Jared couldn't take much more of the aching want Erin kept building tighter and tighter inside him. The hot rushing need drove him wild. He had to act, had to take control of the madness before it claimed him.

"Erin, enough!"

His body trembling with pleasure he didn't want to end, Jared grasped Erin's hips and rolled until she lay beneath him. The warrior in him had to act, had to push this pleasure to its highest level.

He entered her again in a long, hard stroke, holding his weight on his arms, pinning her hips to the mattress. He kissed her deeply as she wrapped her legs about his hips, urging him closer, deeper.

Being inside Erin was unlike anything he'd ever known, greater than any hunger he'd ever felt. He thrust into her until she cried out sharply, clutching him and triggering a pleasure so intense that the very center of his being exploded into a million stars of pulsing light. He'd never known a heaven so great, nor a spirit so beautiful.

He pulled Erin close to his heart, and his spirit soared with hers.

Jared's pulse slowed to a hard thud. He rolled on the bed, pulling Erin tighter into his embrace. She pressed herself to him, head to his shoulder, breasts to his chest, thighs entangled between his. She set her hand over his heart, over the burn scar, as if she wanted to take that pain from him as well. Then she reverently touched his amulet, gliding her finger over the ancient markings.

After making love with Erin, he concluded that being mortal was worth every drawback he'd cursed. In some strange way, he felt alive for the first time ever, even though he'd seen the passing of many millennia.

When he looked into Erin's eyes, he'd seen her soul. Now he'd touched her soul, and the depths and beauty of it were incomparable to any other being. He now understood the reason behind what he'd spent his whole life battling for. He now fully understood what was at stake in the battle Logos waged against Heldon.

Sliding his hand up the soft curve of her back, he threaded his fingers through her lush, sun-streaked hair, breathing in all the fragrant nuances of her—her skin, the taste of it, the feel of it, the scent of her arousal, and the aroma of their joining—a heady sweetness he couldn't seem to breathe enough of. He also breathed in the scent of her Elan blood, and it was stronger than ever now. Though his hunger for her blood had ebbed, he was still aware of the rush of it through her body, the heat of it pulsing against him, the taste of it in her kiss, and the essence of it in her breath. How long before he had no control over the darkness in him? He needed to tell her what he was, what he was becoming, but he also needed to love her again, to feel the cleansing beauty of her arms. To know again the heat and pulse of her body melding with his. She lay half upon him, half at his side with her head cradled against his shoulder. Her fingers absently tracing the star of his amulet that stood for the unity she had just shown him in a way he'd never imagined—a unity he craved to know again. He'd worn the amulet for a millennia and had never really understood the true essence of what it meant.

"Erin," he said roughly, pulling her up to meet his kiss. As he set his lips upon hers, he gazed into the liquid gold of her eyes and lost himself completely.

Erin heard the deep plea in Jared's voice. Even though he'd only spoken her name, she heard so much more, his need of her, his want of her, his secret cry to escape the darkness that had sent him running into the forest. And she answered that cry as his kiss delved deeper and his tongue sought hers. It wasn't the kiss of a man satiated, but one from a man whose desire hungered for fulfillment.

He rekindled her desire within moments. Her pulse raced as he rolled her beneath him, kissing her deeply and then lightly, sliding his tongue sensually against hers, then nipping the fullness of her lips before tasting her cheek, her brow, her ear, and her throat. She threaded her fingers into his hair, luxuriating in the feel of its silkiness sliding between her fingers. She arched herself up to the heat of his questing mouth, willing to give all of herself over to the pleasure of his touch.

He slid between her legs as he moved downward

and sat on his heels, looking at her splayed before him. He slid his hands gently over her breasts, arousing her nipples to feverish points of exquisite pleasure. Her breath hitched as her back and hips arched for more. Then he spread her legs wide, bending her knees out until the fullness of her sex lay exposed and needy.

The fire in his gaze as he looked his fill of her sent a deep burn from the tips of her toes to the crests of her breasts. "Jared, touch me, fill me, love me."

He smiled, and the light and tenderness in his eyes wrapped around her heart in a way nothing had before. But before she could even grasp the meaning of the feeling, he pressed his hot palm against the ache of her wet sex. "You are so beautifully made. So perfect. Everything that I lack to be whole, you are.

"I want to fill you with all that I am over and over again," he whispered as he grasped her hips. Rising to his knees, he pulled her up the long length of his thighs to where just her upper back rested upon the bed and drove his velvet hard arousal deep inside of her. Her blood rushed to her head, and she gasped at the fullness of him spreading fire through her body. She clasped her legs about his hips, arching more of herself to him. He slid almost all the way out, then thrust again, harder and deeper, filling her more than ever before, and she cried out from the pleasure of it, needing more and more.

Her head pressed deeper into the mattress, and she

fisted the sheets in her hands, gaining the leverage that she needed to press herself even closer to him. His thrusts came harder and faster, each time spiraling her higher and higher into a world where nothing else mattered but joining the hot core of her body as closely to his as she could. Her heart raced after his, caught up in the power of his passion as he drove her over the edge of reason. Her gaze locked on his, and the dark desire blazing in his eyes consumed her. She cried out as pleasure so deep and intense filled her and sent her mind, body, and spirit soaring. He drove into her one more time and cried out as his body shook hard and fast against her, telling her that his pleasure had been as great as her own.

Releasing her hips, he slid forward until he could kiss her softly. She wrapped her arms around his neck and pulled the full weight of his body down upon her. The feel of him against her was just as satisfying as all that they'd just shared.

She loved him. She knew it with her heart, even though her mind wasn't able to reason it out just yet. She closed her eyes and had just drifted off to sleep when Jared rolled from her. Lying beside her, he wound his hand into the length of her hair.

"Erin, we need to talk."

The morning had passed with the heaven of making love, and now reality was tearing down the door.

"Erin—"

A sharp blaring cut through his words. The phone.

Erin didn't need her fledging sixth sense to tell her that what Jared had to say wasn't something she wanted to hear. She wished with her whole heart that she could wrap both of them in a cocoon, shutting out the world so that they could have the time to grow, to love, and to be all that they could possibly ever become.

"I have to answer that," she told him, feeling as if something very special was being snatched from her. "It's important."

"It's an annoyance that shouldn't have to be tolerated. Communications should be made spirit to spirit; to do otherwise removes the heart."

"Talk later, phone now." Erin rolled from the bed and crossed to the desk, accidentally bumping the computer keyboard as she reached for the phone. The screen blinked on as she picked up the receiver, displaying the long list of Googled articles about Dr. Cinatas. It was Monday, and somehow she had to get inside the Sno-Med Research and Development Center without him knowing it.

"Hello," she said into the receiver.

"The bleedin' dragon is coming to arrest you," Emerald said. "He won't listen to a word I say. Won't believe that there's more to this bloody world than what's sitting in front of his face. And everythin's goin' to smack him right between the eyes if he doesn't wake up. I'm bringin' you down to the cottage."

"The sheriff is coming? Why? What's wrong?" Erin asked, dreading that Cinatas had found a way to her jugular.

"Some bleedin' clinic in Manhattan burned to the ground Friday. Four bodies were found in the ashes, and you're wanted for questioning in connection to their murders. Sam's going to kill me because I'm to wait for him and his deputy to get here. But I'll be there in a jiffy to bring you here."

Erin felt numb. She'd expected that Cinatas would have eliminated the bodies and all proof of their existence within minutes of her escape. If she had stayed in Manhattan, gone to the police, reported the murders, she had no doubt Cinatas would have not only discredited her story but would have captured her. He had friends in high places. But she never dreamed he would have burned the clinic down with the bodies inside and blame her.

She shivered at his insane genius.

"We'll be ready," Erin said and hung up the phone.

Jared joined her at the desk. She didn't want to let the world intrude, but it was crashing down around her, and she couldn't stop it. She prayed that somehow she'd be able to keep him from the full repercussions of the trouble she was in, which meant she couldn't run from the law. Jared would run with her, and she couldn't stand to have anything happen to him. He stood next to her, totally absorbed in the computer screen.

"I have a problem."

"What is this?" Jared nodded at the screen.

"A computer. It's like a mechanical brain that works faster and holds more information than a human's, or at least my brain. I was searching for information last night on Dr. Cinatas and the Sno-Med Corporation. This is a search engine that compiles information from the Internet—a network of computer communications that connects the entire world. Put in the right words, and you can find out anything you want if someone has posted it on the Internet. Like this article on Dr. Cinatas." She pulled up the one about his near drowning.

Jared glanced at the screen, then frowned back at her. "He too had a near-death experience ten years ago. I would like very much to meet this satanic doctor."

Erin gaped at Jared. "You read that article that fast?" Then her mind sputtered, "Satanic? I thought so, but what made you think—"

Jared pointed at the screen. "Evil relishes to twist things backwards. *Live* becomes that which causes death, *Evil*. *Cinatas* backwards is *Satanic*."

Erin gasped. "And *Sno-Med* backwards is *Demons*." She picked up the list of men she'd made last night. Maybe she had more proof that there was something very wrong with Cinatas than she thought she had. "We have to get dressed and go with Emerald. The sheriff is on his way to arrest me. Dr. Cinatas burned down his clinic in Manhattan and blamed me for it and the murders."

Her hand trembled. She had the urge to run, to get as far away as possible before the sheriff appeared, but that would only endanger Jared. As things stood now, if she gave herself over to the sheriff, then Jared would be free. There was no way he could ever be connected to what happened in Manhattan.

Jared cupped her cheek in his palm, his eyes a clearer blue than they'd been since he woke on the hood of her car. He leaned down to kiss her, but a horn blaring from outside the cabin sent Erin scrambling. She pulled clothes from the closets and drawers, getting dressed and getting clothes on Jared as well—no easy task. The man was a nudist at heart. She dashed out the door with her notepad of names and facts related to Dr. Cinatas in hand. Jared was right behind her.

"Hurry!" Emerald sat revving the engine of her Mini Cooper. Dr. Batista was in the back seat, looking not at all happy or comfortable. The woman clearly did not approve of what Emerald was doing. Erin winced. She hadn't been very truthful with them, even though their generosity and goodwill had been unfailing.

Erin opened the passenger door, frowning. She didn't see how both she and Jared were going to fit in the Mini. "Uh, I—"

"I'm not getting in there," Jared said. "We'll run." He scooped Erin off her feet, and before she could say a word, he took off down the road. Erin thought that she must be getting used to Jared's speed and agility, because she didn't blink an eye as the forest trees passed in a greenish brown blur and the wind rushed past her face. She was beginning to understand Jared's need for space and unencumbered movement.

Once down the long, winding road, Erin could see the white-frosted walls of Emerald's gingerbread cottage. In front, with blue lights flashing, was the sheriff's squad car. Erin's stomach flipped at the thought she would be leaving Jared, trading in the warmth and strength of his arms for the cold back of a squad car and metal handcuffs. Upon their approach, Erin saw that the sheriff was in front of Emerald's cottage, back to the wall by the door, his gun drawn and held up.

Jared didn't make a sound until he set her down and she dropped her notepad.

The sheriff swung, gun pointed. She raised her hands slowly. "Don't shoot."

"Where's Em!" he shouted. "Raise your hands!" he said to Jared.

Jared just fisted his hands, his stance tense. The sheriff might be a mountain, but Jared clearly meant to be the dynamite to bring it down if necessary. He emitted a deep, feral growl that vibrated with threat.

Erin's spine shivered with fear for Jared and apprehension for herself as something skirted the edges of her mind, something that connected Jared with the wolves at the cave that first night in the forest and the sharp howling of the wolves she'd heard last night. Did he have some special communication with the beasts? Did he call, and they answer him? As a Blood Hunter from the spirit world, did he have the ability to commune with animals and nature in some way?

Just then the Mini came into view, flying down the mountain, gravel and dirt scattering as it came to a screeching halt in front of the sheriff's squad car.

"Bleedin' hell, he can fly!" Emerald exclaimed, getting out of the Mini and staring at Jared with appreciative amazement in her green eyes. She didn't even glance at the sheriff. "Not with wings, mind ya, but bloody well close."

"What the hell are you and Nett doing, Em? I told to you stay inside and lock the damn door." The sheriff sounded like thunder and looked like lightning about to strike.

Emerald turned and set her hands on her hips, her bracelets tinkling like a soft wind chime in the face of his storm. "And I told you that it wasn't bleedin' necessary. Now we're all goin' to go inside and discuss this problem, and you're going to listen before it's too late."

"Over my dead body," Sam said. "They're coming with me to the station now."

"I wouldn't be sayin' that if I were you, Samuel T. Sheridan. Your arse is so bloody stubborn you'd tempt a saint to murder."

Erin thought the sheriff was going to explode. She barely resisted the urge to run and duck. The air around them was so charged that it was a wonder it wasn't crackling with lightning.

Surprisingly, Dr. Batista, wearing her customary lab coat and hair knot, moved from the Mini and set herself between the sheriff and Emerald. "I think we ought to hear what they've got to say, Sam." She turned her dark gaze to Jared, an assessing frown knitting her brow. "There are things you don't know, and I've just seen something that can't be explained by anything you or I know. If they were of danger to us, Em and I would be dead despite the pistol in my pocket. And if they were of the mind to run, they would have breezed right by you, and I'm not even sure you would have seen them pass."

"We need to hear what they have to say before it's too bleedin' late," Emerald said again.

Erin's scalp began to tingle. "What do you mean?"

Emerald shook her head. "The Druids weren't so kind, so I can't answer that. I can say we're all going to be somewhere we don't want to be."

Jared inhaled sharply. Erin glanced at him. His eyes were narrowed, and he seemed to be trying to watch the sheriff and scan the area. Erin had to ease Jared's apprehension. "I'm going to lower my hand and hold Jared's hand. He's in pain, and only I can help."

"Pain from what?" the sheriff demanded.

"Poison from a Tsara," Erin said.

"A what?" demanded the sheriff.

Erin slipped her hand into Jared's and plunged herself into his world with no going back. "A Tsara. Jared is a Blood Hunter from the spirit world, a Shadowman warrior for the Guardian Forces who fight Heldon's Fallen Army of the damned. He was poisoned in battle and condemned to our world. If we can sit down and talk, I will tell you all about it and the fact that a doctor is framing me for the murders of four people. Four people from whom he drained blood to transfuse into the king of Kassim, Ashodan ben Shashur. I'm a nurse, and I worked for the Sno-Med Corporation in Manhattan. I'll tell you everything—then, if you want to take me to the station, I'll go. But I have one question for you. I don't know if these four people are the only people Dr. Cinatas has killed or not. How many unexplained deaths or disappearances have there been in this area since Sno-Med moved into Arcadia?"

"Stef," Dr. Batista gasped. "She worked there. What if she discovered something—"

"Erin will not go where I cannot protect her," Jared said.

At that moment several black tubes landed at their feet and exploded, emitting a powder keg of blue smoke. Clouds of it encompassed Erin's face, making the dozen or more gas-masked, black-clad men surrounding them almost seem like a dream. A dream with guns bigger than any Erin had seen outside a movie screen.

Erin's eyes immediately watered and burned. The smoke suffocated her, and no matter which way she turned her face, it was there, burning her lungs.

"Nobody move," a man yelled as if over a loudspeaker. "Drop the gun!"

Through the haze, Erin saw the sheriff swing around. But before he could do anything else, a bullet ripped through his arm with enough force to knock him backward and send his gun flying to the ground. The gunshot was deafening to Erin's ears.

"Sam!" Emerald screamed, running toward the sheriff, sending dread through Erin's heart as she waited for a bullet to plow into Emerald.

The sheriff thought so too, because he threw himself at Emerald, knocking her to the ground beneath him.

Dr. Batista fell to her knees, her lab coat pulled over her face. Erin didn't have a chance to see if the doctor was shot or reacting to the debilitating blue gas. Jared scooped Erin up, pulling her crushingly tight against him as he sprinted toward the line of trees to escape capture. But within five steps a net blasted over them, falling like thick lead ropes, blinding Erin with its gnarling mesh. Jared struggled against the weight of the net, dragging them forward with superhuman strength, groaning with the strain.

His movement only served to bind them tighter into the net. The ropes strained, cutting sharply into Erin's shoulder, pressing painfully into her scalp and face. The blue smoke rose higher, enveloping them in a thick, choking cloud, as if another canister of it had been shot beneath them.

Jared roared with frustration, shoving harder and harder against the net, but gaining no ground.

"No!" he screamed, falling to his knees.

Tears poured from Erin's eyes as the gas stole her ability to see or breathe as well as consciousness.

She knew that whoever was behind this attack had known just how to capture Jared, and had been told how he could run. Only someone with a great amount of money and resources could put together such an elaborate setup, and Erin was very afraid that person was Cinatas. She might have been able to protect Jared from the law, but when it came to Cinatas's evil, she was beginning to think she was powerless against his far-reaching hand.

She wrapped her arms around Jared and pulled him close, even as the world slipped painfully from her grasp.

Chapter Seventeen

AWARENESS CAME SLOWLY in a muddled haze of confusion. Erin tried to move, but couldn't seem to lift her hand or shift her legs. She thrashed her head, fighting against the binding, remembering a heavy rope at the fringes of her mind. Danger. Jared.

She opened her eyes, blinking against the bright lights of a sterile-looking lab, a white one, one very similar to the Sno-Med lab in Manhattan where she'd found the bodies, only this one was much, much bigger. Cold, an icy, bone-chilling cold, surrounded her as if she were lying on a slab of ice. With heart-stopping horror she realized she was strapped to a stretcher, arms, legs, chest, and hips bound tightly down. The IV dripping told her somebody had tapped in to a vein in her arm. A monitor beeped the accelerated pace of her heart and flashed her other vital signs, her rapid respiration and elevated blood pressure.

And she wasn't alone.

She shut her eyes, feigning sleep.

"My patience in waiting for you to rejoin us is wearing thin, Morgan." Dr. Cinatas said. "I've been so looking forward to just a few games before departing the area. You wouldn't want to disappointment me."

Erin snapped her eyes open, catching sight of the dark doctor, who looked more satanic than ever before now that she knew what evil lurked behind his polished facade. The gleam in his eyes that she had first seen as charismatic intensity revealed itself as feral insanity. The slight smile, a cruel twist rather than guarded affability. He had the perfect grooming, his designer suit an expensive casket for a rotting corpse.

"You disappointment isn't very high on my list of priorities at the moment. Where is Jared?"

"Tisk, tisk," he said, holding up a syringe, tapping it, and ejecting a drop of fluid. "My disappointment needs to be your greatest concern, Erin. Your every breath should hinge on it. I owe you an injection, Morgan. Ever read about what a man goes through before being executed? What his last moments are like? What he feels? What he thinks about? Ever wonder what those last moments of a condemned's life are like?"

Cinatas moved closer to the stretcher.

"Where's Jared?" Erin asked again, trying to give Cinatas no reaction to his taunting, but the heart monitor sped to an alarming rate.

The doctor glanced at it and smiled. "Ever wondered what it would be like to die from a lethal injection? The helplessness of being strapped down as a needle of death came closer and closer? Ever wondered what the feel of poison would be like in your arteries and veins as it coursed its way through your body, leaving every cell screaming with pain?"

As Cinatas came at her with the needle, Erin couldn't stop herself from fighting, no matter how futile the effort would be. Beside her, the monitor beeped her skyrocketing pulse. Cinatas laughed as he slid the needle into the port on her arm. He pushed the plunger home, and the vein in her arm screamed with pain that rushed up to her chest, freezing her lungs. Her brain fuzzed, and the heart monitor went silent.

"Erin," Jared whispered as thoughts wavered through his consciousness like fleeting clouds. His wild run through the woods, the campfire bloodbath, his return to Erin, her touch soothing the ragged horror of what he'd become, the indescribable pleasure of her body, the danger . . .

"Erin!" Jared yelled. His eyes sprang open, and he sucked in air, instantly alert to everything about him. The cold dampness, the dank dark oppressiveness of being closed in, bound. He'd split the tape covering his mouth, but chains at his wrists and ankles held him strapped down. He could smell death around him, and the lung-burning scent of acrid chemicals. He could also smell blood—fresh human blood, not Elan blood, not Erin. He could smell the sheriff, Emerald, and Dr. Batista, but not Erin. He could hear their breathing, but not Erin's. He had to find her.

He struggled against the chains for his freedom. He was encased in a metal box that hemmed him in on all sides. He jerked on the chains with bone-fracturing force, but barely felt the solid lengths loosen beneath the full power of his strength. He fell back, chest heaving, body shuddering from the pain of his efforts, the desolate horror that he couldn't help Erin spreading over him. It was as devastating as the Tsara poison eating away at him.

He wouldn't accept that he couldn't get to Erin. He howled with rage, shaking the metal of the box with the shattering volume of his cry.

Cinatas turned from the pleasure of watching Erin's convulsions. A little of this and a little of that had made for a very interesting IV cocktail. The howl coming from the morgue next door had made the glass in the lab vibrate from the force of it. It'd taken one announcement that the lab might have been contaminated with a deadly bio-agent to clear the building of employees and security guards—a problem that would be easily declared as a mistake by his "hazard" team by morning. Besides Manolo, only Shashur, his bodyguard, and his servant were in the building. On the roof he had a gunman and pilot.

Hopefully Shashur, who languished in the penthouse under the first throes of what would soon become a raging fever, hadn't heard the cry. Shashur was sure to recognize that howl, as few sounds could match a werewolf's. Cinatas had heard only one wolf before. Pathos's howl could freeze the heart as effectively as the drug he'd just shoved up Morgan's vein.

Before Cinatas could leave the lab, Manolo rushed in, or ran in as fast as his diseased body would allow. The man was a brittle skeleton of what he'd been two days ago. His scarlet cheeks were sunken, his cracked lips oozed, and his dark eyes were dull with pain and raging fever.

"Did you fail to do as directed to secure the man? If Shashur hears him, it will kill my plans!"

"Sir, I did everything exactly as you ordered. I secured them all in the morgue and set the temperatures very low."

"Good. I'd hate for you to make another mistake. Your service these last two days has been exemplary. It was a shame I had to do what I did, but you're a better man because of it. Stay here. You'll be of no use to me in the morgue." Cinatas left, giving Manolo a wide berth. Even though he thought he'd developed a strain of the hemorrhagic virus that was noncommunicable, medical science did have its failings.

Cinatas moved into the morgue where he accepted and transported medical research cadavers in style to the Sno-Med facility. He had to struggle to slide the drawer open to see the beast-man. Cinatas had hoped to see the werewolf in its wereform rather than the body of a man fighting his binds.

"You are a big one," Cinatas said, scrutinizing the man. "Even bigger than Pathos. If you can do all the things that Pathos can, then this is going to be so good. You, my friend, are going to help me gain control of the most powerful force for evil on earth. The Vladarian Order will bow to me."

"Where is he? Where is Erin?"

"Pathos is coming, but you won't be seeing him for a while, not until you're ready. Three weeks won't be enough time to assure your takeover of the Vladarian Order. Next year's Gathering should be just right.

"And Erin. Well, how she is and where she is will be totally up to you. I get your cooperation, she lives. I don't, she'll live in excruciating pain every second that you thwart my authority and plan. And just so you believe I mean what I say, I'm going to give you a little example of what it will be like. Let me tell you just exactly what I'll be doing to Erin when you hear her scream . . ."

Erin heard Jared's howl, thinking that he was calling her back from the dead again. Only she saw no light, heard no angels, nor was she hovering on the ceiling watching herself on the stretcher. She was on the stretcher; her heart was now beating, her lungs were now breathing, and her mind was working, even if it was a bit fuzzy. What had Cinatas done to her?

She could only assume that Cinatas had injected her with a drug used in the treatment of cardiac arrhythmias, one that stopped the heart for a short interval and then let it beat again. His sheer evil had her palms sweating and her body shuddering with fear. Cinatas didn't seek to eliminate her. His goal was to torture her.

She'd heard what Cinatas had said to the man in the room with her. Didn't the man realize what was happening to him? To her?

"He's done something to you," she whispered. She didn't know how close Cinatas was. "Didn't you hear him?"

Erin heard a shuffling of footsteps, and a man who looked like walking death came into view, his dark eyes so bloodshot that they nearly glowed red, so ill that she feared he wasn't capable of understanding her. His body trembled badly.

"Help me," she said. "I'm a nurse, and I can help you."

He shook his head, his fear of Cinatas too great.

Erin sighed, her heart sinking. "You have to. I was his employee too, but I disappointed him, and now he's going to torture me and the man that I love. Do you have family? Someone you love? He's going to hurt them. He's—"

"Manolo!" Cinatas's sharp command cut through the lab as he approached.

The man turned, his body shuddering horribly, and Erin's dread grew exponentially with the thudding beats of her heart. That she hadn't heard Jared cry out again made her insides wrench with pain.

"Have the pilot on the roof ready to go, should I decide it necessary. Then rest a bit. Once I leave here, you can escort Shashur to the airport and then take your family on a vacation for a week or two while you recuperate. Maybe go down to the island and visit your parents and brothers for a few days. I'll order the private jet to return and take you. You've earned it."

"Yes, sir," Manolo said and stumbled from the room. Erin wondered if the man would live that long.

"What did you do to him?" Erin forced herself to keep her breathing even and calm. She didn't know how, but she was going to do her very best to disappoint Cinatas every way she could. She had to throw him from his calm, force him to make a mistake.

"A little virus in the blood can turn a person into a saint," Cinatas said.

Erin searched her mind. "God! Are you playing God with Ebola?"

"Play God?" He shook his head. "I *am* a god. Ebola is passé, Morgan. There's newer, more potent strains. But I can't have you playing my staff against me. I can't have you casting doubt into their feeble minds. That could be very painful for them, and for you."

Cinatas moved to her side, and the monitor betrayed the increased beating of her heart. He smiled again. "Have you ever studied acupuncture? All of the little places on the body all mapped out, telling you that if you stick a needle here, then this will happen there?" He brushed his finger up her neck and over her temple. She forced herself not to react, even though her skin crawled.

He slipped an alcohol packet from his pocket, opened it, and rubbed the finger he'd touched her with clean. Then he rubbed the skin between her thumb and forefinger with the pad, despite her efforts to twist her hand away from him. Pulling another syringe from his breast pocket, he popped the cap.

Erin steeled herself for what sort of drug he would try next. He stabbed the needle into the muscle of her hand he'd prepped, and the excruciating pain tore a scream from her. Her eyes teared. Her body shuddered and broke into a cold sweat.

"That was perfect, Morgan. Not at all disappointing." He held up a little electronic device, pushed a button, and her scream filled the room. "An hour or two of this, and your big friend will be my little lapdog." He laughed as if he'd said the funniest thing in the world.

"Jared?" Erin gasped, dying to pull the needle from her hand and shove it into Cinatas's face. "Where is he? What have you done with him?"

"He's on ice, learning how to cool his heels to my command. You're proving extremely useful. Now to get you out of here so if he does break free, he won't be able to find you. You're the only thing he will bow to right now. His soul hasn't quite crossed over yet, but it will soon. We'll be an unstoppable force."

Snapping the brake on the stretcher, Cinatas began wheeling her from the room. Erin's mind scrambled, fighting against the pain every jarring move of her hand sent up her arm. She had to do something, say something that would stop Cinatas's mad reign. "They are going to come for you," she said. "The other Blood Hunters, Jared's brethren from the spirit world. There is no place that you can hide when they do, is there?"

"Shut up. You have no idea what you're talking about."

Erin only smiled. "But I do," she said softly. "I also

know the secret to Jared's power. If anything happens to me or Jared, there are a lot of people who are going to find out all about your cancer-treating scam and what you are really doing with Elan blood."

Something she said had struck a nerve. Cinatas paused before a set of elevators and stared hard at her. Then he smiled. "I look forward to extracting all of that information from you at my leisure. Don't try and out-psyche me, Morgan. You'll lose every time."

The elevator doors opened, and Cinatas moved to slide the stretcher in. At the last second Erin screamed at the top of her lungs, "It's a trick, Jared! Don't believe anything."

Cinatas shoved the stretcher so hard that it bounced against the elevator wall, jarring her hand painfully. She fought for breath as the elevator doors closed.

Cinatas hit her in the mouth with the back of his hand, splitting her lip. The acrid taste of blood filled her mouth. He stared down at her hard as if fascinated, then he swiped her lip with his finger, bringing a drop of her blood to his mouth.

He acted as if he were sampling a sweet treat. "Your blood doesn't taste any different than other Elan blood. It will be interesting to find out why you are so special. Why are you under the protection of the Vladarian Order, Morgan? Why did they request that only you administer their transfusions? Why does only Pathos determine your fate?"

The elevator ascended, and Erin shut her eyes. Jared. Somehow they were both connected to the same circle of evil, one that was going to destroy them both.

With the scent of the doctor's corrupted Elan blood gnawing at his senses, Jared waited a few minutes after the man left before making his move. Jared's captor hadn't been able to shut him back into the metal box completely, and that crack proved to be Jared's edge. Twisting his foot, Jared eased his toes into the opening and shoved against the side so hard that the steel drawer he was in slid out, bringing him into the garish light.

He hung out from a row of drawers. Now that he was freed from the tight space, he could sit up, which gave him more leverage against the chains on his wrist. Flinging himself forward, he focused all of his weight and strength on his right wrist and strained to break himself free.

That was when Erin's scream rent the air, cutting through him like a knife. Anger and fear coursed through him, rising with a feral need to destroy Cinatas. The chain broke loose, and Jared set to work on his other arm and his legs, visions of tearing the doctor apart with claws and fangs spurring his anger. He heard Erin's second scream and realized that the quality of the vibrations was different from the first, as if this one had come from the television. Then Erin yelled that it was all a trick. The desperation in her voice had Jared's heart pumping with bloodlust. Once free, he started to run for Erin, but with his heightened senses, he realized that the sheriff, Emerald, and Dr. Batista's breathing had slowed.

Jared jerked open the drawers he smelled them in, pulled off the tape covering their mouths, and broke the plastic binding their wrists before he dragged them off the cold metal slabs to the warmer tile of the floor. The sheriff was starting to stir when Jared ran from the room.

Jared entered the lab next door and followed Erin's scent to two metal doors that he had to pry apart. The scent of her Elan blood lingered more heavily in the air than before. A creaking sound from above gave him the direction he needed to go.

He ran back down the corridor for the stairs, but had to deflect a blow coming from the doorway of the room he'd escaped from.

"Son of a bitch," the sheriff said, shaking his good arm as the metal pole he'd held clattered down the hall. "Why didn't you say something to let me know it was you? Where's Erin?"

Glancing into the room, Jared saw Dr. Batista leaning over Emerald, who moaned groggily. The sheriff had tied a bandage around his arm over his shirt and held his arm close to his side.

"The satanic doctor has taken Erin up. I need to follow."

"Both of you go after Erin," Dr. Batista said.

"I'm not leaving you two defenseless," the sheriff said.

Dr. Batista stood. "I'm in a morgue, Sam. I've got more weapons at my fingertips than you can imagine. Ever had formaldehyde sprayed in your face? And if push comes to shove, my pistol is still in my pocket. But we aren't going to do anything but pull the fire alarm and slip out the back door just as soon as Emerald can run. It should take the fire department less than five minutes to get here. I think we can manage to stay hidden for that long."

"Em is—"

"Going to never forgive you if you don't get your arse movin'," Emerald said as she struggled to sit up, bracelets clinking. "And next time I tell you to bloody listen, you'd better. I don't want to see a bleedin' morgue again as long as I live."

"I must go." Jared turned to leave.

"Wait," the sheriff said. He ran across the room and broke open a glass case. He tossed Jared an ax, then snatched up a red canister. "I hope you know how to swim. Let's go."

Jared ran to the stairs, taking them four at time to the sheriff's frustrating two. They reached the top and slid from the stairwell to the roof, where the loud roar of an engine with a steady whopping beat was deafening to his sensitive ears.

"Shit," said the sheriff. "There must be a helipad on the roof with a copter ready to go." He ran to a metal door and tried to open it, but found it locked. "I bet Erin is either on the copter or about to be. If they take off with her, it'll be hell to find her. We need to stop that bird. Let's find another door."

"Wait." Jared placed a solid kick right next to the knob, busting the door open. He moved out into the whipping wind, ears on fire with pain from the deafening sound. The sheriff dogged Jared's steps. A metal building stood between them and the helicopter. He didn't see Erin, didn't smell Erin, but he saw an armed man pacing in front of a set of glass doors.

Jared skirted the shed, keeping out of sight of the guard. The blinding wind from the helicopter blades stung his eyes, and the roar of the engine sent hot, sharp needles of pain through his head. His teeth bit into his lip, drawing blood, and he growled deep in his throat as a darkness inside clawed to the surface. It was as if his anger and fear had unleashed a beast within him. If the satanic doctor had done to Erin what he said he was going to do, then Jared would rip the man to shreds. He had to know the man paid the ultimate price for hurting Erin.

"We need a back door if this gets ugly," the sheriff said as he tapped Jared on the shoulder. He pointed to two hoses wound on heavy metal spools anchored to the roof. The sheriff grabbed one hose, dragged it to the edge of the roof, and lowered it to the ground. He motioned for Jared to do the same with the other hose.

"You mean an escape," Jared said as he threw the hose over the side.

"Guess you can swim pretty damn well. We make a damn good team," the sheriff yelled. "You distract the guard from the left, and I'll blast him from the right. If we get his gun, we'll be top dog."

Erin could hear the chop of the helicopter blades the second Cinatas wheeled her out of the elevator. She was surprised to see daylight streaming in through the glass windows and doors.

Outside, the dark silhouette of a black helicopter ready for flight stood in contrast to blue sky and white clouds, a brightness that gave an ironic twist to the hell she was in. A guard with a gun paced in front of the doors.

Cinatas stopped in the corridor.

"Why are you doing all of your dirty work?" Erin said. Considering the way Cinatas lived, she expected an entourage of servants at his beck and call 24/7.

"The purity of the act, Morgan. I like to personally handle certain interactions. You wouldn't send a servant or an employee to experience your orgasm and have them report back to you, now would you? I'll be right back," he said. "Don't go anywhere without me." He walked down the corridor, chuckling to himself.

How could a man that mad get where he was in the world without someone realizing his insanity?

Out of the corner of her eye, Erin saw the fevered man she'd spoken to in the lab. He hovered in the shadowed doorway next to her stretcher. If she could get him to help her a little, maybe . . .

"Please," Erin said. "Can you pull the needle out of my hand? It hurts so badly. He won't ever know. I'll tell him it fell out."

The man looked furtively up and down the hall, then at the guard outside the door. He didn't pull out the needle, but, falling to his knees and reaching from beneath the stretcher, he started loosening the straps, freeing her hands.

Before she could pull the needle from her hand or the man could undo more of the straps, they both heard Cinatas returning.

The man slunk back into the room, and Erin slipped her free hand back beneath the binding. Erin swore the first thing Cinatas looked at was her hand, as if finding the needle there told him that nothing had been disturbed since he left.

With a briefcase and a pistol in hand, he pushed her out to the roof.

Erin heard Jared howl. Turning her head, she saw him on the roof running toward her. Then another yell from the opposite direction showed the sheriff barreling at her, too. The guard raised his gun at the sheriff, and the sheriff blasted the guard in the face with foam from the fire extinguisher he brandished.

Cinatas jabbed the gun into Erin's jaw so hard that tears burned her eyes. The doctor faced Jared, laughing. "Shall I shatter her face for you? Will you obey me then?"

Jared paused, but the force of his fury still ran strong in him, and he howled his frustration, making even Cinatas jump in fear. Erin used that moment to jerk her hand free and grab Cinatas's wrist. She wrenched hard, pointing the muzzle of the gun away from her. Cinatas pulled the trigger, and a rapid fire of bullets sprayed the helicopter. Sparks flew.

Cinatas jerked free of Erin's hold, pointed the gun at Jared, and fired. Jared moved like lightning, throwing the ax as he ducked. The ax would have hit Cinatas in the chest, but he twisted and it sliced into his cheek and shoulder, knocking him to the ground, blood spurting as he screamed in pain.

Arms free, Erin pulled the needle from her hand. Then she snatched the IV from her arm before she started grabbing at the straps around her chest and waist.

The pilot of the helicopter must have decided to

leave, as the engine roared louder and the helicopter lifted a foot, wobbling above the helipad.

Cinatas sat up screaming, waving an automatic pistol at the helicopter, then firing a volley of random shots that went wild. Glass shattered in the building Erin had just been pushed from, and the ping of bullets ricocheting off the helicopter filled the air.

Suddenly a shower of sparks erupted from the rear of the helicopter, and smoke billowed out. The helicopter lurched.

"Run," the sheriff yelled, pointing to the rear of the helicopter.

Erin barely saw fire flare from the rear of the helicopter before Jared ripped the straps keeping her prisoner, lifted her up, and ran. She squeezed her eyes shut. They were running for the edge of the building. She knew they were going to jump, and the forty-plus-foot drop ahead turned her stomach.

"Hold on to my neck," Jared yelled, releasing her legs as he bent and grabbed a fire hose. Then, as she wrapped her arms around his neck, he jumped over the edge of the roof. The sheriff, too, grabbed a hose and leaped from the roof, barely avoiding the fireball on their heels as the helicopter exploded in a flash of searing heat. They slid down fast, making Erin's stomach wobble. Once they hit the ground, her gaze locked onto Jared's, finding his gaze on her with a frightening dark intensity. He made her feel as if she was his lifeline from hell. He drew her closer, wrapping his arms around her, bringing her flush against him. Then his mouth descended on hers with ravishing force.

Jared was on fire with the sweet, intoxicating taste of Erin. The trace of her Elan blood from her split lip upon his tongue, and the mind-crazing scent of her blood wafting from the puncture wound on her arm, sent him over the edge. He pressed her to the wall.

The universe could have ended at that moment, and he wouldn't have cared. To have her in his arms was all he wanted, to touch her, to feel her, to smell her . . . he had what he craved, and everything else could go to hell. Erin met his kiss with fervor. She moaned, crushing the full softness of her breasts to him.

All of the pain, the anguish, and the bloodlust that had been building since she'd disappeared from his sight eased, but he had this overwhelming urge to devour her with his whole being, to make himself such a part of her that both of them would cease to exist separately. The kiss came from the dark and light depths of his soul, and he wanted hers in return.

The sheriff jabbed Jared in the back. "We have to find Em and Annette now!"

Erin pushed back, seeking release. Jared wanted to tear the sheriff apart, but caught his emerging growl mid-throat. What the hell was wrong with him?

You're damned. The darkness is out of control. You

tasted human blood last night, and you'll not stop until you've sated yourself on Elan blood.

He groaned. How could he have forgotten last night?

He could no longer stay with Erin. Yet how could he leave her?

One more day. He wanted, needed, one more day with her.

A horn beeped, and a hearse came bouncing around the corner of the building. Emerald and Dr. Batista waved at them from the cushy interior. Emerald brought the hearse to a jerking stop and called out, "Get in. The fire department is driving up. We need to leave before we're seen."

"The hell we do. If that son of a bitch is still alive, I'm going to take his ass to jail and nail him to the wall."

"No." Emerald shook her head. "They find out who we are before we're ready to fight them, and we're all going to be dead. This time you need to have all of the facts before you act, or what happened in Belize will happen again."

"Who told you—"

"The Druids were kind," Emerald said. "Are you going to listen before you act?"

"I'm driving," the sheriff said, cursing as he slid into the driver's seat. "We're leaving the scene of a crime. This is so far over the line of the law that—"

"Evil recognizes no law," Jared said. "You might have to cross a line to bring them to it."

Chapter Eighteen

SHOWERED AND CLEAN, Erin faced the sheriff across the dining-room table in Emerald's cottage with a mug of hot Irish coffee warming her hands. Band-Aids were all that she needed to cover her physical wounds, but she was sure that emotionally and psychologically, she'd never be the same.

It was hard to believe that only eight hours had passed since their abduction. "So that's the whole story, from the time I left early Friday morning after finding the four bodies in the lab with no fire, until Emerald found Jared and me walking down Spirit Wind Mountain from the Sacred Stones."

"Then it's your Tahoe that is torched on State Road Forty-four?" he asked, not looking anywhere near happy with any of the story he'd gotten since returning from the Sno-Med facility. Reports were that the building was still on fire. There were some injured and maybe some dead, but no official report yet.

The hearse sat out in front of the cottage, a grim connection to it all. And the sheriff hadn't heard anything yet that made the price of leaving his integrity worth the ticket.

"The Tahoe must be mine. As I said, I left it in a hayloft. It was not on fire either." She stared down at her notepad. She'd found it where she'd dropped it outside the cottage this morning.

"What about the dead man on the side of the road?" the sheriff demanded.

"I don't know anything about him. Unless Cinatas left one of his discarded men lying about, the man might not have a connection to any of this."

"The Tsara that attacked Erin. The creature that hit her car," Jared said from where he brooded in the shadows. He hadn't said much of anything to support her story, not even reaffirming her account of who he said he was. He'd been quiet and withdrawn since returning, as if the evening shadows darkening the sky outside the windows held more interest than Cinatas.

"What do you mean by that?" the sheriff asked.

Jared turned to him. "Tsaras are spiritual assassins of such virulent poison that one bite condemns its victim to the damned. Heldon cannot create beings, as Logos can. So Heldon must use what he can reap from the mortal realm to serve his evil. The fingerprints identifying the executed man from South Carolina are likely to be accurate. I would expect Heldon to have used one of your worst for his special assassins."

"Are you trying to tell me that some joker from way down under grave-robs executed serial killers? This is just getting too far-fetched to believe. I know Sheriff Slater. All I have to do is call him and tell him what happened, and all of this can get sorted out through the legal channels that it needs to be done through. Do you have any idea of how guilty we look because we didn't stay and report what happened?"

Emerald groaned. "Sam, I told you. The Druid—"

"I don't want to hear about crystals or druids! I want facts!" The sheriff exploded from his chair to pace the room.

"Can you tell me that you have knowledge of all things within this world and within the spirit realm?" Jared demanded of the sheriff.

"Do you?" the sheriff countered.

"Not all, but more than is known to mortals. With so many things that you cannot explain, there is more logical reason for you to believe in what is being revealed tonight than for you to discount it as false. Are you willing to risk the lives of everyone here because you cannot grasp what you can't see? Or are you strong enough to accept your limitations and grant that others can have strengths that you do not have? You can't discredit what I said about Tsaras until you exhume the serial killer's remains. My guess is his casket will be empty."

"Son of a bitch," the sheriff said. Everyone stared at Jared. It was the most he'd said to them since arriving, and he took them all by surprise.

"Did an autopsy report on the man come through yet?" Dr. Batista asked, quietly.

The sheriff nodded. "Not a drop of blood in his body. Burn marks at his temples, on his arms and thighs, no other injuries. No decomposition. If his fingerprints are real, it's as if his body has been on ice for years."

"It has," Jared said. "Hell is a place of burning cold."

"Not hot?"

"Heldon's lie."

"So the man's injuries could be in line with execution in an electric chair," Dr. Batista said.

"This is all supposition, and again, I need facts."

Erin shoved her notepad across the table. "You want facts. Each of those men, along with Ashodan ben Shashur, the king of Kassim, have come to Dr. Cinatas for blood transfusions over the past few months. *Cinatas* backwards is *satanic*, *Sno-Med* backwards is *demons*. I now have reason to suspect these men aren't as human as you and I and belong to a group called the Vladarian Order. They feed on Elan blood. At the expo there was a little girl named Tierney. She had on a white Sno-Med sports bracelet because her blood was 'special.' The two dead women in Manhattan had on white bracelets as well.

"The Vladarians want me. I don't know why, but until I do, I would like to either disappear or lay so low they can't find me. Why don't you check those names out tonight and sleep on it, and we can continue this discussion in the morning? We'll also know more about what the fallout from the Sno-Med facility will be."

The sheriff read the names on the list with widening eyes. "You met Luis Vasquez?" His voice was tight with restrained anger.

Erin blinked, wondering what bone the sheriff had to pick with the Venezuelan oil magnate. "Yes."

The sheriff turned his back and walked to the window. "We'll talk tomorrow. I need to think. Both Annette and I will be staying here tonight. I'll be checking the grounds just to make sure things are safe."

"What do you know about Luis Vasquez?" Erin asked.

The sheriff's back stiffened. "We'll talk tomorrow."

Everyone appeared puzzled by his singling out just one name on the list.

Emerald mouthed the word "Belize."

Erin wasn't sure what had happened in Belize, but the list had given the sheriff the facts he needed. She had the feeling they were finally getting through to him. What happened today was bigger than Cinatas. Bigger than anything any of them wanted to face.

Though the sky stretched a vibrant purple-blue in every direction, and the sun still hovered sweetly on the horizon, leaving only the silhouettes of mountains and trees to shadow the peaceful evening, Erin trembled. The storm and the darkness she feared had come—to Jared's eyes. The stark shadows she'd seen in his eyes this morning were back.

She saw it before they'd left Emerald's cottage, and now that they were alone at the cabin, all pretense had fallen.

"Erin," he said roughly the moment the door shut behind them.

She turned him. "Shh," she whispered, pressing her finger to the lush fullness of his lips. "Don't talk." She kissed the curved corners of his mouth, sucked softly on the bottom swell of his lip, and dipped her tongue into his heated moistness. She tasted him, reveling in the very fact that he was alive and within her reach. He groaned harshly and met her tongue with the hard thrust of his.

She threaded her fingers into the thick of his hair and brought his gaze to hers. "I want you," she whispered, already in her mind making leisurely love to him, trailing kisses over every inch her fingers could explore, seeing his eyes grow dark with the fire of need.

Groaning, he claimed a hard kiss, one that seemed to unleash the storm in his eyes. The thin straps of her dress broke as he stripped her dress down, freeing her breasts to the cupping heat of his hands. He brought her nipples to hard points of need in just a few hot seconds.

She slipped her hands inside his shirt, desperate to feel the supple strength of his rippling contours and the pounding reassurance of his heart. He shoved her dress past her hips, taking her underwear to the floor as well. Buttons flew as he ripped off his shirt, and her pulse raced at the immediate intent in his eyes when he kicked free of his shoes and jerked down his jeans.

He stood hard, rough, and ready. Grabbing her hips, he pulled her against his erection, rocking against her. She met his thrust and pressed her breasts against the hard planes of his chest, wrapping her arms around his neck to kiss him again.

He backed her to the wall in a rush and hiked her knees to his hips. Then he thrust into her wet softness, his breathing ragged and his muscles trembling as he pinned her to the wall. He was crazed, surging into her with hot sexual power that sparked her every erotic nerve to an explosion of sensations.

He groaned deeper than ever before, his muscles quivering with his efforts as he drove into her, moving so hard and fast that her vision blurred. Shutting her eyes, she gave herself over to the pleasure rocketing her. There was no comfort, no tenderness. This was raw passion, and it swept her away in a shattering release that left her more vulnerable than ever before.

Jared shuddered in her arms as his climax ripped through him, and he bowed his forehead to hers. The dark curtain of his hair fell around them, shutting out the world, shutting out everything but the intimacy of them together. She wrapped her arms around him, wanting to stay like this forever, even if it was up against the wall. He was inside her, and the world nowhere in sight.

Suddenly, the howl of a wolf outside cut through the lingering silence, and Jared pulled back from her. Her legs slid unsteadily to the floor as her heart sank.

He'd turned from her, his gaze riveted on the evening shadows creeping into the room. "We have to talk, Erin. Now."

"Okay," she said, drawing a shaky breath. "Talk."

He swung around, looked at her, then began gathering up their clothes. "Get dressed first." He pressed hers into her arms and started pulling on his jeans as she gaped at him. Jared demanding clothes?

"Hurry," he said. "I can't think when you're looking like you want me inside you."

She would have laughed, but the seriousness in his eyes stole the humor from her heart. She quickly dressed, managing to tie the straps of her dress into a kind of halter top. Jared stood at the large windows, looking out at the fading sun.

"Do you remember the Sacred Stones on Spirit Wind Mountain?" he asked, surprising her.

"Yes. Why?"

He took his amulet off. It was the first time he'd ever removed it. He brought it to her and slipped it over her head. For some reason, tears filled her eyes, and her heart felt as if it would break apart.

He set his hands on her shoulders. "Listen carefully. The ancient stones are set in a special pattern, just as you see diagrammed on the amulet. You've four equilateral triangles, each from the four corners of the universe, entwined to form a twelve-point star with a perfect circle in the middle. They are Logos's unity—the coming together of all things, fire and water, positive and negative, male and female, heaven and earth, harmony between opposites—and within the eternal circle at the Sacred Stones no evil can survive. I know, because in just the few minutes I stood within the circle, I felt its killing force. Should you ever be threatened again, go there. Promise me."

"I promise. But what do you mean, you felt its killing force? You're not evil!"

Jared's eyes burned, and he blinked at the unaccustomed wetness clouding his vision. She didn't understand. She didn't know that at this moment he was her greatest threat. He sucked in air, trying to breathe through his teeth so he wouldn't smell and taste the scent of her Elan blood so strongly, but the drop of it he'd gotten in their kiss at Sno-Med had sharpened his hunger even more than before. He wanted to consume her.

Releasing her, he turned and fought for control, fought to strangle the beast trying to rise again inside him. Though the moon had yet to come into view, he could already feel its pull on that beast. Just as the moon moved the tides of the great waters of the mortal world and gave breath to many of the cycles in life, so did it draw the darkness buried within to break free and give into the evil eating his soul.

"Erin, I was a spiritual warrior, true and pure of heart, duty-bound to protect. When I was bitten by an assassin, its evil poison entered me and began infecting my spirit, ripping everything good from the depths of my heart. Though I have fought desperately to hold on to the remnants of what I was, I am nothing but the fading shadow of the warrior I was. But I will not ever cross into the darkness. I will die before I serve Heldon."

"You're not evil, Jared," Erin cried. "I've seen the face of evil, and you are not it. I couldn't love evil, and I love you." She wrapped her arms around him, pressing her cheek to his heart. Tears were streaming down her face. "Can't you see? You may not be what you once were, but that doesn't mean you are evil. You are just different now. You are mortal, and both good and bad are within a human's heart. We're not perfect, and you can't expect to be."

"Erin," he whispered and pulled her close to his heart one more time. "You don't know me. You don't know what's inside of me."

"I know what's important. What matters. That's all I need to know. Hold me, Jared. Please, would you just hold me and make the evil of today go away? Please. I . . . I need you more than ever before."

Any noble intention he had of disappearing into the night before the beast surged through his control died beneath her plea. He couldn't walk away just yet. He swung her into his arms, bringing her close to his heart, and carried her into the bedroom.

Laying her carefully on the bed, he slowly shed their clothes. First his lips and tongue and breath whispered their way from her lips to her breasts, kissing her nipples to sweet points of throbbing need. Then, leaving a solitary kiss upon his amulet nestled between her full breasts, he trailed a path to the fiery heat of her sex, laving the sweet taste of her desire for him. And as he slid the hard need of his erection deep inside of her, he sent his spirit soaring with hers.

Erin woke to a screaming howl of pain and the distant sound of thunder. Night had fallen, and the shadowy light of the moon cut a spidery path over her naked body. She was alone. Jared. Had he screamed in pain?

Rolling from the bed, she pulled on clothes and ran through the cabin, coming to a heart-wrenching stop at the front door. It hung half torn from its hinges.

"Jared!" she yelled, running out onto the porch. Thunder rumbled again. Erin searched the sky, and saw a black shadow nearly obliterating the light of the full moon. She thought about the spirit beings she'd seen before, and the lightning. She moved back to the porch.

"Jared!" she called again.

A scream of pain answered her. She couldn't cower in the house. Not if Jared was hurt and needed her.

"Where are you?" she shouted, moving toward the shelter of the trees, in the direction she'd heard the scream. The sudden chill wind that slammed into her sent a feeling of icy dread racing down her spine. She ran deep into the woods, the dank scents of pine and forest decay closing in on her. Branches slapped at her, and the sting of pine needles pricked her skin as stones bruised the soles of her feet. She didn't care; her only concern was for Jared. The pain in his cry still echoed in her heart. "Jared!"

Rain fell in a sudden gush, pelting her with biting drops of cold and bits of hail. Her skin crawled. Did a spiritual battle wage over her head? Was the rain really iridescent blood falling from the heavens?

Another cry of pain tore shrilly through the night, suddenly sounding like the howl of an agonized wolf. Erin stopped in her tracks. Had that been what she'd heard all along? A wolf, and not Jared?

"There is no hope," Aragon shouted as Jared's ravenous howl reverberated through the forest. "The Tsara's poison has claimed him completely."

The echoing howl sent a sharp stab of guilt through Aragon. He and the other Blood Hunters had gathered on the mountainside, hopeful that the evil thwarted that day had meant salvation to their lost brother.

"We've no choice! He must die! He runs this way with the demons spurring his bloodlust."

"He hasn't taken Elan blood, yet," Navarre said, pacing through the mists, hovering above the mortal ground.

"He will by morning. I feel it. He must die." Aragon stabbed his sword into the ground.

"How do you know?" Sven demanded angrily. "None of us hold Logos's mind. None of us can see into the future. Anything can change in a moment of time."

"No," Aragon said harshly. He snapped his head up. Jerking his sword from the ground, he shifted into a battle stance. "Jared runs this way!"

Minions of the Fallen poured into the clearing,

their gnashing teeth and feral eyes showing their hunger to destroy.

York snatched up his sword and swung around as Jared and a host of Fallen converged on them.

The Blood Hunters fell into circle formation, their backs together, their swords afire.

Upon seeing them, Jared came to a stop and howled painfully. As the Fallen surged forward to attack, he stood watching.

Aragon, Sven, York, and Navarre pressed their backs together, a solid calm center, fighting valiantly as Heldon's minions closed in on them.

Chapter Nineteen

"WHERE ARE YOU?" yelled a deep male voice. "Answer me, damn it!"

It sounded like the sheriff's voice. Erin hesitated, then hurried his way, wondering if the sheriff had hurt Jared. She broke into a clearing just as lightning streaked across the sky in such a display that the entire forest looked as if it were afire.

She saw the sheriff across the grassy field and started running his way. He appeared to be waving his hands, shouting as he ran toward her. She couldn't hear what he yelled, for a sound akin to the thundering roar of a train reverberated around her, causing everything inside her to shake. Shotgun blasts of wind pummeled her and the sheriff. He pointed at the sky above her.

Before she could look, the screeching howl of a wolf cut above the roar, and Erin screamed as an enormous silver wolflike man leaped into the clearing. In a blurring flash, it tackled her to the ground and rolled. Feral fangs and the familiar sight of iridescent blue eyes registered as the wolf-man pinned her body beneath it. A second later heavy tree limbs slammed down on top of the creature and her. The blows were so hard, they pounded her into the wet earth, and the creature screamed.

Erin barely had time to blink before she heard the sheriff digging at the branches and cussing. Forcing her eyes open, she expected to have a dim vision of a silver wolflike creature on her. Instead, Jared's chiseled features met her gaze. He appeared unconscious.

She cried out in shock at the wolf's transformation. She didn't want to accept that Jared and the wolf could be one. Yet she still wrapped her arms around this creature, this man whom she loved.

"Can you hear me? Are you hurt?" the sheriff asked. She couldn't see him through the pine needles yet.

"No, but I think he is."

"The wolf?"

Erin swallowed. "No, Jared. The wolf . . . and him . . . I think are one and the same."

Jared groaned. "Erin," he said. "Hurt."

She saw him shake his head.

"Shh. The sheriff is here. He can help us. I am all right."

Jared tensed. His muscles bunched, and energy poured from him as he planted his hands on the ground and reared back against the tree branches.

The branches cracked loudly as they gave way.

"Shit. What the hell?" the sheriff yelled.

Jared rose up from the branches, breaking their thickness like twigs as he stood. Erin felt the rush of cool air and blinked up at the clear, star-filled night sky. The moon shone full and bright above her, and none of the earlier dark shadows or clouds littered the sky. If she hadn't been soaking wet and covered in pine needles, she would have thought she'd dreamed it all.

She sat up, then stood with Jared's help. He pulled her to his side and stared at the sheriff.

The sheriff looked shaken. "Who are you? What are you? Jesus!" Exhaling harshly, the sheriff turned away. "I suggest we finish this conversation at the cabin. I'd rather not see any more tornados tonight, or encounter another sixty-foot pine tree."

Once at the cabin, Jared single-handedly lifted the front door, bent the metal of the hinges straight with his fingers, and hung the door back in place.

Erin left the sheriff gaping at Jared and fetched dry towels for everyone.

"Let's go to the kitchen," she said. Rather than sitting at the table like a guest, the sheriff searched the cabinets as if he'd been there before and knew what he wanted.

"Em keeps whiskey here somewhere," he said. "I need a drink." He found the bottle and held it up. "Anybody else want any?"

Jared grunted, and Erin shook her head.

The sheriff drew a long drink right from the bottle, then riveted his eyes on Jared. "How long have you been like this?"

"My time on the mortal ground began as Erin said, on the hood of her car."

"And how many of those nights were like last night?" the sheriff demanded.

"Just last night," Jared whispered, closing his eyes.

"What?" Erin said, her heart hammering with dread. She'd found Jared in the hammock. He'd been out all night. "What happened last night?"

"Last night, miles away in the Smoky Mountain National Forest, two men were attacked by a silver creature. They called him Big Foot with fangs. Just about how I might describe what I saw tonight."

"Was anyone killed?" Jared asked. His anguished whisper rang like a convicting gavel through Erin's mind. Her hand froze midair, reaching for him.

"The opposite, so far. Someone was saved. The men had kidnapped a woman from the University of Tennessee who was camping with her college research team. They told her how she would die and how long it would take. They'd raped her once and were going for round two when a silver creature appeared. The woman said the creature tore into the men, looked at her tied up like a sacrificial lamb, then left. With the kidnappers incapacitated, she was able to wiggle to a knife, free herself, and find help from a passing ranger this morning. They found the men, who will be facing charges if they live. Both are under guard in the hospital. You could have damn well told me about it."

"I don't remember anything at all. The woman just happened to be lucky."

"Is that all?" Erin demanded, setting her hand on Jared's arm. She couldn't decide who she was angrier with, Jared for maligning himself or herself for hesitating to touch him.

He turned to face her, pulling away from her touch, his blue eyes burning with self-disgust. No, it was worse than that; self-abhorrence. "A mindless beast roving the forest, craving blood, doesn't care about anything but satisfying its own bloodlust," he said, teeth clenched. He zeroed in on the sheriff. "It won't happen again."

Jared's words curled fingers of dread around Erin's spine. His eyes were those of a man condemned.

"You're wrong," she said, tears gathering in her eyes.

"I don't know about that," Sam said, shaking his head. "You want somebody to die to prove it?"

"No, but you two do." She ran from the room with her heart crying. No matter what she had to do, it wasn't going to happen that way. She loved him.

Jared stepped outside the cabin and scanned the horizon as he waited for the sheriff to shut the door.

He'd asked to speak privately to him, away from any chance of Erin hearing. But considering the depths of her cries, Jared didn't think she would be hearing much at the moment.

All remnants of the battle had cleared from the night's sky, but a swath of destruction from what mortals called a tornado cut along the edge of the forest. The weeping trunks of topless trees dotted the woods like twisted ghosts.

He felt like howling at the pain throbbing inside him. He wanted to run wildly into the wood again, into the frenzied fold of the Fallen who'd found him earlier. He wanted to end the pain, to stop fighting the spread of the Tsara's poison inside him.

More than anything else, he wanted Erin, and he wanted to take the pain in her heart away. But he couldn't. No matter how much he wanted to. And he couldn't go to her again, no matter how much his body hungered for her. He dug his teeth into his lip, determined to stave off his want.

The wolf in him would be back, and he dreaded that.

"What?" the sheriff asked tersely.

"She's going to need protection. And I'm no longer able to do it. I want your vow that you'll do everything you can to protect her, even if it means going against the law you serve."

"You don't ask for much, do you?"

"I don't have a choice."

"You're sure?"

"You saw what I became tonight. It'll happen again, and the wolf has one desire."

"What's that?"

"It wants Erin's blood. It needs her blood. I don't know if the wolf meant to save Erin from the tree tonight, or if it was so crazed for her blood it didn't see anything else. You couldn't have stopped me from harming her either. You were right there and couldn't do a thing. I may not have killed yet. But I am a killer," Jared said, tired of fighting the truth, of fighting the pain inside, fighting his desire for Erin, and fighting the Tsara's poison.

"Jesus. I promise," the sheriff said. "And you aren't getting a greenhorn off the turnip truck. I spent a number of years on a special force."

"Good. Listen to the council of Emerald. She knows many things you've never seen. And keep Dr. Batista close. She has her ghosts, but she'll be a steady hand of reason," Jared said, turning away.

"When?" the sheriff whispered. "How? This just goddamn doesn't seem right."

"At sunrise. What's not right is for evil to walk as freely as it does." Jared went to the deck, looking out at the night, feeling the call of the fading moon. His body shook with the effort to control the roiling needs inside of him. The sheriff left without another word.

Jared had to go to Erin. He couldn't just walk away now. He wasn't strong enough. He opened the front door, and she blasted him with her pain.

"Damn it." Erin glared at Jared, her heart thundering with fear. He looked so far away from her she knew she couldn't reach him, and that was killing her inside. "You have to listen to me, damn it. You're not what you think you are."

He shook his head, eyes bleak with unshed tears. "Forget it, Erin. You're wrong. You're not in my mind. You don't know how far gone I am. I'm telling you what happened last night was just a lucky, random unfolding of events. I likely left the woman untouched because I wanted your blood more than anything else. The little girl at the fair could sense more than you—she wasn't blinded by her own emotions or pain. She knew in a single look that evil is within me. What is it going to take for you to believe that?"

"Why?" She swatted angrily at tears she didn't want to shed. "You can't judge yourself on a child's reaction. You might have just resembled a man she knew was bad. Why can't you at least consider there might be a chance that you're not as damned as you think? What if the wolf in you instinctively knew those men in the forest were evil, and you hunted them down? What if the wolf knew that woman needed help?"

"Then he wouldn't have left her trussed up for another predator, to go after the blood he really wanted. Yours."

"I refuse to believe it!"

He grabbed her shoulders and shook her. "You have to believe, you fool. I am your worst nightmare." Tears fell from his eyes, tears of pain, of shame.

"No, no." Shaking her head, she jerked back, not wanting to see what he was trying to force her to see. It wasn't true. She couldn't be that blind. Her vision blurred with pain and tears. She couldn't love a monster. He couldn't be one.

"Erin, I am so sorry," he said, his voice raw and ragged with a dark despair that scraped her heart. "I should have walked away from you the moment I woke on Earth." He bowed his head, and she reached out, sliding her fingers into the black velvet softness of his hair.. His gaze was so full of regret and pain, so stark with agony, that she finally realized where she'd seen it before.

"It was you fighting the black creature on my car," she whispered. "You were the silver wolf who spoke to me, who fought that horrible evil that was after me."

He sighed. "As a Blood Hunter, I fought against a Tsara. Yes."

"It bit you." She closed her eyes, realizing the full implication of everything that had happened in those few seconds of time.

"Yes," he whispered as if he could barely breathe.

Erin opened her eyes, pinning him with her own pain. "It infected you. That's why you're here now, isn't it? Protecting me is how you were condemned. You sacrificed all that you were for me." Her voice broke on the sharp edge of her pain. "And now you're ready to sacrifice what little you have left."

He sucked in air. "All I did was my duty. That is who I am. I am a protector. I must do what I have to do to preserve that." Anguish filled his voice.

"Duty?" she asked softly. "Duty saved me from lightning? Duty kissed me senseless?" She shook her head. "I think there is more than duty at play, Jared."

"You are wrong, Erin."

Cupping her face in both hands, he looked deeply into her eyes, as he bent down and kissed her. Then he touched the amulet nestled between her breasts, sending a sharp pain right through her heart. "Don't forget. The Sacred Stones will protect you. They are their strongest at dawn."

Releasing her, he moved to the door, and she nearly fell to her knees from the agony tearing her apart inside.

"Jared?" she cried. "Where are you going?"

He didn't answer. He just kept on walking and opened the door. She ran toward him, reaching for him. "You can't do this! You can't just turn into a wolf and walk away from me, damn it. You can't leave me!"

She stumbled, clutching onto the door he left hanging open.

By the time she reached the porch, he was already running into the woods, the breeze blowing his dark hair back from his face, the moonlight shining upon the silver streak, the power and strength of him, so fluid and free. She ached to hold him, ached to touch him, even if it was only for a moment longer.

"Jared," she cried. "I love you!"

He stopped and looked back at her for a moment, but didn't answer before he turned and ran, moving faster than she could ever hope to catch as he disappeared into the darkness.

Chapter Twenty

CINATAS FELT STRANGE. Different than ever before. Agony burned from every cell in his body. He felt weightless, as if floating.

A familiar laugh grated his sensitive ears. He opened his eyes and saw nothing but darkness. No light. No dawn. No glory. Only black. Tiny shivers of dread clawed their way through him.

"Shashur?" The name left a shuddering, bitter taste on his tongue.

"Yes," Shashur said, sounding amused.

Cinatas tried to move, tried to break free of the binds that held him within the piercing cold. "Where am I?" he asked, compelled to ask that which he didn't want to know.

Suddenly agony ripped though his eye, as if some unseen needle had stabbed through the flesh and viscous fluid to penetrate his brain. He screamed, and his

body shuddered from the torturous pain. Then the
pain was gone, as if nothing had happened.

"You're on a long, fiery cold journey," Shashur said
with a soft, grating chuckle.

Another needle-like pain tore through his other eye,
even stronger and reaching deeper and wider, as if
barbs of steel twisted inside of his head.

"I am so going to enjoy you," Shashur said, then
laughed at Cinatas's scream.

Erin forced herself to move, to not give in to the
pain that seared her heart. She had to try to catch
Jared. She couldn't let him go, not as long as she had
breath within her.

She had to stop him. He wasn't the mindless
bloodlusting beast he claimed to be. She ran for her
shoes and shoved her feet into them. Her left heel
caught on the back of the shoe. As she bent down to
jerk the leather free, Jared's amulet smacked her in the
face.

She clutched the amulet in her fist, feeling the
metal warm her palm. More tears filled her eyes, and
her heart thumped painfully as she recalled Jared's
words.

". . . *fire and water, positive and negative, male and
female, heaven and earth, harmony between opposites—
and within the eternal circle at the Sacred Stones no evil*

can survive. I know, because in just the few minutes I stood within the circle, I felt its killing force."

Jared had to be there. She had promised him she'd go there if she ever felt threatened, and the thought of anything happening to him threatened her more than anything else. She ran through the cabin and out the door, praying she wouldn't be too late.

By going through the forest, Jared would reach the Sacred Stones on Spirit Wind Mountain long before she could. The graying edges of dawn had chased away the deepest shadows of the night, sending a stab of fear through Erin.

Don't forget the Sacred Stones. They are their strongest at dawn.

A spirit wind as powerful as Logos's right hand moved over the mountain, whipping through the trees and twisting through the misty maze of spirits that hovered in the twilight between heaven and earth. Dawn broke across the bleak horizon, its light slicing through the shadow, ferreting out the darkness, seeking to wipe it from the face of the mortal world.

"You must stop him, Aragon, before it's too late! He may still have time left for redemption," Sven said, pain lacing every word.

Aragon turned from the outcropping of rocks

where he watched Jared running up the mountain to the Sacred Stones. "No," Aragon said harshly. "He is doing what must be done. He cannot become what Pathos is. Jared should be allowed to die a warrior's death."

"What if you're wrong, Aragon?" Navarre asked. "What if your anger toward Pathos and the betrayal you've always felt that he'd disgraced all Blood Hunters has weakened your judgment? What if Sven is right?"

"Navarre speaks true," York said. "Your anger against Pathos has burned for an entire millennium. Why? Your compassion should be greater that one once so mighty has fallen so tragically."

Aragon turned his back, refusing to let his mind travel back to what was too painful to accept. He shook his head, determined. "Jared cannot become what Pathos is."

"We all agree upon that," said Sven. "But the time to assure Jared's death is not now. Navarre and York agree. You must act with us, for the Blood Hunters are nothing if they cannot fight together."

"A warrior must lead, even though none may follow, or he ceases to be one," Aragon said harshly.

"And a leader who cannot see the wisdom of the council of those whom he trusts and fights beside might be leading all the wrong way. Stop Jared from doing this."

Was he wrong? Aragon reached deep inside himself,

yet could not see any light or truth. Then he heard Jared's scream echoing in the blinding light of the dawn. It was the scream of a warrior dying, not of one damned beyond hope. In that cry, Aragon saw his error.

Sven fell to his knees, groaning, as did York and Navarre.

Aragon planted his sword into the mortal ground before Sven, causing the earth to violently shake. "You must lead now. I am unworthy."

Sven looked up, horror on his face. "I cannot lead."

"You must."

Another cry ripped through the air, and Aragon turned. "Jared!" He turned his back upon his Blood Hunter brethren and ran to the Sacred Stones. Reaching the stone pillars, he found Jared suspended in the air within the center of them, his mortal body convulsing with pain as if every fiber of his being was suffering an unimaginable torture.

"Jared. No! I was wrong." But Aragon's cry didn't reach Jared. Aragon tried to fling himself against Jared, to force him from the ancient stones, but the spirit wind holding Jared within its power was too great. Aragon fell to his knees, his own guilt and Jared's agony ripping through him. He'd made a horrible mistake in believing nothing good remained in Jared. He wasn't fit to lead the Blood Hunters, nor to be a true warrior. He tore Logos's amulet from about his throat and flung it into the air, praying that his spirit would die with Jared's.

Turning down the driveway toward Emerald's cottage, Erin met Emerald flying around a bend in her red Mini. She came to a screeching halt. "Get in," she yelled.

"I've got to get to Jared," Erin said, piling into the passenger side. Dr. Batista was in the back seat, wearing sweats. Her hair hung in wild, long waves, making her looking like a gypsy.

"I know. The fool," Emerald said, whipping the car around and gunning it down the hill.

Erin frowned. "Did the Druids tell you what Jared was going to do?"

"No. Sam just happened to mention it five minutes ago. The bleedin' blatherin' gack tells me it's not my bloody business that Jared's bent on departing. All that 'a man's gotta do what a man's gotta do' is fecked-up blarney. Where to?"

"The Sacred Stones, I think."

Dr. Batista groaned. "I was afraid of that."

Emerald squealed out onto the main road, burning rubber. "I've been goin' to the bleedin' stones at dawn for nine months now. You'd think I'd get a break now that you two were here."

"Where's Megan?" Erin asked.

"Still at Bethy's. They were so close to defeating the Dark Lord last night that I didn't have the heart to make her come home for a readin'."

Clutching the dash, Erin watched the Mini eat up the mountain road. She had to think about something else besides Jared, or she'd go mad with the worry. "What exactly is a reading?"

"Meditating until your mind, body, and spirit are so bleedin' quiet that you can hear your own heart beating like angel wings. If you're listenin', your instincts tell ya the dangers darkenin' yer day. Most folks never hear, too busy blathering nonsense."

Just as if Erin had listened to her instincts Friday morning, she wouldn't have been running for her life. Before now, Erin hadn't quite been able to reconcile Emerald with the whole psychologist persona, not like how Dr. Batista fit so well with hers. But she could see it now. There was a certain solidness about Emerald that nothing seemed to shake.

"Is that something you try and teach your patients to do?" she asked Emerald.

Emerald glanced over in surprise, and nearly ran off the road. Speeding as fast as they were, they would have flipped if Emerald had jerked the car. Instead she gritted her teeth and eased the car back onto the asphalt. Dirt and gravel left a trail of smoke behind them. The shadows of the night were fleeing from the rising dawn faster than the Mini could move.

"Yes," Emerald said. "That's what I teach couples to do with each other. To listen to their hearts and not the noise of the world." Suddenly the blare of the siren cut through Erin's surprise. Lights flashing, the sheriff was hot on their heels.

"The idiot!" Emerald pressed harder on the gas and shot like a bullet along the winding road. Erin gripped her armrest and the dash, getting a very good idea why Jared hated the feel of being closed in a vehicle.

Emerald fishtailed and spun in the gravel as she turned onto Spirit Wind Mountain, then churned up the road. The wind moaned, and the mists swirled so thickly that Erin felt they were trying to keep the car from moving forward.

Now that they were out from the shadow of a neighboring mountain, she could see the sun had already risen. The higher they climbed up the mountain, the harder the wind blew, and she realized that the moaning cries weren't from its whipping swirls, but from a creature howling with pain.

Jared.

By the time Emerald halted at the path to the Sacred Stones, tears were streaming down Erin's face. She leaped from the car and ran into the force of the wind. "Jared!" she cried, but the wind stole her voice.

Heart pounding and lungs burning, Erin sprinted with all her might up the trail. The minute she reached the clearing, she saw him, a wolflike man in the center of the Sacred Stones, howling in agony, its body twisting with the savage pain torturing it.

"Jared! No!" Erin didn't care what happened to her. It didn't matter what they had to do. There had to be another answer besides the one he'd chosen. If he needed Elan blood, she'd give him Elan blood, but he had to live.

As if fighting a hurricane, she forced her way into the circle and threw her body against that of the wolf, trying to knock him from the center of the stones.

He roared, and she could see that his mouth bled where his fangs had gnashed in his agony. His iridescent eyes were dull, grayed with a horrible pain. "Leave now!" he shouted, repeating the very first words he'd ever spoken to her.

"No! Never!" Erin threw herself at him, wrapping her arms around his neck, clinging to him with her whole being as the wind lashed at them.

Jared fell to his knees, his dark despair made worse by Erin's pain. He could have bore his own agony and stood like a warrior until his final moments, but the burden of her pain brought him to his knees, wrenching his being apart. He screamed as his body convulsed and his spirit twisted from him.

He floated up from his body and hovered above the Sacred Stones, seeing the perfection of their design, the harmony of fire and water, heaven and earth, life and death, man and woman, and that which united them all—love.

A strong bright light reached to him, warming him as it pulled him closer. He heard once again the glorious ecstasy of the angels in song and felt a spirit wind flow over him, freeing his spirit.

"Jared!" Erin cried.

The ragged agony in her scream ripped his gaze from the light and he saw her holding his mortal body, her lips pressed to his as she sobbed for him. He reached his hand toward her, wanting one last chance to gaze into her golden eyes, one last chance to feel the pleasure of her spirit soar with his, one last chance to tell her that he loved her.

"Erin!" he cried. But she didn't hear him. He dropped his hand, fisting it as the pain of their parting stabbed through his spirit.

"Jared!" Erin screamed, shaking his lifeless body, refusing to believe she'd lost him forever.

The wind suddenly died.

"Oh, God," Erin cried. She didn't care if Jared was flawed or different. She loved him. Heart breaking with more pain than her body knew how to bear, she pressed the heel of her joined hands to his chest and pumped hard, then placed her mouth on his, forcing the very breath of her soul into his, calling upon all of her training and love to bring him back to life.

She loved him, she'd never give up. Again and

again, she pumped his heart and breathed for him until finally, his body shuddered. His open eyes were no longer a dull, lifeless gray, but shone with a bright iridescent blue that pierced right through her as he met her gaze.

"Jared," she whispered.

"Erin." He pulled her into his embrace, against the solid, steady beat of his heart. "I love you," he said, rolling until she lay under him, and the press of his hard body heated her from the depths of her heart to the tips of her toes.

She threaded her fingers into his hair as it fell in a curtain about them, shutting out the world. "I love you, too."

He kissed her then, long, deep, and hard. What lay in the future didn't matter right then. There would be time to face it together. What lay in the past didn't matter either. They'd conquered it. Only this moment in time, only this man, only his kiss, and only his touch, was all that mattered.

Epilogue

ERIN EASED BACK from Jared's consuming kiss as the world intruded. They were still within the circle of the Scared Stones. She wished they were somewhere else, somewhere where she could share the love bursting within her heart, and share the joy of holding him in her arms and loving him completely. But the world would not go away.

"Calm down, Em. It's not the end of the world," came the sheriff's surprisingly amused voice from the direction of the path to the clearing. Though she couldn't see her friends yet, Erin knew they were almost upon them.

"Don't tell me to calm down, Samuel T. Sheridan. You gave me a bleedin' speeding ticket!"

"A man's gotta do what a man's gotta do," the sheriff said.

"Why don't both of you can it until we see Erin and

Jared. How can you be so sure they're fine, Em? Finding his amulet on the path is a bad sign to me. The metal is still warm from his skin. People disappear from here. You know that."

"She must have seen it in her crystal again. You knew that he was going to be fine all along. So what was that argument this morning all about? I am not anything close to a blatherin' gack," the sheriff said, grieved.

"I didn't see it in my crystal. It's just a logical deduction," Emerald replied. "They're too bloody quiet for anythin' to be bad. Besides, the wind has calmed."

Erin knew the moment her new friends reached the end of the path. There were two shocked gasps and an amused male chuckle at the sight of Jared's naked body.

"Hold on, luv. I've got a yellow towel in the Mini. It's not much, but it'll do."

Erin laughed. "It'll do just fine." She'd developed quite a fondness for Jared clad in that killer kilt.

Upon leaving the Sacred Stones, Jared walked as a mortal, with no regrets for anything he'd left behind in the spirit realm. His willing sacrifice and the cleansing power of the ancients had freed him from the Tsara's poison. He could feel it within him, and in the absence of pain. The fire that had been consuming him since he'd awakened on mortal ground was gone. He knew in his heart he was no longer a Shadowman, but in his heart he was still a warrior, a protector who would go on to fight for that which was pure, and right, and good within the mortal world. His body felt as strong as ever, but different, cleansed.

Just before they reached the path leading to the road, he turned to scan the line of trees encircling the glittering stone pillars. For a moment, he thought he caught sight of a black wolf in the deep shadows, but before he could even say Aragon's name, the vision was gone.

He wondered if this was because of his new life, but feared that it was something more than that. Aragon had lost his amulet, the very symbol that proclaimed him a warrior. Why? Dr. Batista carried the amulet clutched so tightly in her hand that Jared wondered if Logos's emblem wasn't permanently etched upon her palm.

Reaching the road that led from Spirit Wind Mountain, Jared made himself a promise to return to the Sacred Stones soon to look for the black wolf, to use the power of the ancients to help him speak to Aragon. But today his heart was with Erin, as it would be the rest of his mortal days. This woman had gentled his warrior's spirit with the beauty of her own. She'd reached into his darkest despair and grasped his soul. Without hesitation, she had touched the wolf within him and claimed him as hers.

Seeing the red Mini and the sheriff's flashing squad car—bigger, but not big enough—Jared swung Erin up into his arms. He glanced at the sheriff, Emerald, and Dr. Batista. "We'll meet you back at the cabin. Take your time," he said, then took off running.

"Jared!" Erin squealed as he ducked into the concealing foliage of the trees, drinking in the clean fresh scent of the morning air. He sent the mountain mists fleeing from the power of his stride and the passion of his need to be free.

"Jared! Put me down," Erin demanded.

"No," he said. He was anxious to get Erin alone and naked.

"Please," she cried.

"Why?" he demanded, coming to an exasperated stop near a large boulder that sheltered them from the world.

"Because I want to kiss you," she said, wrapping her arms around his neck and bringing her lips to his.

"And I want you," he said. He met her passion head-on, claiming her kiss and demanding more.

Leaning forward to kiss him harder, Erin wondered if Adam and Eve had it so good.

FINALLY
A WEBSITE
YOU CAN GET
PASSIONATE
ABOUT...

Visit
www.SimonSaysLove.com
for the latest information
about Romance from Pocket Books!

READING SUGGESTIONS

LATEST RELEASES

AUTHOR APPEARANCES

ONLINE CHATS WITH YOUR
FAVORITE WRITERS

SPECIAL OFFERS

ORDER BOOKS ONLINE

AND MUCH, MUCH MORE!

13457

Discover the darker side of desire
with bestselling paranormal romances from Pocket Books!

Master of Darkness
Susan Sizemore
She thinks he's helping her hunt vampires.
She's dead wrong.

The Devil's Knight
A Bound in Darkness Novel
Lucy Blue
A vampire's bite made him immortal. But a passionate
enemy's vengeance made his hunger insatiable....

Awaken Me Darkly
Gena Showalter
Meet Alien Huntress Mia Snow. There's beauty in her
strength—and danger in her desires.

A Hunger Like No Other
Kresley Cole
A fierce werewolf and a bewitching vampire test the
boundaries of life and death...and the limits
of passion.

Available wherever books are sold
or at www.simonsayslove.com.

POCKET BOOKS
A Division of Simon & Schuster
A CBS COMPANY

POCKET STAR BOOKS
A Division of Simon & Schuster
A CBS COMPANY

14179